CL.69(02/06.)

The Legacy
of Reginald Perrin

David Nobbs

The Legacy of Reginald Perrin

Methuen

First published in Great Britain in 1995
by Methuen London
an imprint of Reed Books Ltd
Michelin House, 81 Fulham Road, London SW3 6RB
and Auckland, Melbourne, Singapore and Toronto

Copyright © 1995 by David Nobbs
The author has asserted his moral rights

A CIP catalogue record for this book
is available at the British Library
ISBN 0 413 69760 6

Typeset by CentraCet Ltd, Cambridge
Printed and bound in Great Britain
by Clays Ltd, St Ives plc

Contents

1 *A Reunion of Old Friends*

The great November gale killed a plumber in Slough, a lady on her way to demonstrate the boning of a shoulder of lamb to the Bromyard Women's Institute, an aromatherapist from Wakefield, and Reginald Iolanthe Perrin.

Reggie's funeral service bore eerie echoes of his memorial service a quarter of a century earlier. On that occasion he had been present, in disguise. It was difficult for the mourners to realise that this time, at the age of seventy-one, he had gone for good.

'The manner of his death may seem to those who knew him well to be a curiously appropriate full stop at the end of the bizarre sentence that was his life,' intoned the Vicar of Goffley, who hadn't known him at all. 'He was struck by a falling billboard advertising the Royal and General Accident Insurance Company. Ironically, this was the very company with which he was insured. God moves in a mysterious way.'

'Absolutely right,' whispered Reggie's old boss, C.J., who was drawn to clichés like lambs to the slaughter. 'I didn't get where I am today without knowing that God moves in a mysterious way.'

Two months later, Major James Anderson, Reggie's brother-in-law, was also moving in a mysterious way. He was marching with incipiently arthritic care, in order to avoid slipping in the rutted snow, and was keeping to the edge of the pavement, so that dollops of snow sliding off the roofs of the Climthorpe shops wouldn't slip down the back of his neck and arouse his latent sciatica. On these cold, raw mornings he could feel the burden of every one of his sixty-eight years.

He pressed the inside pocket of his patched jacket, to make sure yet again that the letter wasn't a figment of his imagination. It rustled. It wasn't. He knew it by heart:

Dear Mr Anderson,

I am writing to you in connection with the last will and testament of your brother-in-law, Reginald Iolanthe Perrin. If you will present yourself at our offices at 11.30 a.m. on the 12th inst., you may hear something to your advantage.

> Yours sincerely,
> Geraldine Hackstraw (Ms)
> Senior Partner
> Hackstraw, Lovelace and Venison.

Jimmy had always tried to be a good man. He hadn't intended to drive Sheila to drink. He hadn't wanted to be known as an incorrigible sponger. He had regretted his very occasional lapse into incest. How he wished, as he trudged carefully past the public library, closed on Thursdays as an economy measure, that his heart wasn't beating so anxiously, that his stomach wasn't so sick with hope that at last his financial problems might be solved.

'Jimmy!'

In his surprise he attempted too swift an about-turn, almost fell, and slid slowly into the path of a woman who was, did he but know it, the wife of the Chief Housing Officer of Climthorpe Borough Council.

'I'm so sorry, madam,' he said, putting his arms round her ample frame for support, and realising to his horror that he had touched her large, soft, sagging breasts. 'Bit of a cock-up on the swift about-turn front.'

The wife of the Chief Housing Officer disentangled herself hastily, gave him a frightened look, and continued on her way gingerly. It disturbed Jimmy, sometimes, that so many women gave him frightened looks.

'Jimmy!'

At last he identified the source of the voice. It was Tom Patterson, who had once been married to Reggie's daughter Linda. It was with Linda that Jimmy had committed incest, and he was always uneasy in Tom's presence. But then he was often uneasy in the presence of that much greater group of men with whose wives he had not committed incest, so maybe the incest had nothing to do with it.

Tom was standing on the opposite pavement, outside the Climthorpe Tandoori. He did a brief mime of a man crossing the road. Jimmy shook his head in bewilderment. Tom repeated the mime. Jimmy repeated the shake of the head. Tom repeated the mime again, and at last Jimmy thought that he'd cottoned on. Both men started to cross the road and met on a tiny traffic island in the middle.

'I meant that *I'd* cross,' said Tom. There were dark circles under his eyes. His beard was grey and almost entirely free from evidence of breakfast. He was fifty-one years of age.

'Sorry,' said Jimmy, as they shook hands. 'Tricky cove, mime. No damned words. Makes it difficult to understand the blighter.'

'I expect it was my fault,' said Tom magnanimously. 'I expect I did it badly. I'm not a mime person.'

Traffic was whooshing through the slush on both sides of them. At last there was a break long enough to let them step cautiously back to the safety of Jimmy's pavement.

'So what brings you to this neck of the woods?' asked Jimmy as they proceeded up the High Street. 'Not your usual stamping-ground, I'd have thought.'

Tom stared at him in amazement.

'Well, the same thing as you, I imagine.'

Jimmy strove to understand.

'The letter. Reggie's will.'

'Ah!' said Jimmy. 'By Jove, Tom, no flies on you.'

'What?'

A blast of hot, almost edible air emerged from the Climthorpe Cleaners. They passed reluctantly out of its orbit back into the January chill.

'I see you, think, "What's he doing here?" You see me, twig straight-away. Brains, Tom. I'd gone AWOL the day they dished them out. You hadn't.'

'Well, thank you, Jimmy.'

People were pouring into W.H. Smith's to buy lottery tickets. The jackpot had been held over.

'How's the home-made wine?' enquired Jimmy.

'Going along very much as ever.'

'Oh dear. Sorry to hear that.'

Tom gave him a sharp, injured look. His sprout wine had once been one of the most popular lines in Reggie's Grot shops, where everything was guaranteed to be useless rubbish. Its fantastic popularity had both gratified and mortified Tom.

Jimmy tried hard to avoid the subject of the will, but as they passed Spud-U-Like his resolution wavered.

'Can't help wondering, can you?' he said. 'Not being greedy, but . . . "Something to your advantage"! Can't help wondering.'

'It says, "*may* hear something to your advantage",' said Tom. 'Reggie may have one last trick up his sleeve. Not that it bothers me,' he added hastily. 'I'm not a money person.'

'Nice of Reggie to remember the family, though.'

'Jimmy! Tom!'

Again Jimmy's about-turn was too ambitious for his age and the conditions underfoot. He grabbed at Tom, just as Tom was slipping and grabbing at him. The two men just managed to

4

stay upright as they slid helplessly through a complete turn and a half together. Had a panel of international judges been watching from the Halifax Building Society across the street, their ice dance would have been given nought out of ten for style and content.

The sight that met their eyes, when they finally came to rest, was not one that thrilled them. C.J. was standing in front of a boarded-up, empty shop, waving an envelope with indecent enthusiasm.

He manoeuvred carefully over the road to join them. He was seventy-two now, bald and slightly round-shouldered, and no longer quite six foot tall, but he still bristled with the natural authority of a powerful man too insensitive to realise that his powers are waning.

'So you've had the letter too,' he said, clasping their hands with painful vigour.

'Good Lord. Brains on all sides,' said Jimmy in renewed wonderment at their brilliance.

Just before the War Memorial, they came to the Coach and Horses, a large nineteen thirties brick building set back from the road.

'We're going to be early,' said C.J. 'Do you fancy a drink?'

Jimmy looked at his watch. '11.06 hours,' he said. 'Bit early for a snifter. They'll hardly be open. Besides, might look bad if we all turn up stinking of drink. Yes, what a good idea.'

In the pleasant, well-heated waiting room so thoughtfully provided by Messrs Hackstraw, Lovelace and Venison, Elizabeth Perrin sighed deeply. Her hair was silvery now, and her face quite heavily lined, as was only to be expected after fifty years of marriage to Reggie Perrin, but age, while it had taken away the bloom of youth, had given her character, and at seventy she was still a strikingly attractive matriarchal figure.

She sighed again. She couldn't interest herself in the back

5

numbers of *Homes and Gardens*, the *National Geographic* and *Twixt Towns and Downs: The Magazine for Surrey*. A notice pinned to the board above the magazine-strewn table asked, 'Have you made your will?' 'Yes,' she replied silently and ruefully, 'but my will's sensible. What will Reggie's be like?'

Mrs Meaker, her neighbour in Leibnitz Drive, had told her, in the greengrocer's, that she thought it appalling that Reggie should put her through this morning's ordeal, on top of all the other strange events that he had forced upon her. Elizabeth had given her short shrift. 'Might as well have married Attila the Hun and complained that he wouldn't take me on nature rambles,' she had said. 'I've had an exciting life, thanks to Reggie.' Mrs Meaker had changed the subject in spectacular style, peering into Elizabeth's basket and saying, 'I wouldn't know what to do with fennel.' Elizabeth knew that, when talking to other people, Mrs Meaker had been running her down. 'Fancy not inviting anyone back to the house after the funeral. Such bad form.' If she'd said that to Elizabeth's face, she would have retorted, 'Yes. Reggie loved bad form. I did it in his honour.'

Her daughter Linda entered the waiting room almost shyly. Like her mother she had chosen clothes that were sober but not sombre. They hugged each other. It was hard to believe that Linda was forty-nine. You never think your children will grow old.

'I thought I was too early,' said Linda, dropping gratefully into the chair beside her mother. Her feet had been the despair and salvation of her chiropodist, in the days when she'd been able to afford a chiropodist.

'You are,' said Elizabeth. 'I was even earlier. I nearly didn't come in. I thought it'd look as if I'm expecting something and can't wait to lay my hands on it.'

'I thought the same,' admitted Linda.

'Then I thought, "What am I worrying about? Anybody who

knows me knows I'm not worried about what I get from Reggie."'

'Exactly. That's what I thought.'

Linda smiled. When she smiled she looked younger. Her round face had become somewhat gaunt since she'd been to Weightwatchers. She was one of those unfortunate women who put on weight easily and have to make a painful choice between the face and the body as they get older. She was trying blonde hair and wasn't yet happy with it.

The door opened and Joan Greengross, Reggie's former secretary, entered. She was dressed in red, as if she knew that, in Elizabeth's eyes, she had been a scarlet woman. Her hair was auburn now, but her legs still went on for ever, and there wasn't a spare ounce of flesh on her. At fifty-three she remained an attractive woman, and she knew it. She hadn't slept with Reggie often, but it hadn't been for want of trying.

'Hello,' she said. 'I seem to be awfully early. I didn't think there'd be anybody else here yet.'

She smiled. Elizabeth and Linda smiled in return, but I would be failing in my duty to you, dear reader, if I pretended that there was radiance in their smiles.

'I didn't want to get there too early,' said C.J., clinking whisky glasses with Jimmy in the cavernous, unlovely, suburban bar of the Coach and Horses. 'The early bird catches a cold.'

'Absolutely, C.J.,' said Jimmy, whose cheeks were raw with cold.

Tom raised his pint of real ale, but didn't go so far as to clink glasses.

'Not that I'm expecting anything,' said C.J.

'No, no, nor me,' said Jimmy and Tom in unison.

'But you can't help wondering, can you? One is human,' said C.J.

7

There was a brief silence, as if Tom and Jimmy were considering the proposition that C.J. was human.

They were seated at a bare wooden table in the furthest corner from the bar counter. They were the only customers. The barman had two teeth missing.

'I didn't realise you'd be here, C.J.,' said Tom.

'Well, I'm surprised. I didn't always think Reggie liked me,' answered C.J.

'Maybe he's left you something really humiliating.' There was a faintly malicious gleam in Tom's watery, weary eyes.

C.J. grimaced. 'Oh my God, I hadn't thought of that,' he said. The grimace grew worse. His face became contorted. He gasped with pain.

'Are you all right?' Jimmy asked anxiously.

'Yes.' C.J.'s face returned to normal. For a moment Jimmy and Tom had glimpsed an older, frailer man, but the spry seventy-two-year-old had soon returned. 'Yes, ticker's not too good. Nothing to worry about, though.'

The three men fell silent. Their silence clattered loudly through the noiseless bar, and Jimmy felt that he must speak.

'How's the housing market bearing up, Tom?' he ventured

'I haven't the faintest idea,' said Tom.

'What?'

'Wilmot and Pargetter made me redundant three months ago.'

'Don't believe it,' said Jimmy. 'Having me on.'

'I wish I was. They told me I was too old. "I'm only fifty-one," I said. "Really?" they said. "You look older. You don't fit our new thrusting image. These are hard times on the high street."'

'Arrogant bastards,' said Jimmy. 'Argued your case, I hope.'

'No. I said, "I couldn't work with you another day. You can stick your month's notice up your surprisingly spacious, conveniently located backside."'

'Oh dear. You've rather burnt your cakes, then,' said C.J.

'Yes, and not for the first time. My name's mud throughout the profession.' He shook his head sadly. His witty house ads had once, in gentler times, been the talk of the Thames Valley.

The conversation creaked to another halt. The bar smelt of stale beer, furniture polish and . . . something not quite definable. Maybe, thought Tom, the barman had farted, or they were cooking cottage pie upstairs.

'How's Linda?' asked C.J. suddenly, having at last remembered Tom's wife's name.

'I haven't the faintest idea,' said Tom.

'What?'

'I haven't spoken to her for seven years.'

'Oh, I am sorry,' said C.J.

'I'm not,' said Tom. 'I'm delighted.'

Jimmy lifted his glass, and found, to his surprise, since he couldn't remember drinking anything, that it was empty.

'My round,' he said. 'Slight snag. No dosh. Bit of a cock-up on the social security front.'

'Never mind,' said Tom, taking a long swig at his beer, much of which dripped down his grey beard, dislodging a crumb of recalcitrant toast. 'We should be off.' He stood up surprisingly energetically. 'You could do with a legacy, then, Jimmy?'

'We all could,' said C.J., sparing Jimmy the task of answering. 'Not that I'm counting my chickens before they come home to roost. Besides, I don't really want to benefit from Reggie's sad death.'

'Oh no, absolutely not,' thundered Tom and Jimmy hurriedly.

'On the other hand,' said C.J. as they walked to the door, 'there's no point in looking a gift horse in the bush.'

'Absolutely not, C.J.,' said Jimmy.

'I didn't get where I am today by looking gift horses in bushes.'

They didn't say goodbye to the barman, and the barman didn't say goodbye to them.

Joan had plonked herself into a chair opposite Elizabeth and Linda. She had done it instinctively, and now she wished that she hadn't. It looked confrontational. She didn't want to look confrontational. Not today.

'I feel a bit embarrassed, being here,' she said.

'Oh good,' said Elizabeth. Grief had brought a touch of fire to her personality.

'Mum!' protested Linda. 'It's not Joan's fault Daddy included her.'

'You're right,' said Elizabeth. 'Sorry, Joan. Besides, I should look on the bright side. He may have left me fifty thousand pounds and you his screwdrivers.'

In the pause that followed, Joan crossed her long legs, remembered how Reggie had loved her to cross her long legs, thought that the gesture might therefore be inappropriate, and uncrossed her legs again, attempting to make the gesture look natural, and failing. She felt that Elizabeth could read her every thought, and for an awful moment she feared that she was going to blush. Fifty-three years old, and still frightened of blushing. Would she ever achieve poise?

'How's Tom?' she asked, to break the silence.

'I've no idea. I haven't spoken to him for seven years,' said Linda.

'Oh, I am sorry.'

'I'm not. I'm thrilled.' Linda paused, enjoying Joan's discomfiture, then asked, 'How's work?'

'It isn't.' The bitterness showed in her voice as she added, 'For thirteen years I satisfied Mr McCrombie's every whim.'

She regretted the phrase instantly.

'I'm sure you did,' said Elizabeth drily.

'How does he reward my faithful service? Replaces me with a twenty-two-year-old bimbo. Good legs, lousy shorthand.'

Elizabeth tried not to look *too* pleased at this news, and the arrival of Doc Morrissey proved a welcome diversion for Joan.

Perhaps because he had always looked older than his years, the wizened old medico from Sunshine Desserts seemed to have aged less than the others, even though he was now quite bald. It was as if his looks had stood still for more than twenty years, and time had finally caught up with them in this, his seventy-fourth year.

'Hello.' He beamed at Joan. 'Well, this is a surprise.'

'It certainly is,' said Elizabeth. 'How are you, Doc?'

'Much better, thank you.'

'Oh dear,' said Linda. 'What's been the trouble?'

Even as she was asking it she realised that it was a silly question. Doc Morrissey had never known what was wrong with anybody, least of all with himself.

'I haven't a clue,' he said cheerily. 'Some virus, I suppose. Much easier being a doctor now than when I was practising. If you haven't a clue, you just say, "It's a virus." Anyway, rather foolishly, I took six lots of pills at once, and now I've no idea which were the ones that worked.'

He lowered himself stiffly into the chair next to Joan, trying not to make the choice look too deliberate, and fooling nobody. Forgetting for a moment that he was seventy-three, he gave Joan a cheery, frankly seductive smile.

'Do you remember at Sunshine Desserts I kept asking you if you were chesty?' Elizabeth and Linda could hear every word, although he spoke in little more than a whisper.

'You were a naughty boy.'

Joan wasn't offended. Doc Morrissey was too cheerfully frank about his randiness to be offensive. Nevertheless, she felt that she must administer a gentle rebuke.

'I wouldn't have come to you if I had been,' she said. 'You wouldn't have had a clue what was wrong.'

'No, but we could have had a lot of fun trying to find out.' Doc Morrissey laughed, thrilled to be alive and in company and still able to feel desire. Then contrition swept over him. 'I'm so sorry,' he said. 'My levity's completely inappropriate. Nerves, probably. Oh, not that I'm expecting anything.' He changed the subject rapidly, asking after Joan's second husband, Tony Webster, another former employee of C.J.'s at Sunshine Desserts. 'How's Tony?'

'I haven't the faintest idea,' said Joan. 'I haven't seen him for ten years.'

'Oh dear, I'm so sorry,' said Doc Morrissey, but his eyes gave the lie to his words. 'I suppose that's the danger of marrying a whiz-kid. He whizzes off.'

'To New Zealand, in his case,' said Joan. 'Was New Zealand ready for him, I ask.'

Next to arrive was Tony's closest colleague from those old exotic ice-cream days, David Harris-Jones, closely followed by his wife Prue. At fifty, David had cautiously thinning hair with grey streaks that could have made some men look distinguished. It was impossible to tell whether Prue's grey streaks were natural or part of her ensemble, along with her mauve sweater that matched David's perfectly. She had attractive but sensible legs and a sensible but not particularly attractive, rather chubby face. The Harris-Jones's eyes flicked nervously round the room, and they said 'Hello, everyone' in unison.

'Well, at least you two are still together,' said Elizabeth.

'Oh yes. Togetherness is our middle name,' they chorused.

They sat, next to each other of course, at the end of the room, facing the magazine table.

'Elizabeth,' said David, leaning forward nervously. 'I must say that . . . well . . . we were surprised . . . well, very surprised

12

'. . . to . . . er . . . and we don't expect . . . er . . . well, anyway, I thought I'd better say that.'

'I'm glad you did,' said Elizabeth, drily but affectionately.

The clock on the wall above the table showed 11.26. A silence developed. It was one of those awful silences that nobody can break without revealing that they have been the first to crack.

'Well, isn't this nice?' said David Harris-Jones. 'All gathered together like this. Almost like old times. Super.'

Nobody replied. David Harris-Jones wore a fixed, strained smile, and fought against the need to apologise.

'Sorry,' he said.

The door burst open, and C.J. entered, with Jimmy and Tom in his wake.

Tom glared at Linda. Linda glared at Tom.

'Morning, awl, as the leather-worker said to his tool.' Jimmy's words caused bewilderment on all sides and horror on several. 'An awl is a tool in leather-making,' he explained. 'It's used for boring.'

'No comment,' commented Tom.

'So I said, "Hello, awl," instead of, "Hello, all." A little play on words. Lost when you can't see the spelling. Realise that now. Just an attempt to lighten an embarrassing situation. Not that the situation's embarrassing, of course. On balance probably a mistake all round. Joke withdrawn.'

Stunned silence followed the making and withdrawing of Jimmy's gallant but doomed joke. In the silence, Jimmy made a move to sit next to Linda, remembered that he had secretly committed incest with her on more than one occasion, and veered away to sit next to David Harris-Jones, with whom he had never committed anything.

'Sixteen by thirteen,' said Tom suddenly.

Everyone looked at him in surprise.

'Sorry,' he said. 'Once an estate agent, always an estate agent.'

13

C.J. plonked himself down between Joan and Prue.

'So, how are you, C.J.?' asked Joan.

'Well, we're all getting older, aren't we?' C.J. realised that this did not sound gracious. 'Except you. You're looking lovely. Absolutely lovely. You're the exception that proves the pudding. No, my ticker's a bit dicky, but mustn't grumble, though I do.'

'Let's hope Reggie doesn't give you a nasty shock, then.'

'Yes. Quite.' C.J. made a noise like a laryngitic hyena. 'Absolutely.'

'Seat next to Linda, Tom,' sang out Jimmy.

'I'd rather stand, thank you, Jimmy,' said Tom.

'Ah!' Realising that he had been tactless, Jimmy turned to David and Prue Harris-Jones. 'How's young Reggie?' he dredged from the murky depths of his mind. David and Prue had called their boy Reggie in tribute to Reggie, and he was Reggie's godson. 'What is he, must be well into his twenties now? How tempus fooges.'

'He left school at fifteen,' said David.

'He ran away from home at sixteen,' said Prue.

'He got a gypsy girl in trouble at seventeen,' said David.

'He lives with her in a lay-by on the A18,' said Prue.

'Sorry I asked,' said Jimmy.

The clock had reached 11.30. The tension rose.

Tom leant over and spoke to C.J.

'If I'd known you were coming, I'd have brought a bottle of my passion-fruit wine. I'd have valued your opinion.'

'I've no need to taste your wine to give an opinion on it, Tom.'

'Oh! It's kind of you to say so, C.J.'

C.J. stood up, offered Tom his seat, and moved over to sit beside Linda. When Tom took the seat, Linda glared at him, and he pretended not to notice.

14

Jimmy leaned over to C.J. and continued his doomed attempt to lighten the atmosphere with small talk.

'How's Mrs C.J.?'

'Very well. She lives in Luxembourg. I live in Virginia Water. That way our marriage works perfectly.'

'Ah! All-hands-to-pump-of-passion-at-weekends type of touch. Down-to-it-moment-plane-has-landed kind of crack. With you.'

'Oh, no. We never meet at all.'

'Ah. Sorry I asked. Bit of a cock-up on the conversation front.' Jimmy turned towards David Harris-Jones in search of a safer subject. 'How's work going?'

'It isn't,' said David Harris-Jones.

Jimmy closed his eyes. The old soldier was finally prepared to admit defeat.

David Harris-Jones, now launched on his story, expanded on his disaster.

'I rejoined the family firm in Haverfordwest. The . . . er . . . the job wasn't particularly . . . well, it was a bit . . . er . . . but it kept the wolf from the . . . er . . . it was in . . . er . . .'

'Communications,' said Prue.

'Yes. Then the firm was swallowed up by a conglomerate and . . . er . . . they said they thought I . . . er . . . I rather lacked . . . er . . . well I suppose . . . er . . .'

'Dynamism,' suggested Doc Morrissey.

'Yes.'

'Is this the story of our times?' said Linda.

'Don't say you've lost your job as well!' exclaimed Joan.

'Oh no. No. No, I've never even got to the stage of having one to lose. By the time I'd brought up Adam and Jocasta *on my own* . . .' She glared at Tom, who glared at the clock, which said 11.33. '. . . everyone said I was too old even to start.'

'How *are* Adam and Jocasta?' enquired Joan.

'Meant to ask, didn't dare, for fear of more bad news,' said Jimmy.

'Well, it's a pity you didn't ask, because they're fine,' said Linda. 'Jocasta's touring Asia, and Adam's working for the BBC.'

'They're neither of them bringing much money in then,' said C.J. 'Bad luck.'

'Seems as though the lot of us could do with some lolly, then,' said Jimmy. The very worst *faux pas* are those that everyone else is thinking but not saying. Jimmy almost blushed. 'Sorry. Bad taste. Black mark. Shut up.'

'The door opened, and they all half-rose, expecting the summons at last.

A little man with big stick-out ears entered the waiting room.

'Good morning,' he said, sounding as though he had a mouth full of pebbles.

'Morning,' said Doc Morrissey.

Seeing that there were no spare seats, the new arrival went to the table and picked up a magazine at random.

'Nine's company, ten's a crowd,' whispered C. J. to Prue.

'How many more people has Reggie invited?' whispered Doc Morrissey to Joan. 'It will make smaller shares all round.'

'Not that you're expecting anything,' whispered Joan to Doc Morrissey.

'Who's he?' whispered Linda to Elizabeth.

'I've never seen him before in my life,' whispered Elizabeth to Linda. 'Reggie's probably asked hundreds of people. His last great joke.' She cleared her throat theatrically and spoke to the new arrival. 'Excuse me . . . er . . . may I ask you how you knew my husband? I'm Elizabeth Perrin, by the way.'

There was a pause. The new arrival was glancing through an article on kitchens entitled, 'Small needn't mean dull.' As the pause lengthened, it dawned on him that Elizabeth had been speaking to him.

16

'Oh, sorry, were you speaking to me?' he said. 'No, I don't think I did know your husband.'

'You haven't had a letter about his will, then?' asked Elizabeth.

'Oh, no, no. No, I just have an appointment with Mr Venison.'

Now that he was no longer a threat to their inheritance, they all vied with one another to offer him their seats.

'Oh, no, thank you,' he said. 'I can't stand sitting when I'm waiting. I get tense. Coincidentally, I am also here in connection with a will. I'm *making* my will. It's rather amusing really. I'm leaving all my money to the Battersea Dogs' Home.'

The amusement at this intention was entirely confined to the newcomer.

'I just wish I could live to see the horror on the faces of my grasping relatives when they find out.'

He laughed heartily, and he laughed alone.

2   *The Reading of the Will*

'I'm so sorry to have kept you waiting.'

C.J. permitted himself a slight smile. He had always made a point of keeping people waiting, and he was sure that Ms Geraldine Hackstraw also did so. Pretty stunning woman, though. What? Forty-eight? Golden hair, attractively fleshy and eminently kissable legs, full lips, grey eyes as clear as consommé. Stop it, C.J. You didn't get where you are today by allowing your concentration to be diverted by golden hair, eminently kissable legs, full lips and grey eyes as clear as consommé.

The nine people who might hear something to their advantage in the next few minutes settled themselves into chairs facing Ms Hackstraw's neat rosewood desk. David and Prue Harris-Jones sat together as usual, and Tom and Linda took great care to be as far away from each other as possible.

'I'm sorry it's so crowded in here,' said Ms Hackstraw, making a minimal adjustment to one of the two photographs which stood in silver frames on her desk. The photograph showed a white-haired rustic couple standing outside a simple cottage. They weren't actually her parents – she'd bought the picture from a bric-a-brac shop in Petworth – but it did no harm to give the impression that one came from humble, honest stock.

The other photograph was of her husband, from whom she was divorced, but he had a strong face and his presence saved her from considerable sexual harrassment.

18

'Not at all,' said Elizabeth. 'I think we're all pleased to come.'

'I didn't get where I am today without being pleased to come,' said C.J.

They introduced themselves to Ms Hackstraw briefly. 'Elizabeth Perrin, his widow.'

'Linda Patterson, daughter.'

'Charles Jefferson, was his boss, then his employee, then his colleague, then his boss.'

'Doc Morrissey, former medico at Sunshine Desserts.'

'David Harris-Jones, long-term employee.'

'Prue Harris-Jones, David's long-term and adoring wife.' Squeeze of Harris-Jones hands.

'Joan Greengross, Reggie's secretary of long standing.'

This was irresistible to Elizabeth. 'And blessedly short lying down,' she added.

Ms Hackstraw gave her a severe look.

'Tom Patterson. *Ex*-son-in-law. *Ex*-estate agent. *Ex*-asperated by all this drama.'

'Major James Anderson, Harrow (Expelled), Queen's Own Berkshire Light Infantry (Forcibly retired), Founder of Private Army (Disbanded after trusted colleague vamoosed with takings), Managing Director of Narrow Boat Hire Firm (Bankrupt after another trusted colleague ditto), first wife Sheila (Deserted), second wife Lettuce (Squashed by juggernaut).'

'Thank you.' Ms Hackstraw, who was wearing a beige suit so tight-fitting that it was sexy as well as sensible, gave Jimmy a rather wild look, as if she could scarcely believe that one man could pack so much misfortune into his life. It made her one failed marriage seem a mere trifle. Her husband's strong face was deceptive. His morals, income and sperm count had all proved to be lower than expected, and she had left him after seventeen childless years. Jimmy's failures were on an altogether more heroic scale, and indeed, it struck her that there was something heroic about the sadness in his battered old face. She turned her husband's photograph away from her, and picked up Reggie's last will and testament. 'It is now my duty to read Mr Perrin's will to you.'

Slowly, Ms Hackstraw opened the document. The tension was palpable. What last trick would Reggie have up his sleeve?

'"I, Reginald Iolanthe Perrin,"' read Ms Hackstraw solemnly, '"being of sound mind, or as sound mind as ever I was, request Ms Hackstraw, or whoever replaces her in the event of her predeceasing me . . ."' Ms Hackstraw looked up from the document and smiled. '. . . which I haven't, I'm glad to say.' She caught sight of Elizabeth's face. 'Well, not glad. I certainly didn't want Mr Perrin to predecease me, and I'm sure Mrs Perrin didn't. Let's just say . . .'

'Abandon ship,' thundered Jimmy.

'I beg your pardon?' Ms Hackstraw was astounded.

'Rather digging your own grave there,' said Jimmy. 'Oops, sorry, inappropriate metaphor, given the circs. Awkward moment, thought I'd save you by tactful intervention. Tricky wallah, tact. Never quite got the hang of the cove. Interruption over. Carry on.'

'Thank you, Major Anderson,' said Ms Geraldine Hackstraw frostily. She resumed her reading. '"... request Ms Hackstraw to read out this, my last will and testament, in the presence of those persons expressly summoned hereto, to whit, you lot."'

Elizabeth smiled wryly.

'"Battersea Dogs' Home is a splendid organisation."'

Nine people tried not to look horrified. Nine people failed. The snow had begun to fall again, large lazy flakes falling slowly past Ms Hackstraw's immaculately cleaned window like tiny white parachutes.

'"But to leave one's money to it would be a cliché, and to me clichés are like a red rag to a Trojan horse, as C.J. might say."'

20

'It's true,' said C.J. 'I might. It's a failing of mine. I'm drawn to clichés like moths to the water.'

'"I would prefer to leave my money to more original causes . . . to form a society to provide free psychiatric help for the guilt-ridden overpaid bosses of privatised industries, to expand the legal aid system so that it can reach the needy as well as the rich . . ."'

Despite their distress at the thought of money being left to any cause other than themselves, the nine listeners all smiled just a little. It was so typically Reggie, and eight out of the nine of them realised that, to different extents and in different ways, they had loved him.

'". . . and to provide minibuses for the Lords Taverners, so that rich, privileged children can take depressed, underpaid English cricketers to the seaside. I *could* leave money to causes such as these, but I won't."'

They all tried to hide their relief.

'"I leave all my worldly possessions . . ."' Ms Hackstraw couldn't resist a tiny, exquisite hesitation. '". . . to my dear, beloved, lovely wife Elizabeth . . ."'

'Oh!' gasped Elizabeth.

'Hear, hear,' said Jimmy bravely. 'Well, she deserves it. Good girl, Big Sis, and not one to abandon an old soldier in difficulties.'

Ms Hackstraw, who had been waiting patiently, resumed her reading.

'"And to her intellectually deprived, emotionally disadvantaged brother . . ."'

'Oh! Oh, I say,' spluttered Jimmy. 'Thought you'd finished. Well, don't much like the description, but, have to admit, glad of the dosh.'

'"Who will no doubt need it, as there will no doubt have been a cock-up on the pensions front . . ."'

'Got it in one,' said Jimmy. 'Must be psychic.'

'He hardly needs to be psychic to predict that,' said Tom.

'Tom!' said Linda.

'Linda! You spoke to me!' said Tom.

'Well, there's no need to be rude to Jimmy,' said Linda. 'He can't help what he is.'

'Steady on, Linda!' Jimmy's outrage was good-humoured. He was thrilled about his money. 'Anyway, the rest of you, bound to be disappointed, bad luck, but don't worry, all requests for help considered.'

'"And to my dear, dear daughter . . ."' Ms Hackstraw leapt in while there was a chance.

'Oh!' Jimmy had gone quite white. 'There's more. Oh, Lord! Wrong end of stick.'

Ms Hackstraw smiled faintly.

'". . . daughter Linda,"' she continued, '"who has supported me through thick and even thicker, and who will need all she can get after her marriage to that dreadful ass Tom . . ."'

Tom leapt to his feet.

'I see,' he said. 'I've been brought here to be insulted. Well, I've grown too old for that, and I'm off.'

'Sit down, Mr Patterson.' Ms Hackstraw's voice had steely authority. Even C.J. flinched. Doc Morrissey felt a warmth where his erection would have been in palmier days.

'What?' gasped Tom.

'You have to stay,' explained Ms Hackstraw calmly. 'Nobody gets anything unless everybody stays.'

'Oh God!' said Tom, running his hand through his greying hair. 'Bloody hell! Bloody Reggie!'

He sat down.

Ms Hackstraw resumed the even tenor of her reading.

'"And to that dreadful ass Tom. I love him dearly, and was sorry his marriage broke up . . ."'

'Oh!' said Tom. 'Oh! Well, I didn't expect . . . that's very generous. I'm sorry if I was a bit ungracious.'

22

'"It's not his fault he was born a dreadful ass."' Ms Hackstraw broke off her reading to apologise. 'I'm very sorry, Mr Patterson, but I have to read it all. Those are my instructions.'

'It's all right, Ms Hackstraw,' said Tom, rather grandly, rather expansively, now that he was an heir to Reggie's estate. 'I understand about instructions. I too was "in the professions".'

'"In the professions"! Listen to you, Tom,' said Linda.

'You're speaking to me again!' said Tom. 'Is this a new start?'

'Do you want a new start?'

'No.'

'Well then.'

'Shut up!' David Harris-Jones astounded everybody, not least himself. 'Well . . . I mean . . .' he explained. 'I want to hear who else . . . I mean *if* anybody else . . . and if so, who, has been left what. Sorry.'

'Darling!' said Prue. 'You were almost on the verge of being masterful for a moment there.'

'I was, wasn't I?' said David Harris-Jones. 'Super.'

'Do shut up,' said Jimmy.

'That's what *I* was telling people to do,' said David Harris-Jones in an injured tone. 'What's the point of telling me to shut up when I'm telling other people to shut up?'

Ms Hackstraw had put Reggie's will down on her desk while all this was going on. My fees, calculated by the minute, will be coming out of the estate, so I don't mind how long I wait, her expression seemed to say.

The realisation of this may have dawned on everyone else, because silence had finally fallen. Ms Hackstraw picked up the document and began to read again.

'"To Doc Morrissey, who as he gets older will no doubt need to buy more and more medical books to find out what's wrong with him . . ."'

'Nice one,' said the retired medico, whose practice had never

23

made him perfect. 'Always had a sense of humour, dear generous old Reggie.'

'"To my dear secretary Joan, who had so much to put up with from me, and did so much for me . . ."'

'Oh, I wouldn't say that,' demurred Joan.

'I would,' muttered Elizabeth with feeling.

'"To C.J. I hated him once, but time is a great healer . . ."'

'Absolutely. Well said, Reggie,' said C.J.

'"And last, but least, to David Harris-Jones and his wife Prue. I have only one word to describe my relationship with David and Prue."'

'Super,' said David Harris-Jones.

'Precisely. "To them all I leave my worldly goods to be divided . . ."' Ms Hackstraw cradled her moment of power briefly. '". . .equally . . ."'

'Good Lord,' said C.J.

'Equally!' said Doc Morrissey.

'Shame. Scandal. Employees getting as much as relatives,' said Jimmy. 'Oh, not thinking about myself. Thinking of Big Sis.'

'Thank you, Jimmy,' said Elizabeth. 'As usual, well meant. As usual, do shut up.' She smiled at him lovingly, to take the sting out of her words. 'Dignity, Jimmy. Dignity.' She turned to Ms Hackstraw and smiled sweetly. 'Equally. I think that's eminently fair, don't you, Ms Hackstraw?'

'Well, I think . . .' began David Harris-Jones. 'I think . . . well, of course we won't say "no", it would be . . . and it is very . . . very . . . but Prue and I getting two bites at the . . . I think . . . well, it is a bit . . . well, anyway, I've said what I wanted to say.'

'And as David says it was Reggie's wish,' said Prue almost hastily, 'and we should respect his wishes by accepting gratefully, embarrassed though we are.'

'"Counting David and Prue as one unit,"' continued Ms Hackstraw with barely-concealed relish, her grey eyes gleaming,

24

'"which is only correct, as the self-satisfied twerps are always telling us that togetherness is their middle name."'

The snow had stopped. A watery sun filtered shyly into the office, and the snow was melting rapidly on the roofs opposite.

'Well, that's it, then,' said Elizabeth with dignity. 'Thank you, Ms Hackstraw. So, he's divided his money among us all. Shame on those who thought he might have some last trick up his sleeve.'

'"The monies to be dependent on one condition being fulfilled."' Ms Hackstraw dropped her bombshell quite gently. If only all work were as pleasant as this, she thought.

'Ah!' said Doc Morrissey pessimistically, writing off his chances already.

'Condition, eh?' said C.J. gloomily.

'Good old Reggie,' said Joan. 'It would almost be disappointing if there wasn't a sting in the tail.'

'Silence in the ranks,' commanded Jimmy, and for just a fraction of a second the stifling office became the bright, breezy parade ground of his dreams. 'All agog. Well, I'm agog anyway. Carry on, that woman.'

Ms Hackstraw resumed, very quietly, so that they had to hang on to her every word.

'"One very small condition. Each and every one of you must completely satisfy Ms Hackstraw that you have done something that is totally and utterly absurd."'

'That's absurd,' said Tom.

'"Precisely, Tom." It says that here. He knows you well.'

Tom flushed with anger. His emotions were very close to the surface that morning. He fought to calm himself.

'"I know that this condition will cause you all consternation . . ."' read Ms Hackstraw.

'Absolutely,' said C.J. 'I didn't get where I am today by being absurd.'

'I'm just not an absurdity person,' said Tom.

'Oh, I don't know,' murmured Linda, not quite under her breath.

'Please, everybody,' said Elizabeth. 'Reggie had many friends who could have been invited today. Has it struck you why *we* have been chosen?'

'Yes, it has,' said Joan quietly.

'Oh, it has, has it?' said Elizabeth waspishly. '*Do* tell us.'

'Absolutely,' thundered Jimmy enthusiastically. 'All agog again. Well, I'm agog again. Just as agog as I was before, possibly even agogger.'

Everyone looked at Joan, even Ms Hackstraw, who was fingering the photograph of the couple who weren't her parents. The brief sun disappeared suddenly, as if Joan was expected to shed only darkness.

'Well,' said Joan, undeterred. 'We are the people who were closest to Reggie and supported him, in his own words, through thick and even thicker, through the projects that were closest to his heart – his rebellion at Sunshine Desserts, his Grot shops, his community for the middle classes. He wants us, by being absurd, to make our individual memorials to those absurd things we helped him do. He wants us to prove ourselves worthy of him.'

'Absolutely,' said Elizabeth. 'Thank you, Joan. That was beautifully put. No, really, thank you.' She began to cry. 'Oh dear.'

'Oh dear.' Joan had started to cry as well.

Soon Linda was also crying, and even Doc Morrissey wiped away a surreptitious tear.

'This man walked into a bar,' said Jimmy. '"Ouch," he cried. It was an iron bar.'

Astonishment froze tears in an instant.

'Joke, old I know, but all I could think of off the cuff, emotional tension for the relief of,' explained Jimmy.

26

'You shouldn't be frightened of emotional moments, Jimmy. They can be beautiful,' said Tom.

'Now he learns it,' said Linda.

'Well, yes, I admit it. I've learnt from my mistakes,' said Tom.

'I see,' snorted Linda angrily. 'I was one of your mistakes. Terrific.'

'There is still quite a lot to read,' said Ms Hackstraw quietly, and they all looked at her guiltily. They had almost forgotten that she was there.

'"I know this condition will cause you consternation, but you must agree that it is entirely appropriate, since the money you will be receiving will have come very largely from the profits and eventual sale of my Grot shops, sums which have been wisely invested since the late seventies in the Channel Isles, the Isle of Man, Bermuda, Switzerland, Liechtenstein, in fact almost everywhere except Lloyds of London. Who's a shrewdie, then?"'

'I didn't know he'd done all that,' said Elizabeth.

'"I'm sorry, Elizabeth, that I never told you. I didn't want us to live on that money. Life wouldn't have been a challenge any more, and Grot was never intended to make money anyway."'

'Why not give it all away to charity, then?' asked C.J.

'"Why didn't I give it all away to charity, then, I hear you cry, probably asked by somebody who never gave a penny to charity in his life. Because I didn't dare. It was my safety net. I'm human, and therefore I'm weak. The decision as to whether you have been sufficiently absurd rests entirely with . . ."' She hesitated. A faint flush crept over her cheeks. David Harris-Jones thought it delicious, until Prue saw him thinking it was delicious, after which he didn't think it delicious at all. '". . . the beautiful Ms Hackstraw, whose . . ."' Again, Ms Hackstraw hesitated. '". . . cool exterior no doubt hides a seething, passionate nature."' Her disconcertingly penetrating eyes briefly met

Tom's brown, bloodshot ones. Tom gasped. '"She has to read this out, although it embarrasses her – while also secretly pleasing her, because she's quite vain – otherwise all the money *will* go to the Battersea Dogs' Home."' There was the faintest trace of perspiration on Ms Hackstraw's high brow. '"By gamely reading it out, I hope she has shown you that she is not to be feared as your ultimate judge. She will expect regular progress reports and evidence of absurdity achieved. This is the last will, testament and commentary on the absurdity of life of Reginald Iolanthe Perrin."'

There was a long pause. A violent screech of brakes reminded them that there were problems outside their own lives.

As so often, David Harris-Jones proved to be the first not to be able to endure the silence.

'Is it . . . I mean, we didn't expect anything, anyway, so I'm not trying to . . . but would there be any chance of . . . er . . . proving him to be . . . of unsound mind?' he asked.

'What do you think, Doc?' asked David's adoring wife.

'Oh, lorks.' Doc Morrissey waved his hands about, in mock despair and ignorance. 'Haven't the foggiest. Not my area.'

'Elizabeth once asked me to probe subtly whether Reggie was bonkers,' said Jimmy. 'Probed subtly. Came to conclusion he was as sane as I am.'

'There shouldn't be much trouble in proving him mad, then,' said Tom.

'Tom!' Elizabeth was shocked. 'And you, Jimmy. And David and Prue. I'm ashamed of you. My Reggie has made his wishes clear. We should respect those wishes.'

'Not speaking for ourselves, of course,' said Prue. 'We weren't expecting anything. But as a matter of interest . . . I mean, you know, when all's said and done it must be a matter of general interest . . . and I don't know whether you can tell us or not anyway . . . but . . .'

'Oh, darling, do spit it out,' said David Harris-Jones.

Prue gave him an ironic look. 'No,' she said, 'I just wondered
. . . have we any idea how much money there is?'

'It'd be unprofessional of me to suggest an actual figure, but
at a conservative estimate, and without all the information
being in . . .' Ms Hackstraw relished her last great moment of
that memorable morning. How dull lunch would seem by
comparison. '. . . and entirely unofficially, I couldn't be held to
this if it proved wrong, but I'd say it was unlikely to be far short
of a million pounds.'

'A million pounds,' echoed Elizabeth in astonishment.

'Each.'

'Each??' exclaimed Linda.

C.J. fell to the floor and lay there lifeless, a frail, white-haired
old man.

'Oh, my God,' said Prue. 'His heart.'

'Doc? What do we do?' cried Joan.

'Oh, lorks,' said Doc Morrissey.

Ms Hackstraw reached for the telephone. Doc Morrissey
bent over C.J., feeling his pulse. Everyone else except Ms
Hackstraw gathered round behind him, willing him to do the
right thing.

C.J. opened his eyes, saw the wizened old doctor, and closed
them. Then he opened them again, and frowned as if his worst
fears had been confirmed.

'Go away, Doc,' he said. 'I want to live. I've just come into a
lot of money.'

'Yes, so have I, but are you all right?' asked Doc Morrissey
urgently. 'You've just had a heart attack.'

'I haven't had a heart attack, you stupid moron. I fainted,'
said C.J. 'Big sums of money always have that effect on me.'

Ms Hackstraw put the phone down and hurried from the
room.

'Been thinking,' said Jimmy, while she was gone. 'Got to go
for it, million pounds and all that.'

'I suppose I could learn to be an absurdity person,' said Tom doubtfully.

Ms Hackstraw returned with a glass of water. C.J. downed it in two luxuriant gulps. His authority began to return.

'I didn't get where I am today by being frightened of being absurd,' he said bravely.

'Super,' said David Harris-Jones.

3   The Absurdity
of Being Absurd

David and Prue Harris-Jones emerged from their boxy little house on their boxy little housing estate near Haverfordwest, with its cheap, flaking weather-boarding, and scuttled anxiously and uncomfortably through the warm, wet, Welsh air towards the integral garage. David was dressed as Long John Silver, with a tricorn hat, red velveteen jacket and stuffed parrot, all hired from Evans Fancy Dress Hire. The warm, wet wind ruffled his thinning hair and rippled through the parrot's feathers. He had pins and needles in his strapped foot. Prue was dressed as Nell Gwynn, in a lace bodice with a waist too tight for her motherly figure, and with a Jaffa orange stuffed into each cup of her bra. She looked acutely self-conscious as she bounced to the garage, as if horribly aware that despite the Jaffas she still looked irredeemably sensible.

They needn't have looked anxious or self-conscious. A herring gull was the only living creature to witness their attempt at absurdity.

As David had a leg strapped up, Prue drove. She nosed the rusting Ford out into Oak Spinney Close, turned right into Meadow Glade, and right again into Pond Lane. There were no spinneys or meadows or ponds anywhere near, but the houses fetched more money if the neighbourhood sounded rural. Now that *was* absurd.

There were already several cars in the car park of the Leek and Laverbread, and David suddenly remembered that there

31

was a rugby international that day, Wales against Canada, or Romania, somebody they had a chance of beating anyway, and the whole crowd would be gathering to watch it in the upstairs room.

'Oh God,' he said. 'Alun'll be here.'

'So what?' said Prue, reversing nervously into a space between a Renault and a Saab.

'Well, he might give me a job.'

'He never will. He's all talk.'

'Well, I know he seems all talk but he did say he'd bear me in mind.'

David Harris-Jones got out of the car with some difficulty. A small boy in a neighbouring garden watched him incredulously.

'He'll never employ me if I make a berk of myself as Long John Silver.'

'Getting cold feet, are you?' said Prue.

'Well, a cold foot.' David began to hop painfully towards the pub. The pins and needles were excruciating. Alun's Mondeo turned in to the car park at that moment, and David ducked behind their car hastily, pulling Prue down beside him.

'A million pounds, David,' whispered Prue.

'Well, exactly,' he whispered. 'I just don't believe we can qualify for a million pounds as easily as this. I think we should go and ask Ms Hackstraw what sort of thing she'd regard as sufficiently absurd. I'm not opting out. I'm just being sensible.'

'Can one be sensible about being absurd?' asked Prue.

'Well, maybe one can. Would it upset you awfully, darling, if we just went home?'

'No, I'd be thrilled.'

They stood up, stretched, and struggled back into the car. The little boy hurried inside to tell his mum, who smacked him for making things up again.

Prue drove along Pond Lane, turned left into Meadow Glade, and left again into Oak Spinney Close.

They scuttled through the warm, wet, Welsh air from the integral garage to the house. Not even a seagull saw them.

David released his strapped leg and winced as the blood began to flow. Prue deposited her Jaffas in the fruit bowl they had bought in Honfleur. They changed into fawn trousers and pink sweaters, put the hired costumes back in the boxes they had come in, had a cup of coffee, made a shopping list, went to the supermarket, and were happy.

'Do sit down, Mr Jefferson,' said Ms Hackstraw briskly.

C.J. seated himself at the other side of her desk, and gave what he hoped was a relaxed smile. It wasn't. He ran his hand over his pate, as if brushing down the hair he no longer had.

'May I call you Geraldine?' he asked.

Ms Hackstraw widened her astonishingly limpid grey eyes a fraction.

'By all means, but what am I to call you?' she asked. 'I can hardly call you C.J. if you are calling me Geraldine.'

C.J. became unbearably coy and arch. 'My intimates have been known to refer to me as Bunny,' he said.

'Good Lord.' Ms Hackstraw tried not to smile. 'Good Lord. Well, Bunny, what is it you want to see me about?'

'Will you marry me, Geraldine?'

Geraldine Hackstraw's chest heaved, and C.J. was suddenly deeply conscious of her breasts.

'You're a very beautiful woman,' he said.

She smiled and C.J. could have sworn that she almost blushed.

'I'd be failing in my duty to myself, both as a woman and a lawyer, if I didn't remind you that you're married,' she said.

'In name only. We never got round to divorcing. I didn't get where I am today by putting money in the hands of over-paid . . .' He stopped hurriedly.

33

'Lawyers?'

'Yes. So sorry. That was crass.'

'Yes.'

'I can be crass. Geraldine, you are amazingly lovely, and what's a bit of bigamy between friends?'

'Oh,' said Geraldine Hackstraw flatly. The light in her eyes dimmed. 'This is your idea of being absurd.'

'Yes.'

She wouldn't have believed that she could feel so angry, so used. She looked at C.J. fiercely, hoping that he couldn't spot her fury. She needn't have worried. He was far too insensitive to other people's feelings to notice anything.

'Do you really believe that you can ask one absurd question and then claim a million pounds?' she asked. 'Do you really think it's as easy as that?'

'Well, I . . . I hadn't really thought.'

'No, you hadn't, had you? I am the guardian of Mr Perrin's reputation for serious absurdity, Bunny.'

'You're a hard woman.'

'Not at all. In any case, your idea isn't anything like absurd enough,' said Ms Hackstraw. 'All right. Bigamy, yes, but my marrying you . . . does that really strike you as totally and utterly absurd?'

'Yes. I'm an old man.'

'Not old. Mature. Ripe.'

'You make me sound like a cheese. I didn't get where I am today by sounding like a cheese.'

'You were once the big cheese at Sunshine Desserts. You were pretty big, I understand, at Amalgamated Aerosols. You still have an aura of power. Power is sexy. You have money. Money is sexy. Money is very sexy.'

'I don't have a lot of money,' spluttered C.J.

Geraldine Hackstraw hitched her sensible brown skirt a little higher up her undeniably attractive, excitingly fleshy leg.

34

'You'll have a million pounds if you do something sufficiently absurd, Bunny,' she said. 'And I am the final arbiter of that. I think we should take the idea seriously. I'd quite like to marry a very rich man.' There was a humorous gleam in her eye now. C.J. didn't like it. 'You should see Mr Venison, he's our divorce specialist, and in the meantime I think you should ask me out to dinner tonight.'

'Oh. Er . . . oh gosh.'

'You're shy now that it's real.'

'Shy? Me, shy?' C.J. laughed like a goat with a hernia. 'May I take you out to dinner tonight, Geraldine?' he asked stiffly.

'That would be delightful, Bunny,' said Ms Geraldine Hackstraw with a smile.

The spears of rain were almost horizontal in the wind. Empty crisp packets and Macdonald's bags bowled across the tarmac. The crowds were sparse at Speakers' Corner.

Joan Greengross climbed on to the soap box slowly. She was shaking with fear and embarrassment. She had a deep sense of her own futility. She was wearing strappy sandals with high stiletto heels. The sexy effect of her shapely ankles was somewhat marred by her long, green raincoat. One or two people stopped to listen to her, others scurried past, heads down.

She forced herself to begin.

'Nudity is wonderful,' she shouted. 'Nudity is beautiful. We shouldn't be frightened of our bodies. We shouldn't be frightened of other people's bodies either.'

She didn't know why, but images of concentration camps, of vicious tribal conflict in Africa, of the ruthless Russian destruction of Grosny, of the stink of death in the refugee camps, came into her mind.

'We should all set aside one day each week for nudity.' She

ploughed on doggedly, her words torn from her by the wind. 'And it should be a different day for everybody, so that, in every bus and tube train, one in seven people will always be naked.'

Oh, God forgive me, if you exist, for this frivolity. What she was doing was so pathetic, in the light of man's inhumanity to man, man's inhumanity to woman, man's inhumanity to children, man's inhumanity to calves, man's inhumanity to everything weaker than himself. So much for love of the underdog, she thought.

'So many people are unhinged by nudity. They undress people in their minds. They expose themselves. Compulsory nudity would wipe away the need for exposing oneself in a flash.'

A theme-park designer from Dorchester laughed at her unfortunate choice of phrase. She didn't mind. She was warming to her theme. Reggie really believed in the value of absurdity. He really believed that the world was a less safe place because adults invariably lost the sense of the absurd which they had as children.

'Would the Italians have gone to war for Mussolini if they'd regularly seen his private parts dangling in the breeze?' she thundered. 'Would Michael Portillo strike fear into our hearts if we'd all seen his bottom? Would we feel as bad about our bodies if we could see that other people's are even worse? Off with your clothes!'

A gust of wind, which might almost have heard her words, caught her raincoat and sent it billowing out behind her, revealing her long naked legs and the frilly French knickers which were all she was wearing underneath. The theme-park designer fainted, and a sauna salesman from Helsinki called out, 'Why are you wearing your raincoat, then?'

The whole edifice came crumbling down. Reggie believed. She didn't. She was being absurd as a stunt in the hope of qualifying for a million pounds. She hadn't even the courage to admit that she'd worn the raincoat because her nerve had failed her.

'Because it's raining,' she said.

'Will you marry me, Geraldine?' asked Doc Morrissey.

Ms Hackstraw smiled indulgently. This time she was keeping her emotions well in check. And yet . . . she liked Doc Morrissey. She could imagine wanting to mother him, and, oh God, how she longed to mother somebody, how she had to stop herself attempting to mother Mr Lovelace, who didn't clean his fingernails properly, and Mr Venison, whose shoe-laces kept coming undone.

'This is your attempt to be absurd, is it?' she said.

'Yes,' said the wizened balding medico. 'Uttery absurd, isn't it, you and me?'

'Not nearly absurd enough,' said Geraldine Hackstraw.

'What?'

'I think you're kind.'

'Oh!'

'I think you're gentle.'

'Oh!!'

'I think you have a warm heart.'

'Oh!!!'

'I think you and I could have nice times together.'

'Oh!!!!'

'I think you should invite me out to dinner tonight.'

'Oh!!!!!'

Jimmy was wearing a knee-length pink dress, a shimmering green blouse, high-heeled shoes and a fetching little black hat. Overall, it cannot be said that the effect was truly fetching.

He had tried the second-hand clothes on himself.

'Cousin in question, built very much like me, poor woman,'

he had told the surprised proprietress of Barely Used of
Blotchley.

As he turned the corner of Swindon Road, he came face to
face with Brian Deacon, a neighbour in the Mansions.

'Hello, Bri,' he said sheepishly.

'Sorry, I . . . Do I . . .?'

'Jimmy. It's Jimmy,' said Jimmy.

'Jimmy! Good God! Good God, Jimmy! Oh, congratulations.'

Jimmy stared at him in amazement.

'Congratulations?'

'On coming out of the closet. Marvellous.'

'What? What closet?'

'Admitting you're a transvestite.'

'What??' Jimmy was outraged. 'Not!! Good God, man, not a
pervert.'

'I don't like being described as a pervert, Jimmy,' said Brian
Deacon quietly.

A bus bound for Guildford swished through the sodium
gloom, and almost splashed Jimmy as it ploughed through the
puddles left by the recent rains. He didn't notice. He was staring
at Brian Deacon open-mouthed.

'You mean . . . you're a . . . transthingummy?'

'Yes.'

'But you're a quantity surveyor.'

'Yes. So why *are* you dressed as a woman?'

'Been invited to this shindig. Thought I'd go in fancy dress.
Thought I'd try to look absurd.'

'You've succeeded.'

'Are you *really* a transwhatsit?'

'Yes.'

'Well, I'm astounded.'

'Of course you are. I haven't dared come out of the closet.
When I saw you, my heart leapt. I thought, if somebody else in
the Mansions can come out of the closet, maybe I can. I thought

38

perhaps we could pop down to the Balti House together for a chicken tikka in drag.'

'Sorry.'

A cyclist gave Jimmy a wolf-whistle as he swished through the puddles.

'Bastard!' shouted Jimmy in his best parade-ground voice. 'Selfish bastard! You've splashed my tights.'

The cyclist fell off.

By the time Jimmy got to the party his feet were very sore and he'd laddered his tights.

He rang the bell angrily.

The door was opened by Cyril Hardcastle, a friend from the pub. Cyril was dressed as Napoleon.

'Jimmy!' he said. 'Thank God! I was worried I'd forgotten to tell you it was fancy dress. Didn't want you making a fool of yourself.'

Linda certainly felt absurd, shopping in Safeways on roller skates, in a white track-suit that showed only too clearly the sixteen pounds that she felt she still needed to lose. But she suspected that feeling absurd wasn't the same thing as being absurd, and she couldn't believe that a million pounds could be won by doing something so footling.

Her trolley had a pronounced lunge to the left which would have been difficult to control even if she hadn't been on roller skates, so the accident was probably inevitable. It was just bad luck that it happened in the wine and spirits section. The trolley crashed into the wine shelves, knocking over several bottles of Stoneybrook Chardonnay. Several bottles broke. The floor was soaked in full-bodied, smooth, lightly oaked wine. Linda slipped as the trolley spun off across the aisle. As she grabbed at the shelves to save herself, she knocked over some Chilean Cona Sur Pinot Noir from Chimbarango. Out poured the ripe, juicy, velvety liquid. Linda fell. As she fell, she reached out to save herself. She grabbed only more wine bottles. Two bottles of Faustina V Rioja Classica fell with her. Both bottles broke, soaking her white track-suit. She grabbed one of the bottles and lay on her back, holding her trophy, with rivers of red wine all around her.

A horrified assistant hurried up to her.

She sniffed the jagged mouth of the bottle in her hand, and smiled at him.

'M'm,' she said. 'A pleasant traditional oaky aroma, a spicy flavour and a warm vanilla finish.'

As she drove home, in her track-suit stinking of wine, she felt it unlikely that her expedition would win her a legacy of a million pounds, but it had certainly cost her £44.89 in breakages.

More than once, as he sat all alone clutching a bouquet of red roses in that waiting room, the very walls of which seemed to drip with the tension of that other meeting, Tom Patterson was on the point of getting up and going.

Then at last the summons came. 'Ms Hackstraw will see you now.'

Hackstraw! What a beautiful name. So much more subtle than the sentimentality of Lovelace or the gamey chumminess of Venison. And Ms! What a splendidly compact, trim, kempt, neatly beige-suited word.

How perfectly judged was Ms Hackstraw's handshake. Cool, firm, resolute but not aggressive.

'Good morning,' he said. 'You look . . . you look absolutely . . .' He thrust the flowers into her hand. 'For you.'

'Thank you. That's sweet of you.' She indicated that he should sit down. 'So, what can I do for you, Mr Patterson?' she asked. 'As if I didn't know.'

Tom gawped. How could she know? Were his feelings so

obvious? This was madness. She was the most eligible woman in Climthorpe, with the slimmest waist in the whole legal profession, and eyes that could have melted a masonic lodge if she'd ever been allowed in. He was an unemployed estate agent with a grey beard and a paunch.

'Er . . . I was wondering if you'd like to come out to . . . er . . . to dinner with me,' he spluttered.

'Only dinner? You aren't proposing marriage? Tut,tut, Mr Patterson. That isn't very absurd.'

What could she mean? Why was she mocking him? A slow flush crept under his beard and set the hairs itching all over his face.

'I don't understand,' he said.

'You are presumably assuming that I have no feelings and can be used by you in the pursuit of your million pounds,' said Ms Hackstraw, whom Tom had hoped to be able to call Geraldine before his life's span was out.

The awful truth dawned on him. 'You think I'm playing games,' he said. 'You think I'm trying to be absurd.'

'Well aren't you?'

'Ms Hackstraw,' he said, breathing heavily with barely controlled humiliation. 'When we all sat in this room I realised that I might occasionally have seen women who were your equal in beauty, but I had never, ever actually talked to one. Our eyes met, very probably by complete accident, but I could scarcely breathe. I knew that if I telephoned you I would get short shrift, but I hoped that, if you saw me, and I brought flowers . . . oh, Lord . . . oh, stupid, deluded Tom . . . I hoped that you would be so impressed by the intensity of my feelings that . . . and by the force of my personality . . . that love would jump barriers. No, I wasn't trying to be absurd, but I can see that I have been very absurd. I forgot that I'm not a love-jumping-barriers person.'

He gave her a twisted smile.

'I'm so sorry, Mr Patterson,' said Geraldine Hackstraw. 'I'm so very sorry.'

'It's all right,' said Tom. 'It was a very foolish thought, but, you see, I don't look as boring from my side as I do from yours. Goodbye, Ms Hackstraw.'

Elizabeth sat on the Reggie-less settee in the Reggie-less through-lounge/diner of number thirty-eight, Leibnitz Drive, stroking Ponsonby the Third and watching the sun setting explosively in a riot of cruel reds over the dull, square semis of Kierkegaard Crescent. Around her were square hoops in various stages of completion. Her silvery hair was dulled by despondency.

'I miss Reggie so much, Ponsonby,' she said. 'I long for him to make some utterly ridiculous and irritating remark, or to dismay me with some extraordinarily unusual plan. I can think of nothing absurd to do, except to make some more of the square hoops that I used to make for our Grot shops. Reggie used to seek inspiration by talking to your grandpa. Do you think I'll get inspiration from you?'

By way of an answer, Ponsonby just slipped off Elizabeth's lap, and set off towards the door.

'That's right. Abandon me,' Elizabeth cried out. 'Leave me all alone.'

She heard a loud miaow from Ponsonby, and a moment later the cat flap clanged.

Alone! They shouldn't be doing this on their own. They should all be working together.

Had Ponsonby been trying to tell her? The tiny hairs stood up on her neck.

She would give him the benefit of the doubt. Reggie would have done.

She opened the French windows. It was ridiculously mild for

January. The snowdrops were out, and a huge iceberg three quarters the size of the Cotswolds had recently detached itself from the Antarctic shelf.

Ponsonby the Third was staring balefully at the most recent molehill on the lawn.

'Thank you, Ponsonby,' she called out, to the astonishment of Mr Meaker, who was feeding the birds on the next-door lawn. 'You're a marvellous cat, and you're absolutely right.'

Mr Meaker, turning to look at Elizabeth in astonishment, lost his footing and ended up in the goldfish pond.

Elizabeth closed the French windows and reached for the telephone.

4 *A Plan is Born*

There were birds of paradise on the curtains, and roses on the upholstery.

Linda came half an hour before the others, to help prepare the buffet. The setting sun was imploding gently into a vast purple and lavender bruise over the roofs of Kierkegaard Crescent. Slowly, darkness was descending on the molehills that studded the back lawn of number thirty-eight, Leibnitz Drive, Goffley.

'Why did you choose to live here, when you could have lived anywhere?' asked Linda, as she sliced the ham.

'We bought it when Reggie was making one last stab at leading a normal business life,' said her mother.

'Yes, but after he'd left Amalgamated Aerosols under a cloud . . .'

'He didn't leave under a cloud, dear. He left of his own free will, after attending an aerosols smelling and stating that all ten of the aerosols smelt reminded him of Bolivian unicyclists' jockstraps, which nowadays would have been perceived as a very politically incorrect remark, being both racist and unicyclistist.'

Linda stared at her mother in some alarm.

'Find a home for those, dear,' said Elizabeth, handing her daughter a plate of chicken and mushroom vol-au-vents. Oh, and do stop gawping, woman. You're going to have to learn to be less middle-class, Linda. You really are.'

'I should have died, like Mark,' muttered Linda.

'What was that??'

'Nothing.'

Linda's brother Mark had been an actor. He had been killed by Sendero Luminoso guerillas in Peru eleven years previously while touring the Andean *altiplano* with a British Council production of *Rookery Nook*.

'I'm sorry, Mum,' said Linda, realising that Elizabeth had heard.

'I hope so. That was awful.'

'I'm bewildered by you, Mum. I'm out of my depth.'

'Well, don't worry,' said her mother crisply. 'I shall be explaining later to everyone.'

'What? Explaining what? You told me this was just a social occasion.'

'I lied. It's an urgent meeting to discuss how best to continue Reggie's great work. There are some bags of ready-washed salad leaves in the fridge. Make some dressing and toss them, will you?'

'A moment ago you said I was going to have to learn to be less middle-class. Now you want me to make French dressing.'

'Life is such a mass of contradictions, isn't it, darling?'

Elizabeth smiled brightly. The sheen had returned to her silvery hair. Her lines seemed less pronounced. She had an almost regal air.

Linda looked at her in further alarm.

They took their plates and glasses of wine through into the lounge area and seated themselves at random, little realising that the positions they chose that evening would become fixed, over the months to come, and that, at all the momentous meetings that were to be held there, they would sit in the same spots, as if their powers of invention were being so stretched

45

that there was no imagination left over for choosing where to sit.

C.J. and Doc Morrissey sat at either end of the settee, with Tom in the middle. Linda and Joan sat in the two armchairs. Jimmy chose the rocking chair from the kitchen, while Elizabeth, the perfect hostess, settled down on the pouffe. The Harris-Joneses, modest to the last, sat side by side on two Windsor chairs from the dining area.

'I didn't realise there'd be wine, or I'd have brought some of my fig nouveau,' said Tom.

'But you didn't, so you didn't, so that's all right,' said C.J.

'There's no need to be rude,' said Tom.

'No, but it's fun, isn't it?' said Elizabeth.

After they had eaten, Elizabeth rose to address them. Behind her, a coal-effect gas fire flickered merrily. Seven faces looked up at her eagerly. An eighth lolled.

'Wake Jimmy up, would you?' she asked.

C.J. prodded Jimmy violently.

'Rub it harder. The itch is a bit higher. Yes, there,' said Jimmy. He opened his eyes and looked round the room in bewilderment. 'Sorry,' he said. 'Sorry. Dreaming. Asleep. Exhausting wallah, nosh. Always sets the eyelids drooping.'

'Ignoring Jimmy's sexy fantasies . . .' began Elizabeth.

'Oh I say, Sis, bit below the belt,' said Jimmy.

'Yes, it sounded as if it was,' said Elizabeth. 'Ladies and gentlemen, Reggie hated the success of his Grot shops. He didn't want to get rich out of selling useless goods. He wanted to help create a better world. That's why he created Perrin's. After the community failed, he was never quite the same man again. He was tired. So we mustn't see this legacy as cruel, as his attempt to humiliate us. We must see it as our chance to carry on his work. Our real motive shouldn't be the million pounds, welcome though that would naturally be. Our real motive is to repay his trust in us. Oh dear, I've moved myself so much I

46

think I'm going to cry.' She blew her nose on one of Reggie's old handkerchieves. It had his initials, R.I.P., on it. 'Reggie believed that the world is so often so dull,' she continued, 'that to learn to be absurd, to regain the ability to be absurd that children have, would be a deeply worthwhile memorial.'

'I don't think I was absurd even as a child, actually,' said Tom.

'I'm sure you weren't,' said Linda.

'You probably think that's an insult,' said Tom. 'I take it as a compliment.'

'Children!' said Elizabeth. 'Now, we have all tried to be absurd individually.'

'I haven't,' said Tom.

'Yes, you have,' said C.J. 'You've asked Geraldine out to dinner.'

Linda gave a derisory snort as Tom exclaimed, 'How the hell do you know that?'

'She told me' said C.J.

'She told *you*?' exploded Doc Morrissey. 'When?'

'At dinner. At the Oven D'Or'

'You took her to the Oven D'Or?'

'Yes.'

'No wonder she's a bit upset with me. You took her to the most expensive restaurant in Botchley, I took her to the Climthorpe Tandoori.'

'*You've* taken her out?' The two elderly men glared at each other across the discomfited Tom. It was not a happy settee.

'You both asked her out to be absurd,' said Tom. 'I asked her out, because I loved her.'

'Now that *is* absurd,' said Linda. 'Collect your million pounds immediately. Do not pass Go.'

'Children!' said Elizabeth. 'You are abusing my hospitality. Please.'

Silence fell, but it was an uneasy silence. C.J. and Doc

Morrissey were glaring at each other, Linda was glaring at Tom, and Tom was trying to glare at C.J., Doc Morrissey and Linda all at the same time.

Jimmy wasn't glaring at anybody.

'Wake Jimmy up, somebody, please,' said Elizabeth wearily.

Tom prodded Jimmy with unnecessarily petulant vigour.

'Fancy going on top of me now?' said Jimmy. He opened his eyes and looked round the room in some bewilderment. 'Sorry. Dozed off. Dreaming,' he said.

'I wonder if I could borrow your dreams some time?' asked Doc Morrissey.

'Please!' implored Elizabeth. 'May I continue?'

Nobody demurred.

'Have any of you, on your own, done anything good enough to enable you to go to Ms Hackstraw and say, "I claim my million pounds"?'

The silence that followed spoke volumes. A tawny owl hooted, in exactly the manner that might have been expected of it. There is no evidence to suggest that owls have any sense of the absurd.

'I presume from your silence that you don't believe you have,' said Elizabeth. 'I know I haven't. I know I can't. I haven't that kind of personality. But together, supporting each other, helping each other, maybe we can achieve something truly absurd.'

'I don't think Linda and I would be able to work together even for a million pounds,' said Tom.

'I agree,' said Linda.

'Wonderful,' said Tom. 'That's the first time we've agreed for seven years.'

'Oh, don't be so stupid, Tom,' said Linda. 'You know what I meant. I agree that we couldn't possibly agree.'

'I agree,' said Tom.

'Nevertheless you are talking again, and that's something,' said Prue, 'and I don't think we should let Elizabeth down.'

'Well said, that woman,' said Jimmy.

'I agree,' said Doc Morrissey. 'And, I mean, after all, none of us have got anything else to do.'

'All right,' said Tom. 'I'll give it a go.'

'I suppose I owe it to Mummy,' said Linda.

'Well spoken, that highly fanciable woman, though not by me, it would be incest,' said Jimmy.

They all looked at him in horror, but especially Linda.

'Sorry,' he said. 'Carry on.'

Elizabeth topped up their glasses and, despite Jimmy, the atmosphere in the lounge/diner was quite warm and positive.

Then C.J. struck a sobering note. 'I hate to be the one to pour cold water over a wet blanket,' he said, loving it. 'I didn't get where I am today by pouring cold water over wet blankets. Nevertheless, I must ask the awkward question, "All right. We've agreed to work together. But doing what?" That's the fly in the woodpile.'

There was a moment's silence, as everyone considered the fly in C.J.'s woodpile.

'I think the solution to the . . . er . . . the fly in the woodpile may lie in something Doc Morrissey said,' said David Harris-Jones at last.

'May it? Oh!' said Doc Morrissey in some surprise.

'I think you may have solved the problem,' said David Harris-Jones.

'May I? Oh!' repeated the astonished medico. 'Was it something really rather brilliant?'

'Yes, I think it may have been.'

'Oh!'

'Although maybe it . . . er . . . maybe it wasn't, after all.'

'Ah!' Doc Morrissey sounded resigned.

'Please can somebody explain what you're talking about?' asked Elizabeth.

'Yes. Sorry,' said David Harris-Jones. 'No, it was when Doc said, "None of us have got anything else to do." Well, we haven't.'

'Was that it?' Doc Morrissey sounded disappointed. 'Was that my contribution?'

'Yes.'

'Ah.'

'No, but don't you see . . . er . . . some of us are . . . well, not exactly old . . . well, too old to work . . . and the others have been made . . . well, redundant, on grounds of . . . well, age I was told and Tom was told and I don't know about Joan.'

'Oh yes,' said Elizabeth. 'Her boss wanted legs to be crossed by a younger woman.' She closed her eyes in dismay. 'Sorry, Joan,' she said. she looked up at the ceiling. 'Sorry, Reggie, that was petty.'

'Tactful change of subject called for,' said Doc Morrissey.

'Absolutely,' said C.J. 'We'll cross those legs when we come to them.'

'No, but, you see,' said David Harris-Jones, 'I really do have an idea.'

Six faces looked at him in astonishment. One looked at him with love. One didn't look at him at all.

'Wake Jimmy up, somebody, please,' said Elizabeth sadly.

Prue Harris-Jones prodded Jimmy enthusiastically.

'Again? Already? You're insatiable,' said Jimmy. He opened his eyes and looked round the room in surprise. 'Sorry. Must have been in the Land of Nod.'

'In the land of complete and utter fantasy, more like,' said Tom.

'A land you know well,' said Linda.

'Please!' shouted Prue. 'Please! David has had an idea.'

'Good God!' said Jimmy. He realised that this didn't sound

tactful. 'Sorry. Well done, that man. Well come on, then, David. Spit it out.'

'He's trying to,' said Prue frantically. 'He's trying to, but you won't bloody well let him, so shut up!'

An astonished silence fell on the lounge/diner.

'Yes,' said David Harris-Jones. 'Well . . . er . . . no, actually . . . well, it is an idea . . . you'll probably think it pretty feeble, it probably is pretty feeble . . .'

'Oh, stop running yourself down!' Prue forced the words through firmly clenched teeth.

'Well . . . as I say . . .' said David Harris-Jones. 'Er . . . some of us being, as I say . . . well, not old, but . . . oldish . . . and others having been made . . . well . . .'

'Redundantish,' said Joan.

Prue Harris-Jones glared at Joan.

'Exactly,' said David Harris-Jones. 'And, as I say, this probably is feeble, but I just thought . . . er . . . the elderly and the redundant, we could all sort of . . . er . . . well, sort of march on . . . er . . . on . . . er . . .'

'Tiptoe?' suggested Doc Morrissey.

'Westminster,' said David Harris-Jones. 'With placards. Placards saying . . . oh . . . er . . . "Don't get rid of experience. Don't throw us all on the scrap heap."'

'Prue's right. You do run yourself down too much,' said Tom. 'You've shown sound judgement. You said your idea was feeble, and it was.'

'The inadequate are always sarcastic,' said Linda.

'I don't think David's idea was at all feeble,' said Joan.

'Oh!' said David Harris-Jones.

'Well, I mean it *was* feeble, but it was only feeble because he put it so feebly,' said Joan.

'Oh!' said David Harris-Jones.

'But I think he's really on to something,' said Joan. 'I mean, there are so many senior citizens in our society, and so many people are being made redundant well before they become senior citizens, some of them at absurdly young ages, and I think we should really do something about it on a massive scale.'

'A revolution,' said Elizabeth. 'A bloodless revolution. We march on Whitehall. We take over the government on behalf of the redundant and the elderly.'

'It's absurd,' said C.J.

'Precisely!' said Elizabeth. 'We've got our idea! Tremendous!'

And so, in that Home Counties room in Goffley, with birds of paradise on the curtains, and roses on the upholstery, the seeds of revolution were born.

'I think we should leave it there,' said Elizabeth over coffee. 'It's progress enough for one night. Let's go away and sleep on it.'

'Jimmy's sleeping on it already,' pointed out Joan.

David Harris-Jones prodded Jimmy gently.

'Gone!' exclaimed the old warrior. 'Left me! The baggage!' He opened his eyes and looked round the room in puzzlement. 'Sorry,' he said. 'Dreaming.' He smiled ruefully. 'Even my dreams end in disaster. Cock-up on the subconsciousness front.'

5 Cometh the Hour, Cometh the Man

Clement Attlee Mansions did not constitute an elegant memorial to the architect of post-war Britain. It was a yellow, six-storey block with a flat roof, and was generally considered to be a blot on Inkerman Road, Spraundon, which was not an easy road to blot. The paint on the south and west walls, frequently battered by the prevailing winds, was peeling. The guttering on the east wall dipped in the middle, and the resultant dripping of rainwater had caused an unsightly stain above the lounge window of flat twenty-two. The occupant of flat twenty-two was barely aware of the unsightly stain, but was mortified at having to live in a block called Clement Attlee Mansions.

It was the morning after the fateful meeting in Leibnitz Drive. The prevailing winds were exploring the weak points in the paintwork like cats drawing rough tongues over salty skin. Dark clouds scudded across a sky that looked too wild for Surrey. Jimmy and Elizabeth stood side by side at the window, looking out over Spraundon.

'Quite a view,' said Jimmy.

'Extensive,' said Elizabeth.

'Quite. What I meant. See a long way, bugger-all worth looking at. Fancy a coffee?'

'Please.'

'Pity. Haven't got any. Bit of a cock-up on the catering front.'

There were two sagging armchairs, and a cheap, ash-veneer table studded with red rings from wine glasses. On the mantelpiece there was a carriage clock that had stopped. Above the mantelpiece was a very bad water-colour of Jimmy's second wife, Lettuce, who had been no oil painting. On the wall that adjoined flat twenty-one there was a reproduction of an even worse painting of Field Marshal Montogomery. Faced with these two great martial figures, Rommel would have chosen to fight the latter.

'Got vegetable stock cube,' said Jimmy. 'Melt it down, might make a cup of something.'

'Thank you, I'm not thirsty.'

'Little bit in the bottom of a bottle of schnapps.'

'No, really. Thank you, I'm fine.'

'I miss Lettuce. Stout scout. Bloody juggernauts. Blasted European Community. Frogs and Eyeties firing off at thrushes, Spaniards torturing bulls, Krauts putting towels all over beaches we once fought on, fat Belgians sicking up chocolate and smug Scandinavians beating each other with birch twigs. What a rabble.'

'Did you get out of bed the wrong side this morning?' asked Elizabeth gently, seating herself in the better chair.

'Only one side I can get out of it. Wall on other side. Bedroom? Cupboard more like. Anyway, enough of my troubles. How about you?' Jimmy's voice became soft and concerned. 'How are you really, Sis?'

'I'm fine, Bro,' said Elizabeth. 'I'm ... fine. No, I am. I'm fine. Really. Really fine.' Her eyes were watery, giving the lie to her words. For once, she looked like a seventy-year-old woman. 'I mean, of course I loved Reggie, but he wasn't always the easiest person to live with, so in some ways ... no, I'm fine.'

'I miss him terribly too,' said Jimmy.

They sat in affectionate silence for a moment, while the wind moaned in despair at being unable to blow down Clement Attlee Mansions.

54

'Jimmy,' said Elizabeth at last, 'I've come to sound you out.'

Jimmy raised a careful eyebrow. 'Intriguing,' he said.

'You remember what we discussed last night?'

'Bits of it. Kept falling asleep. Embarrassing.'

'You remember that we're planning a bloodless revolution?'

'Yes. Ludicrous.'

'Exactly. Somebody will have to run the show, Jimmy. It'll have to be decided democratically, of course.'

'Oh God, will it?' snorted Jimmy.

'I would suggest you, Jimmy, but there's no point if you wouldn't be prepared to do it. I mean I just want to be sure that you don't feel past it.'

'Because I keep nodding off, you mean?'

'Well, not that particularly. Churchill used to take cat-naps.'

'He woke up refreshed. I wake up knackered.'

Elizabeth leant across and patted Jimmy's leathery hand.

'How's morale?' she asked.

'Bad. Low ebb. Tried to kill myself twice you know. Gas oven, Cornwall, you and Reggie rescued me. Second attempt, lay on railway line. No trains. Bloody bastard Beeching. Recently thought, pity I failed, maybe third time lucky?'

Elizabeth patted his hand.

'You lack a sense of purpose,' she said. 'A sense of destiny.'

'True. No sense of destiny whatsoever.'

'Well, this could be your moment, Jimmy.'

'Not taking this seriously, are we? Thought it was a ruse to get a million pounds.'

Elizabeth stood up and began to pace round the room. She was full of nervous energy. Jimmy had never seen her like this before.

'This is why I'm asking you, Jimmy,' she said. 'We don't have to take it seriously, no, but I would like to. Reggie would have. Imagine if it really took off, Jimmy. A bloodless revolution, led by you. You'd be as famous as Wat Tyler.'

'What tiler?'

'Yes. He led the Peasants' Revolt in 1381. Have you heard of Lambert Simnel?'

'No.'

'Well, you could be as famous as him.'

'Terrific. Think I will have that schnapps. Sure I can't get you anything?'

'A glass of tap water?'

'No problem.'

Elizabeth followed her brother into the kitchen. It looked bare. Jimmy saw her looking into an empty cupboard and said, 'Shopping fatigues 14.00 hours. Major restocking.'

'You were saying?' said Elizabeth, as Jimmy poured her glass of water.

'Yes. Fact is, Big Sis, lost a little bit of confidence lately. Not sure I could pull it off, this leadership thing.'

Jimmy bent down to get the schnapps out of a badly fitted cupboard. His right knee cracked like a rifle shot.

'I won't pretend you're clever, Jimmy,' said Elizabeth, choosing her words carefully, 'but I think you're lucky in a way, in that the brains you have are concentrated in one area.'

Jimmy emptied the schnapps bottle into a glass. There was even less schnapps left than he had thought.

They sat at the ancient formica-topped kitchen table. Jimmy raised his glass.

'Cheers.' He downed his drink in one small gulp. 'Water all right?'

'Very nice.'

'Good. Wasn't with you just then. Haven't the brains to understand what you meant about brains.'

'Well you aren't brilliant with words, for instance. You aren't bookish.'

'Absolutely right. Chap in the Mansions, meaning to be kind, invited me to this arty-farty literati party. Made a fool of myself.

56

Thought Evelyn Waugh was a woman, thought George Eliot was a man. Bit of a cock up on the author-sexing front.'

Jimmy sighed. His battered, leathery face looked like a travelling bag that is near the end of its useful life.

'Your brains are reserved entirely for the great task of your life. The inspiring and leading of men into battle.'

'Well, when you put it that way . . . see what you mean.'

'In this case, it's men *and* women, and it isn't exactly battle, but the principle's the same,' said Elizabeth. 'Cometh the hour, cometh the man.'

'Got you.'

'So, if elected, will you serve?'

''Spose so,' said Major James Anderson. ''Spose so.

'Good,' said Elizabeth. 'It's hardly a ringing call to arms, "'Spose so", but it's the best we've got. Well, I must go. I'm off to Linda's for lunch.'

Jimmy sighed. He always sighed at the mention of Linda.

After Elizabeth had left, he stood at the window of his little lounge and watched her drive off, as if hoping to gain strength from the sight of her departing car. Then he sighed and turned to face the stern, unbending, military figure in the picture. He stood as erect as he could manage.

'I won't let you down, Commander,' he said, saluting smartly, wincing as pain shot through his right shoulder.

Lettuce gazed back at him without pity.

6   *The Goffley Tea Party*

The following Tuesday, over lapsang souchong, crumpets and home-made lemon sponge, they planned the next stage of the Bloodless Revolution of Senior Citizens and the Occupationally Rejected.

Elizabeth's main aim was to secure the election of Jimmy as leader. If it achieved nothing else, it would bring the sparkle back to his deep, sad eyes.

Jimmy was, in fact, the first to arrive, well before the appointed time of two thirty. His days stretched more emptily to the horizon than anyone's.

'Came early,' he said. 'Wondered if I could borrow some nosh. Bit of a cock-up on the catering front. Pay you back, of course.'

'Of course,' said Elizabeth drily, as she hurried to the larder.

'Mean it,' said Jimmy, following her. 'Said it in the past, meant it, been unable to. Coming into some money now. Pay you every penny.'

Elizabeth gave him a Sainsbury's carrier bag containing a free-range chicken, two wild salmon steaks, a tin of humanely slaughtered tuna, and some organic onions, carrots, parsnips, apples and pears. She also gave him a bill, to set against his legacy.

'Bloody hell,' he said. 'Expensive cove, a social conscience.'

Next to arrive were Doc Morrissey and David and Prue Harris-Jones. David looked round the neat lounge/diner, with the nest of tables split up and little slate coasters of Welsh scenes waiting to receive the tea cups, and the coal-effect fire glowing merrily in the tiled hearth. He seemed to be searching for a pithy phrase to embrace the quality of the scene, and he found one. 'Super,' he said.

Tom came next. Nobody needed to ask him what he'd had for lunch. There were unmistakable traces of orange Heinz tomato soup in the grey of his beard. He too looked round the room. 'Twenty-three by fifteen?' he asked. Elizabeth nodded. 'Like to keep my hand in,'

Joan's arrival precipitated them into the first crisis of the afternoon. She was accompanied by a tall, slim, exhausted-looking man with white hair, a floury complexion, a heavily lined baggy face and great black shadows under his bloodshot eyes. He was wearing black jeans and a blue denim shirt. He looked to be in his late fifties.

'This is Hank,' she said. 'He's my chap.'

'Super,' said David Harris-Jones.

'Er . . . I think we have a problem here, Joan,' said Elizabeth. 'I'm delighted to meet . . . er . . . Hank . . . I'd love him to come to dinner some time. But today, this afternoon, is a . . . does he know anything?'

'I know you're inheriting a lot of money if you do something really absurd,' said Hank.

'Yes, well, I'm not sure Joan should even have told you that,' said Elizabeth.

'Hell's bells, Elizabeth,' protested Joan. 'Hank and I are a major item. We're a deeply intertwined entity.'

'I'm not sure we should go into your sex life just now,' said Elizabeth. 'I'm sorry, but I think we have to have a meeting to discuss whether Hank can attend our meeting.'

'Oh, Lord,' sighed Jimmy. 'Complications.'

Elizabeth looked at him sadly. It wasn't quite what she was hoping for from her proposed leader.

'It's all right,' said Hank. 'You discuss it. I'll go and sit in the Porsche.'

'Aren't any seats in the porch,' said Jimmy.

'No, no, the Porsche. It's a car,' said Joan.

'Oh, Porsche. With you,' said Jimmy.

A brief silence followed Hank's exit. It was broken, rather bitterly, by Doc Morrissey.

'Congratulations, Joan,' he said. 'You've got yourself a rich sugar daddy.'

'Hank is only thirty-nine,' said Joan. 'He's my toy boy.'

They tried to hide their shock, but could think of nothing to say.

'His work is very demanding,' said Joan. 'He works on a futures desk in the City. It's high risk, high tech, high tension.'

C.J. entered next, apologised for being late, and said, 'I don't want to alarm you, but there's a very suspicious character sitting in a Porsche outside and casing the joint. Burglar type. I didn't get where I am today without knowing a burglar type when I see one.'

'He's my live-in lover,' said Joan.

'I've always said,' said C.J., 'that you shouldn't judge a book by its silver lining.'

'We're discussing whether we should allow him to listen to our discussions,' said Elizabeth.

'Why not?' said C.J.

'Security reasons,' said Elizabeth.

'Oh God, are we taking it that seriously?' said C.J.

'Yes,' said Tom glumly.

The last to arrive was Linda. She apologised for being late, and said, 'There's a suspicious man lurking in a car outside. I wouldn't be surprised if he's a sex maniac.'

'He is,' said Joan. 'He's my lover.'

Doc Morrissey sighed.

'Where I go, he goes,' said Joan.

'Well, he can't join us,' said Tom. 'He doesn't qualify. He's got a job.'

'He's petrified about losing it,' said Joan. 'He says there's no future in futures. He's terrified of being on the scrap heap at thirty-nine.'

'Thirty-nine!' said C.J. 'Pull the other one.'

'He's a valuable asset,' said Joan. 'He could win us the support of all those who fear redundancy.'

'Do we really want people's support?' asked Tom. 'Can't the nine of us just march on Whitehall and give ourselves up? Wouldn't that be absurd enough?'

'Not for my Reggie,' said Elizabeth.

'Probably not for Geraldine either,' said Doc Morrissey gloomily.

'Ms Hackstraw to you,' said C.J.

'We need the support of everyone we can get,' said Elizabeth. 'If we don't let new people in, this will never take off. I don't like the look of Hank any more than the rest of you . . . sorry, Joan . . . but I think we should have a vote, and I will vote to admit him.'

'Bloody democracy,' grumbled Jimmy.

'I'll vote to admit him too,' said David Harris-Jones. 'I . . . this is probably a bit impertinent, Joan . . . after all, your love life is none of my . . . but I've started so I'll . . . er . . . I'll . . . but I do think he's an improvement on Tony. Sorry, Joan. But I mean at least he doesn't say "great" all the time. He doesn't, does he?'

'He never says "great".'

'Super.'

Elizabeth, Joan, David, Prue and Linda voted in favour of admitting Hank.

Doc Morrissey, C.J. and Tom voted against.

Jimmy abstained.

Joan fetched Hank, and Elizabeth said, 'You're very welcome indeed, Hank, by five votes to three with one abstention.'

'Super,' said David Harris-Jones.

'Wicked,' said Hank.

Linda helped Elizabeth get the tea things. Jimmy hurried after her, caught her in the larder, and stroked her still quite ample bottom.

'No,' said Linda firmly.

'Absolutely,' said Jimmy. 'Black mark, that naughty straying hand. Drummed out of the regiment.'

He gazed at her in misery, slipped a tin of artichoke hearts into his pocket, said, 'Not a word to you-know-who about you-know-what', sighed, and left the larder.

'Why are you walking like that? Are you practising being absurd?' asked C.J.

He had ushered a reluctant Doc Morrissey into the garden for a secret discussion. They were pacing up and down the crumbling, snail-slimy brick path that ran alongside the mole-wrecked lawn. Doc Morrissey's left foot was on tiptoe, but his right foot wasn't.

'Oh no,' said Doc Morrissey. 'No, I have a hole in my sole. I don't want to get my feet wet. You get colds that way.'

'That's a myth,' said C.J. 'Colds are infections.'

'I believe they are, now you come to mention it,' said Doc Morrissey, 'but I still don't want to get my foot wet.'

To their left, a sullen cloud loomed. To their right, a tiny silver aeroplane was making a vapour trail across a sky of brilliant blue. C.J. towered over his rival, even when Doc Morrissey was on tiptoe at the height of his strange, bouncing walk.

'I don't want to hear you refer to Geraldine as Geraldine again,' said C.J.

'Is that a threat?' enquired Doc Morrissey calmly.

'No. Good heavens, no. Just a suggestion. I just wished to make you aware of the situation. I asked Geraldine to marry me. It was a pathetic attempt to be absurd. Yet sometimes, Doc, out of tiny acorns, great molehills grow.'

'Somebody's planted a lot of acorns in this lawn, in that case,' muttered Doc Morrissey.

'I love Geraldine, Doc.'

'Supposing . . . this is purely hypothetical, C.J. . . . but supposing I also loved . . . Ms Hackstraw? And I, don't forget, have no wife. I am free.'

'My wife is perfectly content,' said C.J. 'Luxembourg is a microcosm of European civilisation. I have been on the boards of five companies. You are a faded, failed doctor. I hope you get my drift.'

'Perfectly,' said Doc Morrissey. 'You wish me to call Ms Hackstraw Ms Hackstraw. I'm happy to oblige.'

He turned back along the path, keeping his left foot on tiptoe. Suddenly C.J.'s bald pate glistened in the late afternoon sun. The path began to steam.

Everyone except C.J. and Doc Morrissey praised the home-made lemon cake. 'Delicious,' said Linda. 'Highly desirable,' said Tom. 'Super,' was the epithet favoured by David Harris-Jones and his adoring wife Prue. 'Wicked,' was Hank's considered verdict.

To C.J. the cake had all the charm and taste of a drying-up cloth. He was worried. Where was Doc Morrissey? What was the untrustworthy little bastard up to?

Doc Morrissey was using Hank's car phone.

'Ms Hackstraw?' he was saying. 'This is Doc Morrissey. Will

63

you have dinner with me tonight? Somewhere rather posher than the Climthorpe Tandoori? . . . Splendid! Ms Hackstraw, may I say something rather personal? I love you, Ms Hackstraw . . . Well, I don't expect you to yet, we hardly know each other, but we can work on it . . . I'll pick you up at seven thirty. I think you'll like the Goffley Tandoori.'

When the last crumpet had been eaten, the last crumb of lemon cake consumed, the last sip of lapsang souchong savoured, Elizabeth Perrin stood with her back to the coal-effect fire like a member of the landed gentry warming his backside on a huge log fire, looked round the cosy room, with the birds of paradise drawn against the February night, smiled at the ageing revolutionaries and said, 'We need to appoint a leader.'

'Super,' said David Harris-Jones.

'Wicked,' said Hank.

'I don't think the decision should take too long,' said Elizabeth. 'It seems to me that there is one natural and obvious choice.'

'Thank you,' said C.J. 'I didn't get where I am today without being able to see which way the wind is blowing.'

'I'm afraid you did, actually, C.J.,' said Elizabeth. 'I was referring of course to Jimmy.'

There was a stunned silence.

'You were a businessman, C.J.,' said Elizabeth. 'You will be invaluable to us. But Jimmy was a soldier. A leader of men.'

'He's your brother,' said C.J. 'In my book that's tantamount to nepotism.'

'I must say . . .' began David Harris-Jones.

'Must you? Oh dear,' said Tom.

'Do shut up, Tom,' said Prue. 'Carry on, darling.'

'Thank you, darling,' said David Harris-Jones. 'I must say that Jimmy, while he is an old soldier, well, he wasn't a leader of . . . of very . . .well, was he? . . . and . . . er . . . well, he does tend to . . . er . . . well, doesn't he? . . . and in the last vote he did . . . er . . . which wasn't exactly . . . er . . . well, I mean, was it? . . . so . . . er . . . well, maybe he hasn't exactly . . . well, has he?'

'David means that Jimmy wasn't a leader of very many men,' interpreted Prue, 'and he does fall asleep a lot, and he did abstain on that last vote, which wasn't exactly decisive and there are probably more leadership qualities in David's left sock.'

'Well, yes, sort of,' said David Harris-Jones, 'if not in those actual words.'

'I resign,' said Jimmy. 'I've lost the confidence of my troops.'

'You can't resign, Jimmy,' Elizabeth pointed out. 'You haven't been appointed yet.'

'Well, appoint me, and I'll resign.'

'Well, I believe we should appoint Jimmy,' said Elizabeth. 'All right, he's my brother. All right, he's no spring chicken. All right, his career to date hasn't been an unmitigated triumph. But don't forget that Sir Winston Churchill was quite an elderly man with no great record of success when he led us to victory in the Second World War.'

'I hope you aren't comparing Jimmy to Sir Winston Churchill,' said Tom.

'I didn't get where I am today by comparing Jimmy to Sir Winston Churchill,' said C.J.

'It's all absurd,' said Linda, 'and it's all supposed to be absurd, and we're only doing it in order to claim our inheritance anyway, so let's just do it.'

'I agree. He's promised to resign, anyway, so let's get on with it, we're wasting time and I have a . . .' Doc Morrissey stopped hurriedly.

'A what?' asked C.J. suspiciously. 'Just what do you have, Doc?'

'All those in favour of Jimmy as our leader?' said Elizabeth.

They all raised their hands, including Jimmy.

'I don't think you should vote for yourself, Jimmy,' said Linda.

'Oh. With you. Bad form. Right.' Jimmy lowered his hand.

'You're elected *nem. con.*, Jimmy,' said Elizabeth.

'Thank you very much,' said Jimmy. 'Much appreciated. Your faith very touching. Serve you to the best of my ability.'

'Er . . . correct me if I've got the wrong end of the gist,' said C.J., 'but I thought you agreed that if we elected you you'd resign.'

'Did,' said Jimmy. 'Changed my mind.'

'You bastard!' said C.J.

'Absolutely,' agreed Jimmy. 'Should be glad. Need a bastard for leadership. All good leaders bastards.'

'That really was very naughty, Jimmy,' said Joan.

'Nice of you to say so,' said Jimmy. 'Always nice to get a compliment from a stunning woman with legs that seem to go on for ever. Lucky man, Hank. You are going where many men would like to tread. Well, not tread exactly.'

'I put your name forward, Jimmy,' said Elizabeth, 'but even I think you shouldn't have done that. It's completely undemocratic.'

'Democracy, fiddlesticks,' said Jimmy. 'You need a leader. You've got one. If we're serious about this, democracy, plughole.'

'Well, all right,' said Elizabeth. 'Let's have a vote on whether we should abandon democracy.'

'I find myself on the horns of a quandary,' said C.J. 'I hate the idea of democracy. Frankly, it's a bloody nuisance. But I also hate the idea of Jimmy as leader.'

'Well, abstain, then,' suggested Tom.

C.J. abstained. So did David and Prue Harris-Jones, Doc Morrissey and Joan.

66

Jimmy, Hank and Linda voted that democracy should go down the plughole.

Elizabeth and Tom voted that it shouldn't.

Tom said that the vote was undemocratic, as Hank shouldn't have had a vote.

Joan said it would be even more undemocratic if he didn't have a vote.

Doc Morrissey said that committees were always like this.

Jimmy gave it as his considered view that all committees should be shoved up the rear ends of wart-hogs.

C.J. described a committee as a horse designed by a stable door.

In the end, they decided that there was no way of avoiding having a vote on whether Hank should have a vote.

Joan, Hank, Elizabeth, Tom and Prue voted that he should have a vote.

C.J., Doc Morrissey, Linda and Jimmy voted that he shouldn't.

David Harris-Jones abstained.

Linda suggested that, whether Hank had a vote was not a matter on which Hank should vote, as he was an interested party.

This was agreed unanimously, even by Hank.

The result was therefore four all. David Harris-Jones would have to give the casting vote.

Doc Morrissey looked at his watch.

C.J. asked Doc Morrissey why he was looking at his watch.

Doc Morrissey told C.J. to mind his own business.

David Harris-Jones intimated that he believed . . . well, he thought he believed . . . that, on balance, because a decision had to be reached . . . it was better, though of course he could be wrong, if Hank did have a vote.

It was agreed by five votes to four that Hank should have a

vote, and that the vote that democracy should go down the plughole therefore stood by its original majority of three votes to two with five abstentions. It was also clear that, since democracy had been voted out, there was no longer any point in Hank having the vote that had just been voted in.

'What a palaver,' said Jimmy. 'Introduce a bit of democracy and what does it end up like? Parliament. Not on. You think I'm thick. Two days ago, was. Two days ago, kept falling asleep. You see before you a man transformed, a man vibrated. That's the wrong word, but you see the point. Ladies and gentlemen, this is the turning point. Realise you're only in it for the money, but Big Sis is in it to make a suitable memorial for Reggie. With her all the way. Farewell, apathy. Hail, the bloodless revolution. Wat Tyler? Forget him. Lambert Simnel? A piece of cake. Ladies and gentlemen, we have lit this day such a candle that we will never need electricity again, as Queen Elizabeth the First once said. Ladies and gentlemen, the Wrinklies are on the march.'

Elizabeth looked at Jimmy with astonishment and pride.

'Oh God,' said C.J. and Doc Morrissey and Tom.

7 *Dinner and Disillusionment*

Doc Morrissey had said 'Oh God' that evening because the revolution was a tiresome interruption to the only thing that mattered in his life – the pursuit of his passion for Ms Hackstraw.

For many years he had led a happy, if unexciting, life in Southall, where he was widely believed to be a professor, a view that he had done nothing to discourage. He had given a few English lessons, made many Asian friends, eaten delicious vegetarian curries with his fingers, allowed himself distant dreams about Joan Greengross's chest, drifted slowly towards old age, and generally been happier than ever before. Then everything had changed. It wasn't that he was really greedy, but you couldn't ignore a million pounds. He would be able to go on cruises. He would be able to visit the Taj Mahal, Mandalay and Valparaiso. He would be able to give biryani parties for the whole of Southall. He would be able to buy the books of his dreams. He had visited Ms Hackstraw and proposed marriage in order to be absurd. Over their subsequent dinner he had fallen deeply in love. Where there had been gentle peace there was now a burning ache. Where there had been unexciting content-ment there was now a fierce yearning. He yearned for the touch of her fine, pale, exquisite skin. He yearned for the feel of her tight buttocks. He drew pictures of how he imagined her pubic hair to be, and then deposited them ashamedly in litter bins throughout Southall. And he was miserable.

Ms Hackstraw was looking stunning in gold and orange. Her tapered ankle-length skirt had thigh-length slits. Her loose diaphanous top left little to Doc's feverish imagination. Her golden hair was coiled in an Ivana Trump look. Long gold earrings dangled exquisitely. Doc Morrissey was glad that there were no other customers in the Goffley Tandoori to wonder what she was doing with this balding, wizened man.

'How are your samosas?' he asked.

'Excellent. Your aloo chat?'

'Cardboard. I think only of how you might taste.'

'Doc! I can't keep calling you Doc, Doc. Don't you have an actual Christian name?'

'Well, yes, of course I do.'

'So what is it?'

'Well, funnily enough, ironically enough, it's Gerald.'

'Gerald and Geraldine. How quaint. How . . .'

'Ridiculous. Or are we meant for each other, Ms Hackstraw?'

'Why do you keep calling me Ms Hackstraw?' Ms Hackstraw lowered her voice. Two other customers had entered the restaurant.

'Because I promised C.J. that I would,' said Doc Morrissey in equally low tones.

The waiter arrived at this important moment, as waiters often do. They assured him that their starters had been delicious, and then remained silent until he had cleared their plates.

The restaurant was decorated with crude, brightly coloured paintings of canal scenes in Kashmir.

'You promised C.J. that you would?' prompted Geraldine Hackstraw at last. 'Why? Are you frightened of him?'

'Good Lord, no. Me frightened of C.J.? That's a good one.'

'Then why?'

The waiter brought their main course, and they had to remain silent again until he had gone.

'It amused me to do so,' said Doc Morrissey. 'I can get as

70

much affection into the words "Ms Hackstraw" as I could into
. . . the name I must not name. So I promised the poor old
bugger that unimportant thing.' He leant forward and clasped
her fine, long-fingered, sweet-veined hand. 'I didn't promise
not to take you out to dinner.'

She took a mouthful of her food and chewed delicately.

He took a mouthful of his food and chewed absent-mindedly.

'How's your sag gosht?' he asked.

'Delicious. How's your chicken jalfrezi?'

'Like a face flannel. I can taste nothing.' He clasped her hand
again. 'I didn't promise not to attempt to inveigle myself into
your sheets,' he said. 'I say "your sheets" because my place is so
modest. I know I'm being presumptuous and pathetic and
possibly even offensive, but will you sleep with me tonight?'

Geraldine Hackstraw removed Doc Morrissey's hand quite
gently.

They assured the waiter that their main course was delicious.

'I don't think you're being presumptuous or pathetic or
offensive,' said Ms Hackstraw when the waiter had gone.

'You mean . . .?'

'Precisely. Of course I won't sleep with you. I value your
friendship far too highly.'

C.J. had said 'Oh, God' that evening because the revolution was
a tiresome interruption to the only two things that mattered in
his life – the pursuit of his passion for Ms Hackstraw, and of the
million pounds.

His feelings of desire for Ms Hackstraw were not perhaps
quite as intense as Doc Morrissey's. They had to share space in
his heart with his yearning for the million pounds. But they
were still pretty fierce, and the fact that Ms Hackstraw was
involved in the small matter of the million pounds made them
all the more so. He felt a new potency.

He was feeling this new potency on the evening after the

meeting to elect their leader, when he dined with Ms Hackstraw in La Belle Epoque, which is thought by some shrewd judges to be the better of Climthorpe's two French restaurants.

She was wearing a short, emerald green sarong-style dress which revealed plenty of leg and had a cross-over top which revealed plenty of cleavage. Its slim lines emphasised her narrow waist. Her hairstyle had been transformed. Ivana Trump had disappeared and been replaced by Veronica Lake. Her long golden hair cascaded forward over one shoulder. C.J. ran his hand over his head as if once again he had forgotten that he had no hair to tidy. He was glad that there were so many customers in the restaurant to appreciate what a distinguished couple they made.

Over the poulet de Bresse, which was actually poulet de Sun Valley, C.J. sighed deeply, and said, 'Geraldine! Geraldine!'

'What?'

'I just love hearing your name. In my mind it's shaped like your body. It's my fervent wish, Geraldine, that nobody will ever again speak your name in quite the same way as I speak it. "Geraldine!"'

'So I gather.'

'What do you mean, "So I gather"?'

'Don't be cross with me, Bunny,' said Ms Hackstraw. 'But yesterday I had dinner with Doc Morrissey.'

'What? With that senile oaf?'

'He's about the same age as you, Bunny.'

'Yes, but I'm not a senile oaf. It's a case of the pot calling the kettle a horse of a very different colour.'

'Nothing happened, Bunny.'

'What do you mean, "Nothing happened"? Of course nothing happened. He wouldn't be capable of anything happening. I'd say he was past it except that that would suggest that he had once been capable of it. He was born past it and went steadily downhill from there. He's a quack.'

72

'Don't you like him?'

Laughter sparkled in Geraldine Hackstraw's large grey eyes like sunlight on waves.

'Oh, Geraldine. And I made the bastard promise . . .'

'You made him promise not to call me Geraldine. He didn't.'

'Ah! Did he . . . make suggestions? Did he try any hanky-panky?'

'Surely you wouldn't expect me to reveal intimate details? Any more than I'll tell him intimate details of what passes between us. I *will* tell him I've seen you.'

'Of course. Why not? I'm not frightened of him.' C.J. took a slice from his medallions of venison, and chewed powerfully, sexily. Suddenly an unpleasant thought struck him. 'You'll tell him? How? When?'

'When we next have dinner.

'You'll have dinner with him again?'

'Yes.'

'I forbid it.'

'How dare you tell me what to do?'

'But . . .'

'I enjoy my dinners with him. There's a friendly intimacy which is not a million miles from sexuality.'

'Geraldine!'

'And I enjoy my dinners with you. There's also a friendly intimacy with you which is not a million miles from sexuality.'

'Surely there can be something more?'

'Who knows? It would be a foolish person who said "never". But . . . not yet. Poor Bunny.'

Suddenly C.J. realised that Geraldine held the power and he didn't feel so sexy any more.

The head waiter slid up to them on invisible castors, as head waiters often do.

'Is everything all right?' he smarmed.

'No, it damned well isn't,' said C.J., and the head waiter froze in a parody of hurt astonishment. 'The woman I love insists on sharing me with a bloody old wreck.'

Tom had said 'Oh God' that evening because the revolution was a tiresome interruption to the only two things that mattered in his life – the pursuit of his passion for Ms Hackstraw, and his chosen profession.

Two evenings after the meeting at which Jimmy had been elected leader, Tom found it almost impossible to believe that he was sitting opposite the woman of his dreams in the Bangkok, Climthorpe's first Thai restaurant. What did foreigners think when they tried to find English food?

The woman of his dreams was looking more demure than he had hoped. She was wearing a fine, navy wool suit with a cream blouse. Her golden hair was draped back in a chignon.

I'm so grateful to you for agreeing to come out with me,' he said humbly.

Ms Hackstraw made an irritated little movement with her right hand, as if trying to brush away this unwelcome humility.

'I might have lost my sanity if you hadn't,' he continued.

She frowned, and changed the subject hastily. 'What will you do if you get the million pounds?'

'"If"?' said Tom. 'Will it be hard?'

'It's not my job to give it out without a substantial achievement on your part.'

'Oh, Lord.'

'How's it going?'

'We're all working together. I don't think I should say more at this stage.'

A plump waiter with an infectious smile brought their steamboat fish soup.

'In answer to your question,' said Tom, as the waiter ladled soup and prawns and mushrooms into white bowls, 'I'll open up an estate agent's, called Patterson, Patterson and Patterson.'

He took a sip of his soup, was astonished by its fieriness, and remembered with dismay that spicy food made his nose run.

'Who will the other Pattersons be?'

'Nobody.' He sniffed. Oh God! 'But it wouldn't sound right if it was just called "Patterson's". It'd sound like an Irish pub.' He sniffed again. 'No, I'll do it entirely on my own next time. Then I can guarantee efficiency.'

'An efficient estate agency – that would be something,' said Geraldine Hackstraw drily.

Tom gave her a suspicious look and blew his nose loudly.

'Sorry about that,' he said. 'I'm not infectious. It's just that spicy food always makes my nose run.'

They ate the delicious, fiery soup in silence for a few moments. The narrow, dark restaurant, decorated with bamboo mats and tapestries of exotic temples, was throbbing with conversation, except at their table. Tom could think of nothing to say. His nose streamed. He felt clumsy and inelegant sitting opposite this lovely lady. He was sure there were bits of prawn and lemon grass in his beard. It had all been a dreadful mistake. He took another gulp of wine. He was drinking too fast. Why didn't Ms Hackstraw speak?

At last she did.

'I hear you make your own wine,' she said.

'Oh!' Tom was flattered. 'My fame goes before me. Who told you?'

'Either C.J. or Doc Morrissey. Over dinner.'

Fury swept over Tom. It was not an emotion that he could control. He could feel it distorting his face, and was glad of his beard. Geraldine was looking at him rather intensely. He blew his nose again.

'So you're still seeing them?' he said in a hoarse voice.

'Yes. Am I not entitled to?'

'Well, I . . . yes, but they're old men.'

'You behave like an old man.'

Tom gasped.

'I'm sorry,' said Geraldine Hackstraw. 'I don't want to be rude, but you're sitting there gawping at me like a pregnant duck.'

'I've never seen a pregnant duck gawp, I must have led a sheltered life, but I don't think I'm flattered,' said Tom huffily. 'I'm finding this difficult enough anyway. It's an ordeal for me, if you must know.'

'Then why did you ask me out?'

'Because I love you. I adore you. I worship you. I'm sorry.'

'I should hope you are sorry, Tom. Do you think a woman likes to hear such things from a man she hardly knows? You don't love me. You don't know me enough to love me. You're obsessed by me. It's a most awful intrusion on one's physical privacy to be obsessively desired by a man one doesn't desire.'

'I hope that one day I might persuade you to desire me.' Tom's heart was racing. It needed conversational boldness beyond the range of your average failed estate agent to continue, but he must grab his chance or it would never come again. 'I believe we could have a wonderful rich life together and I could make love to you as you've never been made love to before.'

'That wouldn't be too difficult. My husband was a cold fish and hardly ever even . . .'

Ms Hackstraw's revelations were interrupted by the arrival of the red duck curry and the crab claws in chilli sauce.

'You were . . . er . . . you were saying?' said Tom, when the waiter had gone.

'I didn't have much sex in marriage and I've had none since. It suits me. It's a messy business, I seem to remember. Rather ridiculous really. So our life together would be a fiasco and you would shrivel up physically and emotionally.' She reached across the table and squeezed Tom's hand. 'Put yourself out of your misery now. Learn to forget me.'

The red duck curry made Tom's nose stream again, and the crab claws proved impossible to eat without turning his beard into a dustbin.

'Do C.J. and Doc Morrissey know that you . . . think sex is messy?' asked Tom.

'Heavens, no. I don't want to deny them the pleasure of the chase.'

'But you've told me. Why?'

'Because your feelings are too intense. They need to be weakened or you'll destroy yourself. I'm not that irresponsible.'

'Pretty irresponsible. C.J. or Doc might die of excitement. C.J. has a bad heart and Doc has lots of pain he can't diagnose.'

'Not a bad way to go. Better than a lingering death. Forget me, Tom. Sexless and irresponsible.'

'I believe, Geraldine, that with you I could become a better lover than either you or I ever dreamt of, and I could awaken your latent sexuality.'

'Fantasy, Tom. Fantasy.'

They ate in silence for a while.

'Could you not possibly go back to Linda?' asked Ms Hackstraw at last.

'No. Oh no.'

'May I ask what happened?'

'I discovered she was having an affair.'

'Were you entirely faithful?'

Tom hesitated.

'Yes, but I did once try not to be,' he admitted.

'So why not forgive her?'

'It was incest.'

'Oh.'

'I shouldn't have told you that.'

'With Jimmy?'

'How did you . . .? I'm not saying.'

'With Jimmy.'

'I shouldn't have told you.'

'I promise it'll go no further. There are limits to my irresponsibility. Has it stopped?'

'Oh yes, but . . . I mean, how could she?'

'He has a latent, utterly frustrated strength that she might find stimulating. I do think you should try to forgive her.'

'Maybe I'm not a forgiveness person.' He blew his nose again, and apologised again.

Their conversation continued in an impersonal vein. They discussed the making of wine, the art of pricing houses, the use and abuse of spices. Right at the end of the meal, Tom said, 'I've been awful. I haven't asked you a thing about yourself.'

'Precisely,' said Geraldine Hackstraw. 'All you have for me is obsessive physical desire. The person you love and adore and worship is yourself.'

David and Prue Harris-Jones didn't scale the heights of indifference to the revolution that were achieved by Doc Morrissey, C.J. and Tom, but they faced two problems, one logistical, the other temperamental. Their logistical problem was that they faced a massive journey from West Wales every time they came to a meeting. Their temperamental problem was that they were not of the stuff of which revolutions are made, even bloodless ones. In the years after the sad collapse of Reggie's community, while David worked in the family's furniture business in Haverfordwest, they had become quite confident, able to walk into a pub of a Sunday lunchtime in identical puce sweaters and exchange banter with the best of them. The firm's take-over and David's subsequent redundancy had changed all that. Even at their most confident they would have found that there was a yawning gap between walking into a pub in matching sweaters and marching down Whitehall to take over the government of the nation. Now that gap had become a chasm. Elizabeth provided a solution for the logistical problem. She offered them the use of a bedroom in number thirty-eight, Leibnitz Drive. But the temperamental problem would be harder to solve.

Nor was Linda exactly raring to go down the road to revolution. She was more interested in her usual pastime of wandering round the shops looking at clothes and jewellery that she couldn't afford, and losing weight so that she might attract a man who could afford them.

Joan and Hank showed more enthusiasm for the project than the others. Joan, like Elizabeth, wished to respect Reggie's memory, and Hank thought the whole idea 'wicked'.

Nevertheless, it was clear to Elizabeth that there was a major crisis of enthusiasm, and so, on a cool morning at the end of January, three days after Jimmy had been elected leader, she drove to Clement Attlee Mansions and bearded their new leader in his den.

A *History of England*, borrowed from Spraundon library, was open on the cheap, battered coffee table. Jimmy seemed slightly abashed.

'I'm slightly abashed,' he said.

'Why?'

'Caught with my history book open at Wat Tyler's rebellion. Might seem . . .'

'*Folie de grandeur?*'

'Yes.'

'You could always have closed the book before answering the door.'

'Didn't think of that. Bit of a cock-up on the frontal lobe front. Thick. Do you know how his fracas ended, incidentally? Stabbed to death by a fishmonger's dagger.'

'Jimmy? Your troops need to be inspired. You will have to inspire them. I need that from you as their leader.'

'How?'

'Summon them to a meeting. 08.00 hours prompt. No

79

slacking. Tell them why you're grabbing this opportunity. Give it to them on the chin.'

'With you. On the chin. Will do.'

The winter toyed with Europe, sent snow flurries and a night of frost, then turned absurdly mild again. It rained and rained and rained. There were floods in the West Country and York-shire. There were worse floods in Holland and Germany and France. The European winter games, in Spain, were cancelled due to the complete absence of snow. In cosy pubs, before unnecessary log fires, people talked about global warming and did nothing.

On a Wednesday in early February, Major James Anderson, leader of the Bloodless Revolution of Senior Citizens and the Occupationally Rejected, drove his eleven-year-old jeep through driving rain to Goffley, turned right into Wittgenstein View, left into Sartre Rise, and left again into Leibnitz Drive. It was 07.58 precisely.

And so, on the dot of 08.00 hours, the old soldier, his back almost as stiff as a ramrod, his shoulders barely bent, all the morning gunge removed from the corners of his eyes, marched into that temple of upholstery, the through-lounge/diner of number thirty-eight, Leibnitz Drive, and saw . . . absolutely nobody.

Elizabeth hurried in, carrying a half-consumed cup of coffee.

'Bit of a cock-up on the date front?' enquired Jimmy.

'No.'

'Well, where the hell is everybody?'

'David and Prue are finishing breakfast. They had a long day yesterday moving all their stuff from Haverfordwest and I suggested they lingered over coffee till you came.'

'Lingered over coffee? Thought this was a parade.' Jimmy raised his voice. 'David! Prue! Let's be having you.'

David and Prue Harris-Jones entered rather blearily. Charcoal grey was the colour they had chosen for their sweaters. Prue yawned.

'Sorry,' she said. 'We had a long day yesterday.'

'I'll give you long day yesterday!' said the disgruntled old soldier.

The doorbell rang at 08.07 hours. It was Joan. 'Sorry I'm late,' she said. 'The traffic was terrible.'

'Traffic terrible!' exclaimed Jimmy. 'Never heard anything so ridiculous. Sorry I missed the battle, Monty. Got behind a milk float at the Alamein crossroads. Start earlier, Joan.'

'Yes. Sorry. Hank's at work, incidentally, but he sends his love.'

'Oh, that's all right then,' enthused Jimmy sarcastically. 'So long as he's sent his love.'

Doc Morrissey arrived at 08.13 hours.

'I'm sorry I'm late,' he said. 'Prawn vindaloo, I'm afraid.'

'Prawn vindaloo!' yelled Jimmy. 'Prawn vindaloo! What kind of excuse is that? Probably find Tom's late because his sparkling cauliflower chardonnay gave him wind.'

Linda arrived at 08.16 hours.

'Sorry I'm late,' she said. 'I couldn't find the right earrings.'

Jimmy opened his mouth twice, like an asthmatic brill, but he couldn't bring himself to rebuke Linda.

'Tricky little blighters, earrings,' he said. 'So I've heard, anyway. Little tip from an old soldier. Try choosing earrings the night before.'

Tom arrived at 08.21 hours.

'I do apologise,' he said. 'I didn't sleep well. My sparkling cauliflower chardonnay gave me wind, and then I dropped into a deep sleep at about six, and overslept!'

'I'll give you wind before you're through,' said Jimmy.

Tom looked at him sourly. Then he looked at Doc Morrissey sourly.

'Had any good dinners lately, Doc?' he said.

'I haven't a clue what you're talking about,' said the old medico calmly.

It was 08.28 when C.J. arrived.

'I'm sorry I'm late,' he said, not sounding at all sorry. 'I had a dinner engagement that dragged on somewhat.'

'I'm so sorry it was a drag,' said Doc Morrissey bitterly.

'Oh absolutely,' said Tom. 'What a shame.'

'It wasn't a drag at all,' said C.J. 'I should have said we lingered in the candlelight.'

'Never mind lingering in the fucking candlelight,' said Jimmy. 'Oops. Sorry. Ladies present. Forgot. Er . . . don't know what's going on, but time to forget all this guff about dinners.' He paused, and looked at Elizabeth hesitantly.

'Jimmy has summoned you all here to read the riot act,' she said. 'You were called for 08.00 hours. We are not joking. We are not playing at this.'

C.J. sighed.

'It's no use sighing, C.J. There's a lot of money involved. And Jimmy is going to explain to you why there's a lot more than money involved. So, we'll have no talking, no smoking, no sighing, no yawning . . .'

Doc Morrissey belched.

'I am so sorry,' he said. 'It really is a most persistent vindaloo.'

'And no belching,' continued Elizabeth remorselessly.

'Had your vindaloo all on your own, did you, Doc? What a shame,' said C.J.

'Please!' said Elizabeth. 'Please! Our leader is about to address us.'

Jimmy stood up and faced his motley crew.

'Wat Tyler has gone down in history,' he said. 'Lambert Simnel has gone down in history. They led rebellions, and they've had streets named after them. I missed the war. Too blasted young. Sacked from Queen's Own Berkshire Light Infantry. Too blasted old. Never had any glory in my life at all.

Got my chance now. Chance for me to go down in history. Chance for me to have streets named after me. So, get your fingers out.'

The chattering of an angry magpie in Bertrand Russell Rise sounded like gunfire, so deep was the stunned silence in the lounge/diner.

'That wasn't exactly what I meant, Jimmy,' said Elizabeth softly, sadly.

'Told me to tell them why I'm grabbing this opportunity,' said Jimmy. 'Did.'

'You didn't strike quite the right note, Jimmy,' said Elizabeth the next day, accepting his offer of a coffee and handing him the jar of Nicaraguan coffee that she had brought

'Concentrated too much on my own side of things?' asked Jimmy, as he filled the kettle.

'Yes, frankly, slightly.'

Elizabeth began to wipe the condensation off the inside of the window with a piece of kitchen roll that she had also brought.

'Thought as much afterwards,' said Jimmy. 'Should have made more of the lolly. That's all those bastards care about.'

Elizabeth dropped her wet kitchen roll into the swing bin, which had no liner.

'I didn't want you to talk about the money either,' she said. 'I wanted you to appeal to their idealism.'

'Not with you.'

Elizabeth removed the soggy kitchen roll from the swing bin, got a roll of liners from her carrier bag, pulled one off, fitted it on to the swing bin and dropped the kitchen roll back into the bin.

'Needs a woman's touch, this place,' admitted Jimmy. 'Fancy a biscuit?'

'Why not?'

83

'Brought any?'

'Yes.'

'Good girl.'

They took their coffee and biscuits into the lounge. Elizabeth again chose the better of the armchairs.

'Idealism, you said,' prompted Jimmy.

'Yes. I want you to call another meeting, and explain why the revolution's a good idea.'

'Ah.'

'Explain the philosophy behind the concept.'

'Ah.'

'Our plan has sprung out of our experiences. It's absurd, but it isn't arbitrary. It has some basis in logic, however subverted. We must explain the bones.'

'I see. You want me to explain philosophy behind concept, explore basis of logic, appeal to their sense of idealism.'

'In a nutshell, Jimmy.'

'Oh, my God.'

8   A Timely Arrival

Afterwards, everyone agreed that the meeting at which Jimmy explained the philosophy behind the concept had been the turning point.

Before the meeting, apathy reigned, though with powerful pockets of enthusiasm.

After the meeting, enthusiasm reigned, though with powerful pockets of apathy.

What caused this sea change? Was it the leadership of Major James Anderson? Plunge ever onward, gentle reader, and judge for yourself.

Jimmy stood with his back to the coal-effect gas fire, and addressed the bizarre gathering in the chintzy suburban room.

'Right,' he said. 'Elizabeth will tell you why we've gathered you here.'

'Oh,' said Elizabeth. 'Will I?'

'Yes,' said Jimmy firmly.

'Ah,' said Elizabeth. She flashed Jimmy an angry 'How-like-a-man-not-to-say-a-word-about-this-beforehand-and-then-announce-it-in-public-so-that-I-have-no-alternative-but-to-agree-but-don't-think-I-won't-have-a-word-with-you-after-wards' look. 'Right. Jimmy feels you aren't giving enough thought to the philosophy behind the concept, you haven't explored the basis of the logic behind our absurdity, so today he's going to take you through that aspect of things and give you a chance to feel . . . er . . . more involved.'

'On the nose,' said Jimmy. 'Spot on. Now, in this country, at this juncture in our history, we . . . er . . . we . . . er . . .'

'We have an ageing population, with a very large proportion of senior citizens,' said Elizabeth, 'yet we remain essentially a youth culture.'

'Precisely,' said Jimmy. 'And this state of affairs . . . er . . .'

'Must stop,' said Elizabeth. 'It really is ridiculous. Films, fashion, adverts, they're all directed towards the young. The bodies that we see on adverts are lithe and lissom and lovely.'

Doc Morrissey sighed.

C.J. leant forward and glared at him.

Tom smiled at them both, appeasingly.

'Precisely,' resumed Jimmy. 'And that is absolutely . . . er . . .'

'Fatal to the morale of the nation,' said Elizabeth. 'It means that those of us who were never lithe and lissom and lovely in the first place . . .'

'As you certainly were . . . are . . .' said David Harris-Jones.

'Thank you, David,' said Elizabeth. 'Those of us who were never like that wish we were, and those of us who still are like that dread ceasing to be. Supposing we idealised wrinkles, and sagging breasts, and hollow cheeks. We'd all be moving towards our ideal, not away from it. Is that roughly what you . . . er . . . Jimmy?'

'Absolutely,' said Jimmy. 'It's time we . . . er . . . er . . .'

'Put a value on experience,' said Elizabeth. 'Presumably we learn something in our journey through life. Presumably we are a little wiser at sixty than at twenty. We should look up to experience, use it, not just give it a choice between golf in the Algarve or life in a retirement home. How do we intend to achieve our aims, Jimmy?'

'How indeed?' said Jimmy. 'How indeed?'

There was silence, then, but it was soon broken by Linda.

'I agree with a lot of that,' she said, leaning across to pat her

86

mother's hand. 'No, I really do. I'm not a political type. I think about practical things – clothes, my children, my home. But I'm no chicken any more.'

'Nonsense,' said Jimmy gallantly, and Linda actually thought that she could see him blush.

'Well, I'm not, and I realise that very little in the fashion world is really aimed at me. At my age I'm not a desirable object any more. I've been a bit lukewarm so far, but I'm beginning to see the point. I mean it's true what . . . er . . . Jimmy said. I've been going through the motions for the money, but I'd like to get properly involved.'

'Me too,' said Tom.

'Careful, Tom,' said Linda. 'We might end up agreeing with each other.'

'The cause is too important to be messed up by personal quarrels,' said Tom loftily. He glared at C.J. and Doc Morrissey. 'This is no time to be petty. I'm not a pettiness person. I listened carefully to what . . . er . . . Jimmy said, and there was a lot of sense in it.'

'Oh! Thank you,' said Jimmy.

'I'm too young to go on the scrap heap,' continued Tom. 'I've too much to offer the world.'

Several retorts sprang to Linda's mind. To her surprise, she found herself biting them back.

'I don't find commitment easy,' said Tom. 'I've never really been a commitment person. Why not? What have I got that's so wonderful that I can afford to stand aloof? I give my commitment to the cause, unstintingly. I commit myself publicly, irrevocably, utterly. What else have I got? Failure and fantasy. I'm yours, Jimmy.'

'Oh! Well . . . thank you very much, Tom,' said Jimmy. 'Er . . . glad to accept you.'

'If this means being on the same side as Linda, agreeing with her, marching shoulder to shoulder . . .'

87

Linda closed her eyes. There was no way she could avoid hearing the sarcastic punch-line, but it might be less painful if she couldn't actually see Tom.

'If this means talking to Linda and being forced to co-operate with her,' continued Tom, 'then that's an added bonus.'

Linda opened her eyes and looked at him in astonishment.

He smiled. It was a stiff, awkward, shy smile, but it was a smile.

Linda gave him a faint smile in return.

Elizabeth felt the hairs on the back of her neck stand up, and David and Prue Harris-Jones came out in synchronised goose-pimples. No words could add anything to this dramatic moment, least of all the words, 'The night is always darkest before the mast.'

'Thank you, C.J.,' said Elizabeth.

There was another less poignant, altogether emptier silence then. A silence into which C.J., or Doc Morrissey, or Joan, or David and Prue Harris-Jones might possibly have thrown some positive comment, some personal commitment. None came, and the doorbell rang.

It was Hank. He looked even whiter than ever, as if he'd chalked his face and hair. His eyes were dark pools of suffering.

'Hank!' said Joan, delight giving way rapidly to concern. 'What are you doing here?'

'Joining the club,' said Hank. 'Joining the revolution.' He gave a lopsided smile. 'I was told I'm losing my grip. Not sufficiently "on the ball". Too old.'

'Hank!'

Joan went up to him and flung her arms round him.

'Oh my darling,' she said. 'Oh my poor baby. How could they do this to you?'

'Very easily, without a qualm,' said Hank.

Jimmy coughed.

'Predicament understood,' he said. 'Moment of emotion

overlooked. Don't want to be tactless, but moment of emotion over, meeting continues.'

But Joan continued to cling to her City-suited lover in the middle of that crowded room.

'Sit down!' barked Jimmy.

Joan and Hank looked at him in amazement.

'Jimmy!' said Elizabeth.

'Sorry,' said Jimmy. 'Thought we were having a revolution. It's obviously only another tea party. My mistake. Bring on the toasted tea-cake.'

'Jimmy's right,' said David Harris-Jones. 'I mean, not right to shout "Sit down" but right. We must go on. Hank proves that. I mean . . . we're sorry about the job. Well, I'm sorry, anyway. But it's just like what happened to me. I mean, they're ruthless bastards.'

Elizabeth fetched an extra chair from the kitchen, and put it beside Joan's. Hank sank down on to it, and clutched Joan's hand. They both looked severely shaken.

'No, but, heaven knows, I'm no revolutionary,' said David Harris-Jones. 'Let's face it, I'm not a Che Guevara.' They faced the fact that he wasn't a Che Guevara in thoughtful silence. 'I mean, I care about things, I've written to the Prime Minister twice, had very nice replies from his secretary, but . . . rebellion, revolution, taking over the government, I'd never have thought I could really be a part of that.'

'Me neither,' said Prue. 'I . . . er . . . I listened very carefully to . . . er . . . Jimmy, and I was impressed.'

'Thank you, Prue,' said Jimmy modestly.

'I thought, "Yes, there's more in this than . . ."'

'. . . hits the nail on the head,' said C.J.

'And then I thought, "Yes, but I don't know, am I really going to take part, can I really be any use?"' said Prue.

'Yes, and I thought, "Will there ever be enough fire in my belly?"' said David Harris-Jones.

'And then in you came, Hank,' said Prue.

'And I thought, "It's an outrage. Count me in",' said David Harris-Jones.

'Turned out to be lucky you came in when you did, Hank,' said Doc Morrissey.

'Well, that's all right then,' said Hank bitterly. 'So long as I lost my job for a reason.'

9   *On the Road*

The following Monday, in number thirty-eight, Leibnitz Drive, a leathery old warrior made a stirring call to a small group of middle-aged and elderly revolutionaries.

'Time for thought is over,' he said. 'Time for action has come. I have fixed the date of the revolution. Sunday, August the twentieth.'

Jimmy explained that the date had been chosen because Members of Parliament would all be away on holiday, and London would be stale and drowsy. What he didn't explain was that this had been Elizabeth's idea, not his.

'Put it in your diaries,' he told them excitedly.

'No,' said Elizabeth hastily. 'There must be nothing on paper. Security.'

'Don't put it in your diaries,' Jimmy told them excitedly.

And indeed there was an air of excitement in that incongruously chintzy suburban room. Excitement mingled with awe and fear. Now that the date was fixed they all felt that it was actually going to happen. David and Prue Harris-Jones clasped hands. Their pulses raced. They were afraid. Elizabeth looked up at the ceiling as if she were looking far beyond the ceiling to Reggie in Heaven, as if she were saying, 'We're going to do you proud, darling.' Jimmy could smell cordite, even though there was no cordite. Whole minutes passed without Linda wondering what she would buy when she had her million pounds. She looked across at Tom, and he smiled.

Hank had a streaming cold. It was twenty years since he had last had a cold, twenty years of vibrancy, of adrenalin, of excitement. Now he felt completely adrift. The moment he had stepped out of the world of the City he had felt that it had all been deeply boring, utterly meaningless, the excitement totally spurious. He had given his best years to an illusion. He had been conned. He would do anything to get back at the bastards, if only he didn't feel so tired.

Tom had enjoyed smiling at Linda. He had decided to give in to the idea of the revolution not because he believed in it, but because it presented him with an alternative to Ms Hackstraw, and also . . . yes, also, and to his surprise . . . because Linda had committed herself to it. Now that he had committed himself, he was beginning to believe in the cause. Hank's dismissal had cemented his feelings, and he saw the force of Elizabeth's point. It really would be rather wonderful if we were all moving towards the best years of our lives, rather than away from them. Sometimes he almost forgot that he was an embittered, failed estate agent.

Only C.J. and Doc Morrissey felt nothing of the excitement of the new forces that were shaping their lives. Each was trapped in his absurd love for Ms Hackstraw, and in his hostility to the other. Never had the adage, 'There's no fool like an old fool' seemed more true.

'I want you all to go out there,' Jimmy said, 'to . . . er . . . to the . . . er . . .'

'Old people's homes, retirement homes, sheltered flats, golf clubs, impotence clinics, Saga Holidays and prostate wards of our ageing island,' said Elizabeth.

'Absolutely. Spot on. Tell them what we plan. Get them to put August the twentieth in their . . . well, not in their diaries. Security. In their minds.'

'Is it safe to give them the date?' asked Linda.

'Is it safe to tell them anything?' asked David Harris-Jones.

'Quandary,' said Jimmy. 'Don't know the answer. Confusing wallahs, quandaries.'

'Oh, do be sensible,' said Tom. 'We can't go up to people and say, "We're going to do something, can't tell you what, on a particular day, can't tell you when, will you join us?" We have to take the risk and tell them.'

And so, there was much thumbing through the *Yellow Pages* and much reading of maps, and the revolutionaries set off on their great task.

Major James Anderson rattled round Surrey and Berkshire in his old jeep, sniffing the premature spring, scenting the cordite, feeling the sap rising. All right, it couldn't compare with killing people, but he had long ago abandoned hope of ever actually killing anyone, and he had the open road ahead of him, his map beside him, and his schedule on his clipboard. If only Linda could be beside him, legs still slightly plump, if regrettably less so nowadays. Oh, Linda. Down, soldier's friend.

His first port of call was the Evergreen Residential Home just outside Coxwell. A long drive led up to a stern Georgian stone house, softened by creepers. He parked beside an Audi and marched purposefully up the steps, carrying his clipboard. A nurse greeted him. In the foyer an old lady opened her arms and shouted 'Daddy!', which upset him, but he scurried on and found himself in a large lounge, which smelt of furniture polish and daffodils. White-haired people were reading books and newspapers, arguing over law and order, gossiping about sex, and playing bridge and Scrabble.

'Good morning,' he said, addressing them all. 'Anderson's the name. Don't know you, you won't know me, so hello.' He gave them what he thought, mistakenly, would be recognised as a smile.

'Do you need some Rennies?' said a retired fishmonger.

There was laughter.

93

'No, I don't need any Rennies,' said Jimmy gamely, and he tried another smile, to show that there was no ill feeling. 'I'm here on a rather unusual mission. Top secret. Should be fun. We're planning a revolution. Take over Britain on behalf of the elderly and the redundant, that kind of crack. How about that, eh?'

'You're mad,' said the widow of a pest control officer.

A matron entered and ordered Jimmy to leave. He contemplated grappling her in a half nelson, but thought that this might frighten the old folk. He left quietly, cheeks blazing, and thinking furiously, which he never found easy.

Things were little better at his next port of call, the Verruca Foundation's Home for Retired Chiropodists on the outskirts of New Blagdon. Here he made his address more pithy. 'Ageing population. Youth culture rampant. Bad show. Remedy – revolution. March on Whitehall. Take over government.'

The elderly chiropodists looked at him in astonishment.

'March?' exclaimed one. 'At our age? With our feet?'

'We know about feet,' said another.

'We value feet. I don't think we'd attempt it,' put in a third.

'Where's the spirit that won an Empire?' asked Jimmy sadly.

'Locked up in my room,' said a good-looking, well-endowed lady chiropodist from Clacton. 'Fancy coming up and sharing it with me, handsome?'

Jimmy fled.

Elizabeth decided to start with the gentlemen's clubs of London's West End. If anywhere was full of old people, they would be.

She began at the Reliance Club. The porter was on his knees, looking for a ten-pence piece, so she just walked straight in and up the long staircase, past all the portraits of old actors and judges, very few of whom had actually been members, though nobody was to know that.

With every step her reluctance increased. She wasn't Reggie and it was hard work pretending that she was. But she wouldn't let him down. She would go through with this absurdity to the hilt.

She could hear a hum of masculine conversation, and had no difficulty finding the bar. Men in dark suits, with round shoulders and hideous old school ties, were three deep at the counter. As she entered, the conversation faltered and then stopped, and everyone turned to look at her.

Suddenly they all spoke with one voice.

'I spy with my little eye, something I hoped not to see e'er I die,' they thundered.

An old gentleman with hair as silvery as hers and a face the colour of a 1986 Margaux approached her, smiling.

'Don't look so abashed, my dear,' he said. 'It's only tradition. It's nothing personal.'

'I just wanted to talk to some people,' said Elizabeth lamely.

'My dear lady! No woman has ever crossed the threshold of the Reliance at lunchtime, even during the hostilities.'

He looked so old that Elizabeth wasn't sure which hostilities he meant.

'Let me lead you out, my dear.'

He led her down the stairs, past all the stern faces, which might have been painted for just such a moment as this.

At the front door, standing with her back to the paintings, and longing to walk out into the comparative sweetness of the street, she felt as if the eyes of all the portraits had turned to follow her. Her flesh crawled. Give me strength, Reggie, she cried out silently. It was important to rescue something from the wreckage of her first public confrontation.

'How would you like it if the elderly were truly respected in this country?' she asked.

'My dear lady,' said the silvery-haired old gentleman in a

slightly doddery voice. 'I have all the respect I need. I'm a High Court judge.'

I don't think I need tell you, gentle reader, that C.J. didn't get where he is today by asking old people if they would join a bloodless revolution. He hadn't the slightest enthusiasm for the cause. All he wanted was the money. He was the only one who didn't need the money at all, and so he wanted it more keenly than any of the others.

C.J. visited no retirement homes, no sheltered flats, no twilight villas. In fact, he didn't go anywhere near a euphemism at all. He sat in the panelled study of Expansion Cottage, his substantial five-bedroomed house in Virginia Water, in its acre and a half of rhododendrons and silver birch, and filled in a log book of unsuccessful calls on behalf of the Bloodless Revolution of Senior Citizens and the Occupationally Rejected. Why did he not sprinkle his failures with the occasional encouraging fictional success? Because he wanted the whole nonsensical business to be abandoned as soon as possible.

After he had recorded twelve unsuccessful visits, he went into the bathroom and cleaned every corner where Ms Hackstraw might put her exquisite limbs that night. Then he went into the master bedroom, pulled back the nine-tog duvet, pressed his lips to the sheet that had been thus revealed, planted several sweet kisses on the sheet and gasped, 'Oh, Geraldine. Oh, Geraldine. How your Bunny loves your pussy.' As he raised his lips from the sheet, he saw the window-cleaner gazing at him in amazement.

As he paid the window-cleaner, he could hardly bring himself to look him in the eye, but the window-cleaner said, 'Don't worry, mate. What I've seen through windows could fill a book, if I could write. Yours was nuffink. Nuffink. I done some pretty crazy fings myself when the sap's been rising in the spring.'

'Thank you,' muttered C.J. grimly.

He lunched carefully, on things that couldn't taint his breath.

After lunch he filled a couple of hours by walking, and then he had a bath. He washed every crack and crevice twice, and then he had a cold shower, because the bath had made him hot. He shaved for the second time that day, and anointed himself with deodorants. He concealed his ageing body in an immaculate and expensive Italian suit. He looked at himself in the mirror and almost purred. He looked dapper

He picked up Geraldine promptly at six thirty. She was looking stunning in green and pink.

His libido and his Bentley purred on the run to the Hog's Back. He kept noticing retirement homes. That was the racket to be in.

Models of a Spitfire, a Mosquito and a Lancaster stood on the wide window-sills of the Dissipated Kipper. Aeroplane propellers hung on both brick chimney pieces, and a third concealed the florid wrought-iron grille above the bar. A fourth, smaller, white propeller adorned the upper lip of mine enormous host.

'Hello, Tiny,' said C.J.

'Hello, C.,' said Tiny. 'Long time no see, C.'

'I've been busy,' said C.J.

'So I see,' said Tiny. 'So I see, C.' He winked. 'Are you dining?'

'Oh yes.'

'Whacko.'

C.J. bought drinks and carried them to a wooden table overlooking the car park.

'What an awful man,' said Geraldine Hackstraw. 'I *hate* men who wink.'

'My brother,' said C.J. 'He's had this pub for twenty-seven years.'

'I'm sorry.' Geraldine Hackstraw smiled wryly. 'Cool Lawyer Loses Poise in Wink Slur Disaster.'

'I don't mind,' said C.J. 'I'd forgotten about his winking. I don't know why I brought you here. But the food's good.'

C.J. was lying. He had taken Geraldine there because it would not be out of the question to drive her home from the Hog's Back via Virginia Water and say, 'Gosh. We're not far from home here. Would you like to pop in and have a dekko at my little place?' To which she would reply, 'I'd love to.'

And that, after decent, crisp devilled whitebait and a disappointing beef Stroganoff – 'I haven't had a good beef Stroganoff since 1981' – was exactly what C.J. did.

But Geraldine Hackstraw did not say, 'I'd love to.' She said, 'You must think I was born yesterday, Bunny,' and C.J. said, 'I admit the intention. The bed's ready and waiting. There's nothing like striking while the bird in the hand is hot,' and Geraldine said, 'This bird is not hot and is not going to be in your hand,' and C.J. said, 'Are you ever going to come to bed with me? That's seven dinners I've bought you now,' and Geraldine said, 'That is the most terrible, crass, insensitive thing that any man has ever said to me, and that includes Mr Venison. I never want to see you again, Bunny. You're a monster,' and C.J. had driven her from Virginia Water to her small but luxurious flat in the very best part of Climthorpe in silence.

David and Prue Harris-Jones decided that they would work separately for the revolution.

'We shouldn't do things in unison on this one,' they said to each other in unison as they prepared for bed on the night of Jimmy's call to action.

They laughed at that one, and then they both said, 'I agree,' and then they laughed again.

'I don't expect any dramatic change in our personalities overnight,' David said, 'but we have to learn to be . . . I don't know . . . er . . .'

'More confident. Bolder.'

'Yes. I'll tell you what . . . no, it's silly . . . well, perhaps it isn't so silly . . . I mean, it seems very petty, but it sort of could be . . . sort of symbolic.'

'I know what you're going to say,' said Prue.

'Oh good,' said David, 'because I'm feeling shy about saying it, so it'll help me if you say it. Oh God, I don't seem to be changing very dramatically, Anyway, tell me what I was going to say or we'll be here all night.'

'We should wear different-coloured sweaters tomorrow.'

'Yes!'

So David Harris-Jones came down to breakfast, on that first day of the recruitment drive, in a blue sweater, and Prue came down in a green sweater. They felt a bit uncomfortable, but also a teeny bit proud of themselves, and Elizabeth gave them an extra round of toast as a reward for their boldness.

They tossed for the use of the car, and David won, so Prue took a train to Reading, where there were bound to be lots of old people within walking distance of each other.

As she walked past the bus station, she saw a group of mildly excited senior citizens filing on to a bus. It must be a Saga holiday. Her heart began to race. Her blood began to pump. Or was it her heart pumping and her blood racing? She wasn't sure. In any case, she knew what she must do. Quiet little Prue must transform herself into impulsive, extrovert Prue.

She jumped on to the bus. Up and down the aisle people were preparing to sit, discussing who they would sit beside, laughing and making sexy insinuations. They were so uninhibited! Prue felt empty suddenly, useless, a wraith, a void. The uninhabited among the uninhibited. People were trying to let her get past, holding in their cheerily ample buttocks to let her through. 'Is my great arse in the way, ducks?' called out a cheery lady, and everybody laughed.

'No, no, not at all,' mumbled Prue, and she felt very middle-class and dreary.

'Er . . . I wonder if I can interest you in our project,' she said.

The people around her at the back of the bus became wary. She had felt, even as she spoke, that she sounded like a cross between a double-glazing salesman and a Jehovah's Witness.

'I wonder if you're happy with your status as senior citizens,' she said.

'Course we bleeding are. We're going on holiday, darling,' said the wife of a retired signalman.

'Do us a favour, love. I'm only fifty-six,' put in a line-worker from a biscuit factory.

'Yes, well, I'm not just speaking of senior citizens,' said Prue. 'We aim to improve the lot of the redundant as well.'

'Well, that's me out, then,' said the line-worker. 'They'll never make me redundant. I'm . . . I'm indis . . . not indisposed, the other fucking thing.'

'Sidney! Language! This lady's a lady,' said the line-worker's wife.

'It's all right,' said Prue bravely. She knew that her face was bright pink. 'I'm quite used to four-letter words. Our leader sometimes uses them.'

'Indispensable. That's what you meant, Sid,' said his wife. 'Ignorant bugger.'

'That's right,' said the line-worker. 'I'm indisbleedingpensable, aren't I? Chocolate bonbons as we know 'em would cease tomorrow if I was made redundant.'

'"Our leader"!' said the signalman's wife. 'What is this organisation, then? 'Ow are you planning on improving our lot?'

'We're . . .' Oh God. 'We're . . . planning a bloodless revolution. We're going to march on Whitehall and take over the government.'

There were peals of laughter. Prue was almost jerked off her feet, and she realised that the bus was moving. Her cheeks were blazing. The signalman's wife had gone down to the front of the bus and was talking to the driver.

'The driver'd like a word with you,' she said on her return.

Prue made her way down the aisle to the front of the bus. She was aware of being an object of great curiosity. She was hating this.

'I believe you wanted to speak to me,' she said, feeling as out of place as a Conservative MP at a miners' gala.

'That's right,' said the driver. 'I believe you've been attempting to . . . I dunno, convert, recruit . . . my passengers to some cause or other.'

'Well, yes,' said Prue. 'I wasn't asking for money or anything, though.'

'No, well, that's good,' said the driver. 'That's good. But my passengers is my responsibility, they're on holiday, and their welfare is tantamount. Understood?'

'Yes.'

'I don't like interference with my passengers' welfare.'

'Yes, and I can understand that. Could you just let me off and I won't bother anybody any more.'

'Sorry, love. Can't do that. Regulations. My passengers is my responsibility "from point of departure to destination". Sorry, love. More than my life's worth.'

'Oh,' said Prue. 'Well . . . er, where are you going?'

'Bognor.'

Not often in her life had Prue Harris-Jones uttered the same words as a King of England, but she did so now.

'Bugger Bognor,' she said.

She turned away, to find the signalman's wife bearing down on her.

'"Bugger Bognor"! I like that,' said the signalman's wife. 'You're all right, gel. You just need to let your hair down a bit, that's all. Follow me. We'll see you're all right. We got a crate of Guinness!'

As Prue followed her down the aisle, the signalman's wife lifted her skirts, to great cries of delight on all sides, did a little dance, and sang, 'Didn't we have a lovely day, the day we went to Bognor?'

Tom Patterson and his former wife Linda decided that they would work together, for the revolution.

Tom telephoned Linda on the evening of Jimmy's call to action.

'It's me. Tom.'

There was silence.

'Are you still there, Linda?'

'Yes, I'm just . . . astonished.'

'I don't like talking on the phone. I'm not a telephone person. But . . . could we meet and talk?'

'Why not? I think we should talk. Why don't you come over and have a drink?'

There was silence.

'Are you still there, Tom?'

'Yes, I'm just . . . astonished.'

So Tom set off, pausing only to collect a bottle of fig nouveau, and a bottle of elderflower champagne, and drive his rattly old Peugeot in his inimitably ponderous way to Linda's flat.

Tom had never seen Linda's flat before. It was a restrained, rather anonymous affair on the ground floor of a four-storey modern block in what had once been the large garden of a large house on the edge of the ribbon development that had eaten into the green belt between Climthorpe and Goffley.

The sitting room had white walls, and the three-piece suite was upholstered in oatmeal. Two scarlet lampshades introduced a touch of colour. Above the mantelpiece, over the gas fire, was a portrait of Reggie, painted by John Bratby. Reggie had felt honoured and even moved, until he had discovered that John Bratby had painted everyone who was even remotely well

known. Anyway, there he stood, looking scornful of the oatmeal upholstery.

The gas fire was on, but turned low. There was a chill in the
air, but Tom and Linda both sweated easily, having very open
pores.

'Eighteen by thirteen, including the alcove?' ventured Tom,
looking round the room thoughtfully.

'Eighteen by twelve.'

'Close.'

He handed Linda his two bottles of wine. She was simply
dressed in black trousers and a white blouse. The trousers clung
very closely to her legs, which were distinctly less plump than
they had been at their peak. Her blouse was unbuttoned enough
to reveal the beginning of what, if people were described by
estate agents, would be called her 'ample cleavage'. She had
abandoned her new blonde look almost immediately, and now
her hair had been dyed a reddish brown by Pierre of Goffley.
She wasn't yet quite confident with it.

'What would you like to drink?' she asked.

'Well, how about what I've brought?'

She smiled bravely.

'Terrific,' she said, 'but which?'

'Well, the elderflower champagne is excellent, though I say it
as shouldn't, though it may be a bit frisky after the journey.
The fig nouveau's very interesting, nouveau doesn't last for
ever, it's nearing the end of its shelf life, so logic points to the
fig. On the other hand, and I know what you're going to say
when I say this, sentiment might suggest the champagne.'

'What am I going to say?' Linda said. ' "But, Tom, I've never
seen you as a sentiment person"?'

'Precisely. The fig nouveau does have a bit of sediment, so, in
a way . . .' Tom became coy and rogueish, which was the usual
prelude to one of his rare jokes. '. . . it's a choice between
sentiment and sediment.'

'Oh, I don't know.'

'That was a joke, incidentally.'

'Oh! Right. Yes, of course. Huh! Well, what sentiment do you feel, Tom?'

'Nothing very sensational. Just . . . I just feel rather over-whelmed by the thought that it might not be necessary to go on hating you.'

'Well, I don't enjoy hating you either, so I think that calls for champagne.'

'The champagne it is.'

Tom's prediction of friskiness proved correct.

'It doesn't matter. It's an old table,' said Linda. 'Cheers.' She took her first sip cautiously, then looked up in surprise. 'It's good. No, it is. Really good.'

'There's no need to sound so surprised. I do have occasional successes.'

They talked about their personal lives. Tom said that he had remained celibate, passing swiftly over his feelings for Ms Hackstraw. Linda said that she had not remained celibate, but didn't explain why none of her four affairs had lasted. They finished the bottle of elderflower champagne, Linda made scrambled eggs on toast, and they sat in front of the fire, with the plates on their knees, and Tom said, 'It's extraordinary that I should be doing this. I'm just not a plates-on-knees person,' and Linda said, 'It's all extraordinary after all these years,' and they discovered that fig nouveau doesn't go brilliantly with scrambled eggs, or indeed with anything, and they reminisced about Reggie, and the amazing success of Grot, and the sad failure of Perrin's, and Tom realised that he'd drunk too much to drive, and Linda said, 'You can stay here,' and their eyes didn't meet, and Tom said, 'I haven't any pyjamas,' and Linda said, 'You didn't used to be a pyjama person,' and Tom just managed to stop himself saying, 'You shouldn't say "didn't used" it's "used not", and instead he said, 'I'm still not a pyjama person, but . . . well . . . you know,' and Linda said, 'I think the bed in the spare room's aired,' and it was, and Tom spent the night there. He didn't sleep very much, and neither did Linda. In the morning he made nasty bathroom noises, to his great embarrassment, because elderflower champagne gave him wind, and he was a wind person, but he didn't mention the wind to Linda. He drove her over to his flat, which was a masculine affair on the second floor of what had been a Victorian mansion, set in wooded country four miles outside Blotchely. He gave her a cup of coffee which she drank in his bare, unloved sitting room, while he shaved and changed.

They started their recruitment efforts at a block of sheltered flats in Botchley. They didn't ask the warden's permission.

'You take the even numbers and I'll take the odd,' said Tom. 'We'll get through them quicker that way.'

'You always were . . .' Linda stopped hastily.

'What were you going to say?' Tom asked.

'Brilliant at stating the obvious. But then I thought I wouldn't say that.'

'I'm glad you didn't.'

Tom didn't have much success with the odd numbers.

'The people were odd,' he said. 'I wonder if people are odd who live in odd numbers.'

'I think they're pretty odd even in even numbers,' said Linda. She hadn't had much success either.

Joan Greengross and her burnt-out lover Hank Millbeck also decided to work together for the revolution. They began their recruitment campaign in Ibsen Ward at Climthorpe Hospital. Why the wards at Climthorpe Hospital were named after European playwrights was just one of life's many unfathomable mysteries. Why the patients in the wards should come to resemble the playwrights after whom they were named was just one of life's many bizarre facets. Anyway, it was generally believed that if you were put in Ben Travers Ward you were soon smiling your way back to health, but if you landed up in Strindberg Ward you'd come out feet first or raving.

Just before they entered Ibsen Ward, Hank had a coughing fit and Joan had a sneezing fit. She had caught Hank's cold.

The atmosphere in the ward was grave and forbidding. They approached the first bed nervously. The blood-flecked bottle attached to the catheter indicated that this was a prostate case.

'You aren't vicars, are you?' asked the prostate.

'No. Why?' said Joan.

'It's one of the bugbears of hospitals, vicars. It's very painful peeing through a tube. You don't need vicars on top. Yesterday, C of E at 9.15, Catholic at 10.10, United Reform at 11.05, rabbi at 11.50. "Take a peek, rabbi," I said. "I'm not Jewish. Wish I was today, be less painful." That got rid of him. I rang the bell. I said, "Excuse me, nurse, I'm not one of your troublemakers, your ring-the-bell-every-ten-seconds merchants, but will you instruct them not to send me any more vicars? I'm an atheist and proud of it." She only sent the chaplain, didn't she, to find out why I'm an atheist. So you're not vicars. Well done. What are you?'

'We're revolutionaries,' said Hank.

'Come again?'

'We're planning to take over the government on behalf of the redundant and the retired. This country will be a haven for old people,' said Joan.

'Sod off,' said the prostate. 'You're worse than vicars, you are.'

Three more prostates expressed similar feelings. A hernia listened more sympathetically, then said, 'It's interesting, but it all seems a bit wishy-washy.'

'Wishy-washy? A revolution! A bloodless coup!' said Joan.

'Well, yes. You don't seem to have worked anything out,' said the hernia.

As bad luck would have it, three things happened at that moment. Hank coughed, Joan sneezed, and the matron entered and threw them out for spreading germs among the post-operative.

The first call made by David Harris-Jones was to Dr Swarthy's impotence clinic in Bracknell. David had read an advertisement for the clinic while waiting to have his hair cut, and it had struck him immediately that it should be a fertile field for his endeavours.

All round the walls there were upright chairs, discreetly spread so that the patients needn't be embarrassingly close to one another.

In the middle of the room there was a low rosewood table, on which there were back numbers of *Hello!* and *Reader's Digest*, and user-friendly sex manuals with titles like *The Beauty of Sex*, *Conquering Your Inhibitions – It Can Be Fun* and *Premature Ejaculation – A Ray of Hope from Sweden*.

There were three men sitting in the waiting room, each one with his back to a different wall. All three were reading *Hello!*, which was full of details of people who were too successful, too rich, too arrogant and too insensitive to need to visit an impotence clinic.

David Harris-Jones sidled across to a chair, picked it up very carefully, took it towards one of the men, put it down very quietly, and sat on it very gently. The three patients were being so careful to avoid any embarrassing eye contact with anybody that none of them noticed him. *Hello!* may never have had such rapt readers.

'Er . . . you won't know me,' began David Harris-Jones in a low voice, and the patient, who had had no idea that David was there, almost jumped out of his foreskin.

'I won't ask you who you are,' continued David Harris-Jones in a near whisper, running his hand nervously through his thinning hair, 'because I imagine that privacy and discretion are bywords here. I . . . er . . . I represent an organisation which . . . er . . . which might be able to help you, and you might be able to help us . . . oh, I'm not asking for money, I'm just . . . er . . . our aim is to . . . er . . . create a better world for the old . . . I mean not that you're old . . . and the redundant . . . which you probably aren't . . . but . . . oh!'

His surprise was at the abrupt departure of the man. He sighed, plucked up his courage, and took his chair over to another patient, put it down very gingerly beside him, and sat on it.

'Hello,' he said.

The man transferred his attention from the *Hello!* magazine to the 'Hello' conversation with difficulty.

'I represent an organisation called the Bloodless Revolution of Senior Citizens and the Occupationally Rejected, or . . .' He hesitated as he worked out the acronym. '. . . BROSCOR. That's not bad, actually. I'll just . . . er . . . yes, we could use that . . . oh, sorry, just thinking aloud. We aim to . . . I mean, I'm being presumptuous in assuming that you have any . . . er . . . any problems with modern living, but . . .er . . . if you didn't, you wouldn't . . . well, would you? . . . so . . .'

A nurse entered.

'Mr Ingleby-Fitzpatrick?' she called.

The man to whom David Harris-Jones had been speaking sighed, stood up, and followed the nurse out of the room.

The man to whom David Harris-Jones had first spoken re-entered the room, glared at David, picked up another copy of *Hello!* and sat as far away from him as possible.

David Harris-Jones dredged up another little spurt of moral courage and took his chair over to the third patient. He had decided to try a more direct approach, in case he didn't have much time before the man fled.

'Having . . . er . . . difficulties in getting it . . . as it were . . . or in keeping it . . . as it were . . .?' he began. The man glared at him. 'I . . . er . . . I mean, since you're here I assumed . . . er . . . that you couldn't . . . er . . . or not as often as . . . er . . . anyway, how do you feel about sticking it up the government, as it were, instead of . . . or rather, hopefully, as well as . . . and I speak metaphorically, and . . . er . . .'

The nurse returned. She fixed a fierce glare upon David.

'Are you the man who's badgering our customers?' she barked.

'Well . . . er . . . yes, I . . . though I would dispute the use of the word "badgering" . . . but . . . I mean I'd call it chatting to and trying to help rather than badgering, but, yes, it's me,' said David Harris-Jones.

'Then I must ask you to leave immediately,' said the nurse.

'I . . . er . . . I apolgise if I . . . and I won't . . . I won't talk to anybody any more if it's . . . as it obviously is, though I don't think it need be . . . but anyway, I won't . . . but as for leaving, I . . . er . . . I do actually have an appointment with Dr Swarthy at 10.45,' said David Harris-Jones, handing the nurse the appointment card.

He picked up a copy of *Hello!* and sat down.

Doc Morrissey didn't give in to his apathy about the revolution quite as easily as C.J. He made one call before resorting to fiction and filling in a ledger of imaginary calls. His one visit was to the West Middlesex Golf Club. He didn't tell any of his Asian friends about his planned visit as he hated to seem too English in their eyes, and he knew that there wasn't the faintest risk of his meeting them there.

He did give in, however, after speaking to just one member. In his defence, I would point out that he made a spirited attempt to recruit that one member, and that the member made a reply so pithy and so devastating that, if you are as compassionate and understanding as I believe you to be, gentle reader, you will sympathise with the discouraged old medico.

'I've got involved in a new organisation. We're planning a bloodless revolution to take over the government on behalf of senior citizens and the redundant,' was Doc Morrissey's spirited attempt.

'Why?' was the pithy and devastating reply.

Doc Morrissey went home, told his Asian friends that he had to consider some abstruse points of philosophy, seated himself in a comfortable, if sagging, armchair in his shabby attic above an oriental spice shop, and wrote up the details of eleven more unsuccessful calls. Like C.J., he was eager to precipitate the abandonment of the project.

He had a troubled sleep that night, partly because he had eaten a particularly fiery dish of Bombay potatoes, and partly because of his dream. He dreamt that he had killed C.J. and was on the run, that he was on an island, naked with a naked Ms Hackstraw bronzed and glistening with sea water beside him, and even in his dream he didn't call her Geraldine. And then C.J. emerged naked from the sea, and he had a sword, and his expression was unfriendly, and he advanced towards Doc Morrissey, and Doc Morrissey woke up.

He spent a leisurely day, drowsing, showering, anointing himself with sweet-smelling oriental fragrances. He cleaned his teeth twice, used dental floss three times, and dressed himself in his absurdly unseasonal crumpled off-white canvas suit. The last traces of mutton dopiaza had almost gone from the lapel.

'The professor's going a-hunting,' he told his friends.

That evening he took Ms Hackstraw to the Taj Mahal in Flickley. The Taj Mahal in Flickley had remained firmly in the era of flock wallpaper. Several bright stars were painted on the ceiling. Ms Hackstraw, whose golden hair outshone those painted stars, wore a long shimmering, pale yellow dress into

110

whose folds Doc Morrissey longed to plunge his face. From her ears there hung stainless steel fishes of striking Nordic design. For once, Doc Morrissey took no raw onion with his poppadam. He wished to keep his breath sweet.

After the meal, as they sipped their coffee, which soothed and pricked their raw throats, Doc Morrissey leant forward and spoke very urgently to Geraldine Hackstraw, in a quavery voice.

'You are incredibly beautiful, my sexy darling,' he said.

Geraldine Hackstraw blushed slightly and raised her eyebrows.

'I never promised C.J. I'd not say that,' said Doc Morrissey.

'You really are a wicked old man,' said Geraldine Hackstraw.

'When given the chance,' said Doc Morrissey. 'Will you ever give me the chance to be wicked, Geraldine?'

Geraldine Hackstraw slid her hand across the table and clasped Doc Morrissey's hand.

'No,' she said.

'Why not?' said Doc Morrissey. 'Why not, most lovely of all lawyers?'

'You don't mind sounding ridiculous, do you?'

'Not in the slightest. Why not, my angel?'

'I prefer it as it is.'

'More coffee, sir, madam?' asked the waiter.

'Yes, please,' said Geraldine Hackstraw.

'No, thank you,' said Doc Morrissey. He hadn't yet abandoned all hope, and didn't want to consume so much liquid that he'd feel the need to pee in the middle of things. That had happened to him once, in Oslo.

He smiled ruefully, in recognition of the absurdity and complexity of life, in which a man could think such mundane, calculating, practical thoughts while uttering florid romantic compliments in the verbal equivalent of flock wallpaper.

'But *I* don't prefer it as it is,' he said. 'I was content in Southall. Content rather than happy, admittedly, but very content. Now I am sometimes happy and often miserable, but never content. Stop seeing C.J. He only wants one thing.'

'And you?' asked Geraldine Hackstraw gently, holding her coffee cup to her full lips. 'Don't you also want that one thing?'

'Yes, of course,' said Doc Morrissey, 'but with me it's the culmination of a whole pyramid of desire, my sweet-skinned vision. It's the expression of my utter love for you. My attic flat is modest but very clean. Come back to Southall with me.'

'I really don't think that's wise,' said Geraldine Hackstraw.

'"Wise"? What has "wise" got to do with it? Be foolish tonight. I will love you utterly, perhaps briefly, because I have rather disturbing palpitations – don't know what they are, but don't like the feel of them – but I will love you utterly. And I'll be rich. You must give me the million pounds now. What I've said tonight is so utterly absurd.'

'All this isn't still a trick to get the money is it?' asked Ms Hackstraw quietly.

'No!' shrieked Doc Morrissey desperately, and so loudly that a psychiatrist and his physiotherapist fiancée turned to stare at him in some alarm. 'How could you even think that?' He swung round and glared at the psychiatrist. 'Mind your own business and eat your dinner,' he told him. He turned back to Geraldine and tried to smile. 'Better get the bill.'

He paid the bill in silence, then turned a carefully seraphic smile on Geraldine Hackstraw and said, 'I can't take it, you see. I shall go back to Southall and try to recapture my contentment. This is goodbye, Ms Hackstraw.'

He stood up, gave her an altogether less studied, less successful, more twisted smile.

'Goodbye, Ms Hackstraw,' he said again. 'I'm sure they'll get you a taxi.'

He raised his head towards the crude stars on the ceiling, and realised fully for the first time how Reggie must sometimes have felt. He gave an astonishing cry of pain of animal longing and despair.

Everyone in the restaurant turned to stare at him, except Geraldine Hackstraw, who sipped her coffee serenely, and the physiotherapist, who concentrated hard on her dhansak in her embarrassment, a reaction which the psychiatrist would analyse at length later that night.

At that moment, however, the psychiatrist was following Doc Morrissey to the door.

'My card,' he said. 'At your service if you need me.'

The next day, they all reported the failure of their efforts at recruitment.

There was laughter when Prue told how she had woken up in a police cell in Bognor, with a screaming hangover and no recollection of how she had got there.

When Joan and Hank told of their efforts in Ibsen Ward, Tom said, 'I was in that hospital once. I had a vasectomy in Shakespeare Ward. I asked the surgeon how it had gone. "Is it *Love's Labours Lost* or *All's Well That Ends Well*?" I asked. He said, "From what I've seen, it was *Much Ado About Nothing*."'

When the laughter had died down, Tom said, with an air of wonderment, 'I've made a joke against myself.'

C.J. and Doc Morrissey won praise for the number of calls they had made, and for their persistence in the face of rejection.

David Harris-Jones made them laugh with his tale of the impotence clinic. He didn't tell them that he had himself seen Dr Swarthy, who had recommended testosterone and prayer.

But there was a slightly hysterical quality about the laughter, as if they were trying to hide from themselves the gloom that they were feeling.

Jimmy, however, surprised them with his optimism.

'Excellent progress,' he said. 'First rate.'

'But we've failed utterly,' said Elizabeth.

'Yes, but people are upset that they failed. Means they're taking it seriously,' said Jimmy. 'Got under your skins. Good show. Well done. Besides, think I know what we've done wrong.'

This remark, sad to relate, was greeted with a degree of incredulity which spoke volumes for the legatees' opinion of their leader's mental powers.

'Oh,' said Tom. 'So you think you know what we've done wrong, do you?'

'Yes,' said Jimmy. 'We've done things the wrong way round. Got our tactics wrong. Tricky wallahs, tactics. Should have sat down, worked out our policies, what we stand for, how we should put our message across, then gone recruiting.'

There was a stunned silence in the lounge/diner.

'You're stunned,' said Jimmy. 'You think I'm talking nonsense.'

'No,' said Elizabeth. 'We think you're talking sense. That's why we're stunned.'

'Charming,' said Jimmy. 'Bloody charming. Bloke makes a sensible suggestion, bloke gets ridiculed. Charming.'

'It is indeed a sensible suggestion, though,' said C.J. 'That's exactly what we've done. We've put the horse before the egg.'

10 *Tricky Wallah, Leadership*

March winds tweaked at precocious bulbs, and the Children of the Bloodless Revolution of Senior Citizens and the Occupationally Rejected began to plan their strategy in earnest.

Their leader had begged them to think long and hard over the weekend.

The fruits of their thinking varied considerably.

David and Prue Harris-Jones thought long and hard without coming up with much, even though they were sadly uninterrupted by the results of David's early doses of testosterone and prayer.

Joan and Hank came up with nothing, because they were still full of cold and Hank was overcome with lethargy after twenty years of frenetic tension.

C.J. and Doc Morrissey didn't even try to think of anything.

Linda spent long hours looking round the shops to find something nice for Tom, while Tom spent long hours sitting at home, furrowing his brow, achieving nothing. Yet when Tom had his idea it came suddenly and without a furrowed brow. He had taken Linda to La Bella Napoli in Bagshot, for dinner. 'Eureka,' he said suddenly, over the parma ham and melon.

'What?' said Linda.

'I've had an idea. It's very absurd. It's very Reggie.'

'What is it?'

'Young age pensions. Instead of old age pensions. Everybody has a pension from the age of eighteen to twenty-eight, so that they can learn about life and won't be wet behind the ears when they start working.'

'That's brilliant, Tom,' said Linda. 'That's really stupid.'

'Oh!' said Tom. 'Well, thank you.'

After the meal, he drove Linda home, and she didn't quite dare ask him in for a nightcap, which was probably just as well, because he wouldn't have quite dared to go in. He kissed her on the cheek, said, 'It is nice not hating you any more, Lindysquerps,' and waited to make sure she wasn't attacked on her way up her drive, as one does these days, even in semi-rural Surrey.

Jimmy sat in flat twenty-two, Clement Attlee Mansions, in increasing terror of Monday morning.

Elizabeth thought long and hard, and called out to Reggie for guidance, and maybe she got some guidance from him, for certainly she had a few ideas, and she wrote them down, and on Sunday afternoon she took them over to Clement Attlee Mansions.

'How are you?' she asked.

'In mortal dread,' admitted the old soldier. 'Bayonetting the enemy, no terror. Avoiding snipers' fire, iron nerve. Seriously injured in battle, equilibrium barely dented. Not that I ever had any of those experiences, chap reaches puberty, blasted peace breaks out. But, point is, no terrors if I had had. Addressing meeting on Monday morning, everyone listening to my thoughts, quaking in my boots. Reason – haven't got any bloody thoughts.'

'No, but I have,' said Elizabeth.

She handed him what she had written.

He read it slowly, then stood up abruptly, marched to the window, and stared out over a snowy, slushy landscape. The light was fading.

'Look a real prat when you read this brilliant stuff out and I've got the square root of bugger all,' he said, dreaming of

116

leading his men bravely across the frozen tundra, with not a thought in sight.

'No, no. You're going to read it out,' said Elizabeth, joining him at the window and linking her arm through his. 'I give it to you. It's yours.'

'Why? I mean, damned decent of you, Big Sis, but why?'

'I want us to do well, for Reggie, and it'll be bad for morale if nobody respects their leader.'

'Oh well, if you put it that way . . . thank you.'

'A pleasure. Now get me a glass of wine. I need it.'

'I haven't got any wine.'

'I've brought some.'

'Good scout.'

And so, on a cloud-scudding, washing-tossing Monday morning, grey Tom sat between bald C.J. and balding Doc Morrissey on the sad settee of the sexually starved; David and Prue Harris-Jones, with their matching grey streaks, and back again in matching sweaters, held hands on the Windsor chairs; auburn Linda and long-legged Joan sat in the armchairs; pale baggy Hank sat on a reproduction rustic Victorian kitchen chair, holding Joan's hand; silvery Elizabeth sat selflessly on the pouffe; and the rocking chair awaited their leader.

At exactly 09.30 hours, Jimmy marched in from the kitchen, and seated himself in the rocking chair, beside Linda.

C.J. was glaring across Tom at Doc Morrissey, and Tom had the impression that Doc Morrissey might have leapt up and hit him, if he hadn't been trapped in the softness of the settee like a bluebottle in a teasel. Jimmy tried not to look at Linda, and felt a surge of incestuous desire. The birds of paradise were pulled wide. A few desultory spears of rain flicked on to the French windows. There was a fresh molehill right in the middle of the lawn.

'Before we start,' said Tom, 'I wonder if you'd change places

117

with me, Jimmy. I'd rather like to sit next to Lindysquerps.'

Linda blushed, and Jimmy's heart went to his boots.

'If Lindysquerps doesn't mind, that is,' said Tom.

'Lindysquerps doesn't mind,' said Linda. 'She's even prepared to put up with being called Lindysquerps.'

Jimmy stood up and tried to smile.

'Good show,' he said. 'Well done, those divorcees.'

Tom sat down in the rocking chair beside Linda's armchair and clasped her hand, rocking gently as he did so. David Harris-Jones squeezed Prue's hand, and Joan squeezed Hank's hand.

'What an affectionate gathering,' said Elizabeth with just a touch of dryness.

Jimmy plonked himself down between Doc Morrissey and C.J. and only then realised that it wasn't the ideal position for a leader to be in.

Elizabeth stood up and addressed the meeting. She had tried to make herself look bland and dowdy in order not to deflect any of their leader's glory. It hadn't worked. Age had given her a patina of distinction.

'Our leader tells me he's had a few thoughts over the weekend,' she said. 'He'd like to put them to you now.'

Elizabeth sat down, and Jimmy stood up. He stood with his back to the coal-effect fire, removed Elizabeth's notes from the inside breast pocket of his Harris Tweed jacket, put on his glasses, and cleared his throat. There were patches on the elbows of his jacket, and a small Band-Aid under his left ear, where he had nicked himself shaving.

'Thank you, Big Sis,' he said. 'Yes . . . er . . . I've had the odd notion.' He began to read. '"I'm not going to be too specific at this stage. I just want to lay down the broad parameters."'

'Good Lord!' said C.J.

'What?' said Jimmy.

'I didn't think you knew a broad parameter from your backside,' said C.J.

118

Jimmy searched for an icily witty retort. 'Belt up,' he said. '"I believe that we should set up a Think Tank to work out the broad sweep of our policy, and a Policy Research Unit to fit the nuts and bolts on to the Think Tank's efforts.

'"I think our broad aim must be to create a society that looks forward to old age, not back towards lost youth. We should be aiming to replace a youth culture with an age culture. Wrinkles should be deemed desirable. Baldness should be a privilege, keenly sought. Areas to look at are advertising, film-making, popular music and the club scene.

'"One of the main areas to explore should be work. Seven per cent of the population can produce the food we need. Sixteen per cent can produce the goods we need. The other seventy-seven per cent can't *all* become lawyers. We need a completely new work ethic, otherwise people will simply become redundant younger and younger – at forty-five, forty, thirty-five. There won't be room in the Algarve for them all to play golf. There won't be enough money in pension funds to support them in the manor that they've bought at great expense."'

Jimmy looked up from the notes. 'That's manor as in big house,' he explained. 'Joke!'

They looked at him in astonishment, all except Elizabeth.

'"On recruitment,"' resumed Jimmy, '"I believe we're wrong to confine our efforts to the elderly and the redundant. Our most fertile breeding ground may well be among those still at work but frightened of redundancy.

'"I look forward to a day when age and maturity are eagerly awaited and universally respected.

"'I look forward to a day when women will lie about their age by discreetly adding a few years to it.

'"I think that'll do for now, Jimmy. It's a bit vague, but it'll give them something to chew on. Good luck." Oops! Sorry! Shouldn't have read that last bit.'

Elizabeth buried her head in her hands.

Tom tried not to laugh.

C.J. smirked.

'Oh dear,' said Doc Morrissey. 'How embarrassing!'

'You don't make it any less embarrassing by pointing it out,' said Joan, coughing as she spoke.

'Bit chesty, are we?' said Doc Morrissey. 'Come and see me afterwards, Joan, if you like, and I'll get my old instrument out.'

Joan looked at him in astonishment, and Hank frowned.

'I still have my trusty stethoscope,' said Doc Morrissey with practised innocence. 'Happy to give you a good going-over.'

'Thank you, Doc, but I think we'll forego the good going-over,' said Hank.

'As you wish,' said Doc Morrissey.

'I apologise for my deviousness,' said Elizabeth. 'I can promise you I had no ulterior motive. I only wanted you to respect your leader.'

'Tricky wallah, leadership,' said Jimmy.

'Anyway, they were super ideas,' said David Harris-Jones. 'Super.'

'Thank you,' said Elizabeth. 'I think we should throw it open to the floor now. Any ideas?'

Linda nudged Tom, and he began to wind himself up to speak, but before he could do so, Doc Morrissey plunged in.

'I do have the occasional flash,' he said.

'I'm not at all surprised,' said C.J.

'Little things please little minds,' snapped Doc Morrissey.

'I'd heard it was little,' countered C.J.

'I shall ignore your childishness,' said Doc Morrissey loftily. 'An old man making a fool of himself for love is pathetic. As I say, I do come out with the occasional idea.'

'January sales, in July, with the price of everything going up,' said Linda.

120

'Absolutely,' said Doc Morrissey. 'Well I've come up with another one. Just came to me. Young age pensions.'

Everyone gasped, none more so than Tom.

'Super,' said David Harris-Jones.

'Wicked,' said Hank.

'Pensions from the ages of eighteen to twenty-eight,' said Doc Morrissey. 'Let them learn about life before they try to administer it.'

'That's what I was going to say,' said Tom. 'I had that idea on Saturday.' He was beside himself.

'We could all say that,' said C.J. 'How do we know you're telling the truth? Theft of invention is the mother and father of a lie.'

'He did,' said Linda. 'He told me it. Just the same.'

'Too late, Tom. Too slow. Bad luck,' said C.J.

'You all like to mock Tom,' said Linda. 'He's an easy target. Well, I think he's worth ten of you.'

'Linda!' said Tom, amazed.

'I love you, Tom,' said Linda. 'I realise now that that's why I thought I hated you so much.'

'Well . . . good Lord . . . I . . . I don't know what to say,' said Tom.

'Oh, don't worry if you don't love me,' said Linda. 'I can cope.'

'I'm not saying that I don't love you,' said Tom. 'I'm saying I'm astounded that you love me and I'm working out how I really feel, which is a matter of . . . well, I suppose I'm not an impulsive person. I'm an estate agent.'

'Touching scene, but this is a meeting, not a marriage guidance clinic,' said Jimmy.

'Absolutely,' said C.J. 'I didn't get where I am today by confusing meetings with marriage guidance clinics.'

'I thought of that twenty-eight-year-old in Singapore, and that merchant bank that collapsed,' said Doc Morrissey. 'With

121

my idea he'd just be starting out. There wouldn't ever be too much power too young. I just thought it was a good idea. I'm sorry it's caused so much trouble.'

'It hasn't,' said David Harris-Jones. 'It's caused Linda to say she loves Tom and, okay, maybe she would have done eventually anyway, but who knows? But the point is, it's a terrific idea.'

'It's a great idea,' said Hank. 'Young people are encouraged to be greedy by old men who sit back and exploit their greed. It seems like freedom, but it's really exploitation. I realise that now.'

'So I think,' said David Harris-Jones, 'that we should say, "Congratulations, Doc," and "Congratulations, Tom," brilliant both of you and it doesn't matter who thought of it first.'

'Bloody creep,' said C.J.

'How dare you?' said Prue Harris-Jones. 'How bloody dare you? David is trying to make peace, because he's a lovely man.' She went pink and said, 'Sorry.'

David Harris-Jones clasped her hand.

'Anyone else want to declare their love?' enquired Doc Morrissey, not without a touch of bitterness. 'Hank? Do you wish to tell us of your adoration of Joan?'

'I love her very much,' said Hank. 'And you can keep your rusty stethoscope off her.'

'I think,' said David Harris-Jones, 'I think . . . and it's terrific that Hank loves Joan, and that Linda loves Tom, and that Prue loves me, and if that makes me a creep, then I'm a creep, but . . . oh, and that I love Prue too, nearly forgot, oh, Lord . . . but it does make us seem a bit self-satisfied and that's difficult for those who're lonely and starved of . . . not that I'm saying that C.J. and Doc . . . oh, or Elizabeth or Jimmy . . . are starved of affection, I don't expect they are, but I think all this is a red herring and we should get back to basics, well, no, not back to

122

basics, that's a discredited phrase, but I think we should forget the red herrings and get back to the meat, and, yes, C.J., I know I'm speaking your language.'

A yellow dustcart, crunching tins violently, only emphasised the silence that greeted David Harris-Jones's speech in the cosy lounge/diner.

No further memorable ideas were put forward, and they moved on to the next business, the selection of a Think Tank and a Policy Research Unit.

The selection process proved easier than anticipated.

'Bloody lovey-doveys should be separated or everyone'll just be mooning and holding hands all day,' opined C.J.

'I dislike the way C.J. put that, but he has a point,' said Elizabeth. 'We are setting up these organisations in order to work.'

'I'm not joining anything that vain old cockerel's in,' said Doc Morrissey.

'Ditto that dried-up heap of camel dung,' said C.J.

'Blasted well go where you're told, you bastards,' said Jimmy.

'I agree with Jimmy in principle,' said Elizabeth. 'In practice, we can't have internal warfare, so C.J. and Doc will have to be separated.'

'Doc Morrissey's idea should win him a place on the Think Tank,' said Prue.

'I had that idea too,' said Tom.

'Yes, so you should be on the Think Tank too,' said Elizabeth hastily.

'I'm not having Joan on the same group as that randy old stethoscope,' said Hank.

'Then you must go on the Think Tank, Hank,' said Elizabeth. 'That's Doc Morrissey, Tom and Hank on the Think Tank, and therefore, that's C.J., Linda and Joan on the Policy Research Unit. Excellent.'

123

'The Think Tank's all male so far,' said Prue, 'so I'll have to go on that, so therefore David has to go in the Policy Research Unit.'

'I think Reggie would like me to be on the Think Tank,' said Elizabeth. 'I ought to know better that anyone else what would be in his mind if he were here doing this.'

'So the Policy Research Unit is less important, is it?' said C.J.

'Not at all,' said Elizabeth hastily. 'There'd be no value in our ideas if we didn't know how to apply them. The two are interlocked in a web of indispensability.' There was silence. It seemed that agreement had been reached. 'So that's it, then. Think Tank – Doc, Tom, Prue, Hank, me. Policy Research Unit – C.J., Linda, David, Joan.'

'Super,' said David Harris-Jones.

'Wicked,' said Hank Millbeck.

'Wait a minute,' said Jimmy. 'I'm the only one not on anything.'

There was a long pause. Ponsonby the Third miaowed loudly on the patio.

'We have to have somebody to report to,' said Elizabeth.

'We're all just joint members of organisations, but you have the responsibility of being reported to all on your own,' said Tom. 'It's a great honour.'

'But I'm your leader,' said Jimmy, 'and I'm the only one not deciding what we do.'

'Well, that's very democratic,' said David Harris-Jones. 'It avoids the possibility of your becoming a dictator.'

'Fat chance with you lot around,' grumbled Jimmy. 'Thought we'd scrubbed democracy, seen the little runt off, now he's back. You're all dictators, I'm the blasted typist.'

'The point is that you need to conserve your energies for the big push,' said Elizabeth. 'We decide, corporately, what we want to do. You are going to have to lead us into action *on your own*.'

124

It was Doc Morrissey, to C.J.'s obvious fury, who found the key to the mollification of Jimmy.

'Wat Tyler didn't involve himself in the tedious day-to-day details,' he said.

11 *The Strange Behaviour of C.J.*

The first meeting of the Think Tank took place the next morning. The venue was the lounge/diner of number thirty-eight, Leibnitz Drive. The meeting was not an enormous success.

Perhaps Elizabeth, who had vacated the pouffe for the rocking chair, was trying too hard to fill Reggie's shoes. She was anxious to be swept away on a tide of inspiration and invention.

Hank was still recovering from his cold, and hadn't even begun to recover from the lethargy which had enveloped him. The comfort of an armchair was probably a mistake.

Tom kept hearing Linda saying, 'I love you.' And he had too much room to loll, now that he was sharing the settee only with Doc Morrissey.

Doc Morrissey was so busy trying not to think of Ms Hackstraw that he had little room in his head for anything else.

Prue feared that she was not made of the stuff from which great ideas spring.

'Well, somebody must have some ideas,' said Elizabeth after half an hour of fruitless discussion.

'I'm really trying,' said Hank. 'I think the whole concept's wicked, I really do, but I'm just so tired all the time.'

'I'm worried that my flash may turn out to have been a flash in the pan,' said Doc Morrissey.

'I'm beginning to wonder whether I'm a Think Tank person,' said Tom.

'I know it was right in most cases to split up loving couples,' said Prue, 'but I'm not sure that David and I function very well except as a team. Togetherness is our middle name. On our own we feel naked.'

Smug cow, thought Doc Morrissey, but he was far too polite to say so.

'I keep wondering what Reggie would say if he were here,' said Elizabeth.

The first meeting of the Policy Research Unit was held the next afternoon. The venue was the lounge/diner of number thirty-eight, Leibnitz Drive. The meeting was not an enormous success.

Joan was still recovering from her cold, and she was deeply worried about Hank and his lethargy. Would he ever be her old Hank again?

Linda kept hearing Tom say, 'I'm not saying that I don't love you. I'm saying I'm astounded that you love me and I'm working out how I really feel, which is a matter of . . . well, I suppose I'm not an impulsive person. I'm an estate agent.' Dear Tom. Would he ever be able to commit himself to her again?

C.J. was so busy trying not to think of Geraldine that he had little room in his head for anything else.

David Harris-Jones, freed from his hard chair, found the luxury of the settee inimical to hard thinking, and feared that he was not made of the stuff from which great policies spring.

'Somebody must have some ideas,' said Joan, after half an hour of fruitless discussion.

'I suppose it's because I'm so emotional at the moment over Tom,' said Linda, 'but I'm in an absolute lather. Is anyone else too hot?'

They all shook their heads.

'It's just me then,' said Linda. 'I do sweat easily. I have very open pores.'

'I know it was right in most cases to split up loving couples,' said David Harris-Jones, 'but I'm not sure that Prue and I function very well except as a team. Togetherness is our middle name. On our own we feel naked.'

'Smug bastard,' said C.J.

'I keep wondering what Reggie would say if he were here,' said Joan.

That evening, Tom called round to take Linda out to dinner. She invited him in for a drink first.

'Two double radiators!' he said. 'And four power points. I didn't notice them last time. I was too nervous.'

'Are you nervous now?' asked Linda, handing him a Ricard.

'Of course I am,' he said. 'I keep saying to myself, "Did she really mean it when she said, 'I love you'?"' He took a sip of Ricard. He'd forgotten how much he liked it. It brought back the scent of their house in the early, happy years – a pot-pourri of aniseed, squid Provençale and dirty nappies. 'Did you mean it?'

'Of course I did. Did you mean it when you said, "I'm not saying that I don't love you. I'm saying I'm astounded that you love me and I'm working out how I really feel, which is a matter of . . . well, I suppose I'm not an impulsive person. I'm an estate agent"?'

'Well, yes, I suppose I did. I'm not a very exciting person, am I?'

'I'd settle for you, Tom. Cheers.' They clinked glasses.

'Cheers.'

'Tom? Do you really want to go out?'

'What do you mean?'

'We could just stay in. We could . . . we could go to bed.'

128

'I'm hungry. I mean, that sounds very nice, but . . . *very* nice, but . . . I'm very hungry.'

'I could knock something up.'

'It sounds tempting. But we've booked.'

'We could cancel.'

'Well, yes, but . . . I don't like cancelling. It isn't really fair. It's quite a struggle running a Greek restaurant in Camberley.'

'They'll be grateful if we bother to cancel. Most people these days just don't turn up.'

'Well . . .' Tom sipped his Ricard. 'I mean . . . I'd love to go to bed, but . . . love to . . . but I do rather fancy a taramasalata and moussaka and a bottle of retsina. Actually, Lindyplonks, I'm very nervous. Why don't we compromise? Go and have the meal and then, after a nice night out, when we've built up to it and we're feeling really amorous, then I think I'd rather like to go to bed with you.'

Linda sighed.

'I mean this is a momentous moment in our lives, Lindyplops. Terribly important. We must be careful to do it right.'

'Oh yes, Tom. We must be careful.'

'Well, I suppose I'm a carefulness person. Sorry.'

So they went to the Villa Daphne in Camberley, and Tom proved that he wasn't quite as careful a person as he thought by deciding on the spur of the moment to have the afelia instead of the moussaka.

They talked about the old days, about Adam and Jocasta and their disastrous trip to the safari park, when Adam had done biggies in his pants and Reggie had got out of the car in the lion enclosure and almost been killed; about their appalling family holiday during the wettest summer in Dorset's history; about the reluctance of the housing market to recover; about open pores and closed minds; about central heating and cassoulet; about best end of lamb and loneliness.

There was Greek dancing, English style. They danced with careful Home Counties abandon. Tom strained his knee.

'I'm not really a dance person,' he said breathlessly, as they sat down.

When they got back to Linda's flat, she said, 'Right. Let's go to bed.'

'I'm not sure if it's wise, with my knee,' said Tom. 'I mean, it's been nearly ten years. Another few days won't matter. I mean, why choose a moment when I've got a limp?'

'A limp what?' asked Linda. 'Sorry. You don't like *double entendres*, do you? I'd forgotten what a prig you are.'

'I am not a prig, Lindyflops.'

'And I don't like being called Lindyflops. Goodnight, Tom.'

While Tom and Linda were having an evening that didn't quite fulfil all their hopes, Joan and Hank were also hacking their way through the tangled thickets of romance.

They were sitting on the floor in front of the gas fire in their gleaming, high-tech, split-level living room. On the hearth was a half-finished bottle of 1990 Côte de Rully.

'I've lost my appetite, my capacity for drink and my sexual drive,' said Hank. 'I'm an empty husk.'

'You're just reacting to twenty years of never daring to let go for a moment,' said Joan.

'I feel middle-aged.'

'Well, good. That's what the revolution is all about. Not feeling frightened of growing old.'

'You won't want me if I'm old.'

'I will. I'll still be older. I love you. More wine?'

'I don't really want any more,' said Hank. 'I daren't tell you what I really want.'

'Oh, Hank. You don't need to be shy with me. What do you really want?'

'A mug of cocoa.'

Joan went into the gleaming, high-tech kitchen, pressed the touch panel on the ceramic hob, thus setting the far left front ring to the temperature at which milk would heat without boiling, and returned to her lover.

She put on a Nina Simone CD. They sipped their cocoa, and allowed lassitude to overcome them.

They were in bed by ten o'clock. They put their arms round each other, and cuddled gently beneath the duvet.

'I like cuddles,' said Joan. 'I like not having to prove oneself. I like the idea of growing old together. I love you, Hank. And since you haven't got the energy to ask me, my darling burnt-out case, *I'll* ask *you*. Will you marry me?'

But Hank was asleep.

While Joan and Hank had been sitting on the floor, C.J. was storming round Expansion Cottage in Virginia Water like a fart in a colander.

Every now and then he would exclaim out loud. His words echoed dismally in the large, empty house.

'Your attitude to Ms Hackstraw is all wrong, C.J.,' he thundered in the great panelled drawing room.

'You're behaving like a square pig in a round poke, C.J.,' he told himself in the square dining room with the round table. 'You're going to have to change your attitude.'

'I didn't get where I am today by changing my attitude,' he told himself in the handsome panelled study, where the pages of the complete works of Dickens had never been cut.

'Where *are* you today? All alone in Virginia Water,' he admitted in the master bedroom with built-in Scandinavian-style wardrobes.

He poured himself a treble malt whisky – his fourth of the evening.

Slowly, very slowly, the whisky gave him courage. At five past ten, he picked up the cordless telephone and dialled.

131

Oh God, he thought, she'll be out. I'll get the answering machine.

Oh God, he thought, she'll be in. Please let it be the answering machine. It wasn't.

Her voice made him go weak at the knees.

'Hello, Geraldine. It's C.J. here,' he said.

'I've nothing to say to you.'

'Right. Fair enough. Don't say anything. Just listen,' he said. 'I . . . er . . . I . . . er . . . what I said the other evening . . . it was . . . unforgivable. I . . . I . . . I apologise, Geraldine. I apologise unreservedly.'

'Oh. Well, thank you. That wasn't easy for you, was it?'

'No. I didn't get where I am today by apologising.'

'I imagine not.'

'However many dinners a person gives a woman, it doesn't give him the right to expect to take her to bed, and slowly take all her clothes off, and kiss her sweet bottom and give her a real good seeing-to.'

There was a click, and then silence.

He dialled again.

Her voice made him go weak at the knees.

'I'm so sorry,' he said. 'I . . . er . . . I apologise again.'

'Is it getting any easier with practice?'

'Yes. My mistake was, I was sitting on the edge of my bed, and bed made me feel sexy. Association of ideas, I suppose. I'm in my kitchen now, at the antique Breton refectory table, so I'm hoping that I'll be able to confine my thoughts to food. Association of ideas again, you see.'

'Yes, I . . . I do see.'

'Geraldine, will you come out to dinner with me again, absolutely no strings attached, truly no strings attached?'

'You're very persistent, aren't you?'

'Well, yes I am. If at first you don't succeed, the mountain must go to Mohammed, that's my motto.'

132

'All right. Let's try again, but absolutely no strings attached.'

'How about tomorrow?'

'Oh no.'

The first day on which Geraldine Hackstraw admitted to being available turned out to be Thursday week.

After he'd put the telephone down, C.J. had a cold shower.

Doc Morrissey climbed the stairs slowly. Behind him was a most delightful evening, sitting on the floor with his Asian friends, eating chicken masala and bhindi bhagee with his fingers.

Ahead of him was his door, with its plate that announced, 'Professor G. F. Morrissey, BA, Eng. Lit., Cantab.'

The memory of the delightful evening didn't cheer him. He had felt sick at heart throughout it. Contentment didn't make him happy any more.

The thought of his bookish attic did not excite him. It no longer pleased him to be the only white man in the street. His battered, lived-in, well-thumbed books no longer comforted him.

The attic flat looked pitiful. The leather armchairs were shabby. The portrait of him at medical school served only to remind him what an undistinguished career he had had. He could feel the symptoms of at least three diseases and had no idea what any of them were.

He opened his wallet and took out the psychiatrist's card. Not for the first time, he was on the verge of telephoning for help.

He didn't need help. He needed Ms Hackstraw. He would take her on any terms he could get. He would take her on her terms.

He looked at his watch. Seven minutes past ten. Not too late to ring.

He dialled her number. It was engaged.

*

The next morning, Doc Morrissey threw himself into the work of the Think Tank with a new enthusiasm. They were meeting at Tom's flat, on the second floor of the converted mansion, Elizabeth having decided that they were becoming stale through over-familiarity with number thirty-eight, Leibnitz Drive.

Tom's sitting room, seventeen by fourteen, two double radiators, five power points, was a rather dark, very masculine room, furnished with a black leather suite. The five members of the Think Tank sank squeakily into its well-worn depths. The room smelt of garlic and pipe tobacco, although he'd given up the latter some time ago, and looked out over handsome gardens shared with the other seven tenants. Around the lawn was a row of tiny gravestones, where the original owners had buried their beloved pets.

'I have an idea,' said Tom. 'An incentive. A bottle of my mangetout '94 at twelve thirty if we feel we've earned it.'

There was a long silence.

'Well, anyway,' said Doc Morrissey at last, 'despite that, I've had another idea. Fashion shows.'

'Yes,' said Elizabeth. 'Well done, Doc, far be it from me to criticise anybody who comes up with anything at all. But I think it has actually been done.'

'For the over-fifties,' said Doc Morrissey, 'and modelled by the over-fifties. Lots of old people about, all need glamorous clothes. Young people don't need glamorous clothes. Old people have bits of nice flesh on them, so it's silly that all the clothes should be modelled by young people built like walking sticks.'

Everybody congratulated Doc Morrissey on his idea. He smiled, basking in their esteem. He was discovering that it really was quite nice to bask in esteem. In some ways it beat sexual intercourse into a cocked hat. It lasted longer, for instance.

'I could try to come up with some pithy advertising slogans, like I did at Grot,' said Tom. 'Adverts geared to old people. The role model for the ideal body should be mature and achievable.'

'People could have face drops instead of face lifts,' said Hank.

'Good. Excellent. Well done, Doc, Tom. Well done, Hank,' said Elizabeth. 'On a more practical note, supermarkets and shopping malls are very difficult for old people.'

'Perhaps we could ask the Policy Research Unit to prepare draft legislation to make them more age-friendly,' said Prue. 'I mean, we must give them something to do.'

'I've had another idea,' said Doc Morrissey, and Prue, Hank and Elizabeth looked at him with something approaching awe.

Tom was too busy thinking to look at Doc Morrissey at all.

'I've had another idea,' he said.

'Doc was just going to tell us his idea,' said Elizabeth.

'Oh, sorry,' said Tom. 'I was so busy thinking about mine that I didn't hear. Well, mine's such a corker it can wait. You first, Doc. Age before beauty.'

'Ah, but in the new order we won't be able to say that,' said Elizabeth, 'because age will be beauty.'

Hank had fallen asleep.

'Shall I wake Hank?' asked Prue. 'He oughtn't to miss Doc's and Tom's ideas, ought he?'

Everyone agreed that she should wake Hank. She shook his shoulders and for a dreadful moment she thought he wasn't going to wake. At last he groaned, opened his eyes, and looked round the room. Panic roused him from his lethargy.

'You're part of the Think Tank,' said Prue gently.

'Oh yes. Oh, sorry. Oh God, this is terrible,' said Hank.

'We'd have let you sleep on,' said Prue, 'but Doc and Tom have had ideas. Tom's is a corker. We don't know whether Doc's is, but anyway Doc thought of his first, so he's going first.'

'Wicked,' said Hank.

'Doc, the floor is yours at last,' said Elizabeth.

'Yes, and I feel nervous now,' said Doc Morrissey. 'You've waited so long, my idea's been built up so much, and mine isn't a corker at all. I wish Tom'd go first with his corker.'

'No, no, you go first,' said Tom magnanimously.

'Right. Well, it's just a little thing,' said Doc Morrissey, 'and it's another example of substituting age for youth, I'm afraid. Age hostels. Places where senior citizens can stay cheaply, while they're walking or cycling.'

'I don't believe it,' said Tom. 'He's done it again. He's stolen my thunder again.'

'Oh no! That wasn't your corker, was it?' said Doc Morrissey.

'Yes, it was, and I feel embarrassed now at calling it a corker,' said Tom.

'It was a jolly good idea. Congratulations, both of you,' said Elizabeth.

'Wicked,' said Hank.

'Cheer up, Tom,' said Prue.

'It's all very well to say "Cheer up",' said Tom, 'but you don't keep getting your thunder stolen.'

'I suggested you went first,' said Doc Morrissey, 'when I thought your idea was a corker.'

'Well, it wasn't, was it?' said Tom. 'It was a silly, lousy idea like yours. You knew it wasn't a corker. I thought it was. I'm just a bag of wind, a pompous priggish conceited twit. All right, I know this doesn't compare with war in Chechnya and famine in Rwanda and earthquakes in Japan. It registers pretty low on the Richter scale of human misery. But I still can't help feeling put out. I've a good mind to cancel my incentive offer.'

'You'd be fully justified,' said Doc Morrissey eagerly.

'Absolutely,' said Elizabeth. 'Constantly having your thunder stolen, you'd have to be a saint to offer us free wine.'

'But, no, I can't be petty,' said Tom. 'Things are stirring in my life. Linda loves me. I have a chance of happiness again. I must learn to become a better human being. We'll have a bottle of the leek and potato as well as the Mangetout '94.'

*

136

The Policy Research Unit met the next day at C.J.'s house. C.J. ushered David Harris-Jones, Joan and Linda into the vast, panelled drawing room with a beaming smile.

'What an amazing room, C.J.,' said Linda.

'Super,' said David Harris-Jones.

'Well, it's all too big, of course,' said C.J. 'I rattle around rather on my own. Coffee and biscuits?'

He pulled a bell-rope and a deep bell boomed in the distance.

'I do love this view,' said C.J., looking out through the wide windows across a well-wooded garden studded with urns. 'The squirrels are such fun to watch. I love to see them nibbling at their nuts.'

Joan, Linda and David gawped. They would never have believed that C.J. had got where he was today by watching squirrels nibbling at their nuts.

A large lady with bow legs and thick glasses entered.

'Ah! Could we have coffee and biscuits for four, Mrs Wren?' said C.J. 'Thank you so much.'

When Mrs Wren had left, C.J. said, 'It's touching, don't you think, that such a very large woman should have the name of such a very small bird? These little things are the very stuff or life, are they not? Do sit down.'

They seated themselves in vast reproduction armchairs, upholstered with sombre tapestries of mediaeval hunting scenes. The chairs made gruff, embarrassing noises like badgers farting. C.J. roared with laughter.

'A memento of olden days,' he said. 'I love nostalgia, especially for the past. Now, we have a very good report from the Think Tank, don't you think?'

'Super,' said David Harris-Jones.

'They've done very well,' said Linda. 'I think I can see Tom's hand in a lot of it.'

'I think Prue had a lot to do with it,' said David Harris-Jones.

137

'I know I shouldn't say it myself . . . and yet, why not, because I'm proud of her . . . but the lovely thing about Prue is, if you don't mind my being personal, but I have to say it, is . . . she's so sensible.'

'I don't think Hank had much to do with it,' said Joan. 'Apparently he kept falling asleep.'

'He's a living example – well, just living – of what we're about,' said C.J. 'He's been used and discarded like an old sock. I didn't get where I am today by using and discarding people like old socks. Well, I did, actually, but not any more. Oh look. It's climbing that tree. Isn't it lovely?'

'Grey squirrels are actually members of the rat family,' said David Harris-Jones.

'So what? You're Welsh, but you're delightful,' said C.J. 'As I say, an excellent report. Any thoughts about it?'

'Well, yes,' said David Harris-Jones. 'And, incidentally, I wish you wouldn't make cheap cracks about the Welsh.'

'I'm very sorry,' said C.J. 'I like the Welsh enormously, actually. They're musical, witty, and they cook seaweed wonderfully. I like Belgium too. Beautiful cities, friendly people, wonderful beer and food. Why do certain people mock certain people? It's cruel. Sorry. Carry on.'

'Well . . .' David Harris-Jones had lost his thread, such was his amazement at C.J.'s remarks. 'Sorry, I've forgotten what I was going to say.'

'But it would have been brilliant,' said C.J. 'Well done. There would have been plenty to chew over there.'

'I think there are two areas we need to explore,' said Joan. 'First, the question of supermarkets and their unsuitability for the elderly. Second, and even more important, our retirement policy.'

'Absolutely,' said C.J. 'What an intelligent woman you are. I always thought so . . .' He raised his voice. 'So, I thought we

138

could prepare a pictorial record of the squirrels' year.' He lowered his voice. 'Security. Mrs Wren approaches.'

The door opened, and Mrs Wren entered with a tray of coffee and biscuits.

'Thank you so much, Mrs Wren,' said C.J. 'You're a treasure.'

Mrs Wren looked at him in astonishment.

'Doesn't usually say things like that,' she said. 'Usually says I'm a bleeding nuisance.'

C.J. laughed heartily, stood up, and took the tray off Mrs Wren. His chair made no noise.

'What a wag you are, Mrs Wren,' he said. 'And what lovely biscuits. Do feel free to go home early if Mr Wren's feet are playing him up again.'

Mrs Wren gave him another astonished look, and left the room.

'Salt of the earth, the Mrs Wrens of this world,' said C.J. 'Do come and get your coffee.'

Their chairs made noises like farting badgers as they stood up and as they sat down. C.J. made a noise like a manic depressive jackal in its manic phase.

'Ah, humour!' he said. 'Where would we be without it? Item one. Supermarkets and the elderly. Anybody got any ideas?'

They decided that the Children of the Revolution, when they formed the government, would make it an offence not to stock small wrapped portions for one person whenever such a thing was possible. They would also bring in a compulsory delivery service, trolleys attached to drive-on electric buggies, packing facilities at all check-outs, minimum aisle width, and ensure that you didn't have to be an Olympic weight-lifter to open jars of marmalade and individual pats of butter.

By eleven o'clock, after a second cup of coffee – 'Just as nice as the first, Mrs Wren, and that's saying something' –

they were on to the main item of the morning, their employment policy. By lunchtime they had decided that there would be young age pensions from eighteen to twenty-eight; a thirty-hour week from twenty-eight to forty, reducing to a twenty-five-hour week until the age of forty-five, but at the same salary; and then, still on the same salary, a twenty-hour week until the age of fifty, a fifteen-hour week until the age of fifty-five, and a ten-hour week until the age of sixty. Voluntary retirement could be taken at any time, but nobody could ever be forced to retire except on provision of a doctor's certificate or on rigorous proof of incompetence or misconduct. After the age of sixty, people would be able to continue to work up to ten hours a week on half salary for as long as they were able to. This work would be consistent with their physical condition, and of such a nature as to call on the experience, judgement and knowledge that they had amassed over a lifetime. There would be no old age pensions at all. People would be able to make their own arrangements in the certain knowledge that they could never be made redundant if they didn't misbehave.

'Won't it be difficult to sell to the young?' asked David Harris-Jones.

'If I was young I'd love to have ten years to see the world,' said Linda.

'We might even end up with a work-force that weren't insular and knew a few foreign languages,' said Joan.

'Besides,' said C.J., 'the young will themselves benefit because, whatever they may believe, they are not immune to the ageing process.'

'There'd be no more schoolteachers, policemen and social workers so young that nobody ever takes any notice of them,' said David Harris-Jones. 'I mean, even in business that happens. Nobody took any notice of me until I was about thirty.'

'And not much, then,' said C.J., his new geniality slipping.

140

'Sorry. That was a joke. Well, I think we've had a wonderful morning. I think we deserve some champagne.'

That afternoon, emboldened by four glasses of champagne, Joan scurried home to the high-tech modern flat, and found Hank fast asleep on the adjustable orthopaedic bed that folded into the wall electronically when they had parties.

She woke him up, very gently.

He groaned, moaned, screwed his eyes up against the impact of existence, saw Joan and smiled.

'Hello, darling,' he said, with more energy than he had exhibited for several days. 'Big kiss for your burnt-out case?'

'Something even more important than a kiss,' said Joan. 'Something even nicer than a kiss, I hope.'

'I don't think I have the energy for anything nicer than a kiss.'

'Not that, Hank. A question. I asked you it a couple of days ago, but you were asleep.'

'Oh God. That figures.'

'Will you marry me?'

'What??'

'Will you marry me, Hank?'

'My God! Marriage! With me in this state?'

'In any state I love you. I want to spend the rest of my life with you.'

'Wicked.'

'Does that mean "Yes"?'

'Yes, of course.'

'Good. Shall I make you a nice cup of tea?'

'Wicked.'

Also that afternoon, also emboldened by four glasses of champagne, Linda made her way, heart beating like the wings of a bee-eater, to Tom's desirable second-floor flat.

'Linda!' said Tom, opening his desirable oak door. 'Come in.'

He led her through the hall. She didn't notice the double radiator, the telephone point or the attractive recess.

Linda was wearing a pair of Cerutti jeans which emphasised her desirable bottom. Tom had forgotten how nice her bottom was.

'I've got a bottle of leek and potato wine open,' he said. 'Would you like some?'

'No, thank you. I've been drinking proper wine. Oh God! Why did I say that? Because I'm nervous. Oh, all right. Yes, please. It'll probably go very well with champagne.'

Tom poured the wine. They clinked glasses and said 'Cheers'.

It was a bit like drinking iced vichyssoise soup, but not seriously unpleasant.

'Very nice,' said Linda, exaggerating.

Tom invited her to sit on the black leather settee, and she needed no second bidding.

'This is a surprise,' he said, sitting beside her.

'I came round to apologise,' said Linda.

'What for?'

'For calling you a prig.'

'I am a prig.'

'Maybe you're a bit on the priggish side, but I wouldn't even contemplate loving you if you were a copper-bottomed prig.'

'No-one could call you copper-bottomed,' said Tom. 'You're luscious-bottomed.'

'Tom! That was almost risqué. How's your knee?'

'Much better, thank you. In fact . . .'

'Yes?'

'Look, I . . . about going to bed together . . .'

'Yes?'

'Well, you did suggest it the other night.'

'I did, yes.'

142

'I don't think my knee will incapacitate me if we go to bed this afternoon.'

'Oh. Gosh, Tom.'

'There's only one thing.'

'What?'

'It's been a long time. It may not be like the old days straight away. I mean . . . I may not be feeling very confident. I may not be very good.'

'So what? You weren't very good in the old days.'

'Linda!'

'You weren't very sexy, Tom.'

'Oh! Oh, I see.'

'I don't love you because you're sexy, Tom. I love you because you're . . . slow and pompous, but kind and gentle.'

'Oh! Oh, I see.'

'I love you because you're as comfortable as a pair of old bedroom slippers.'

'Charming!'

'Yes, it is charming, Tom. I've tried Gucci loafers. I've tried Church's brogues. I want my bedroom slippers.'

'Tremendous! What a turn-on!'

'It doesn't have to be a turn-on this afternoon, Tom. It just has to be . . . togetherness. Comfort.'

'Well, let's go off and be comfortable, pompous bedroom slippers together. It sounds wonderful.'

'Oh, Tom. I do love you so when you're grumpy.'

Tom was pleased that he'd changed the sheets two days before. The sun peeped through the windows of the masculine, unloved room. He kicked his bedroom slippers under the bed.

They undressed quickly, nervously. Tom hopped into bed first, and was astounded by Linda's shapeliness as she joined him. He suddenly felt a great warmth of affection and memory and with it came a keen sexuality that made him gasp.

They were in bed for over an hour, and Linda admitted afterwards that Tom hadn't once reminded her of a pair of bedroom slippers.

'He did what??'

'He talked about squirrels nibbling their nuts. He was very nice to his cleaning lady. He said he liked the Welsh *and* the Belgians. He told Joan she was intelligent.'

'Do you think he's sickening for something?'

They were seated at the dining table in the lounge/diner, eating pork casserole. In the garden, Ponsonby the Third was sitting beside a molehill, listening intently. Elizabeth was deeply alarmed by David Harris-Jones's description of C.J.'s behaviour.

'What's he up to?' she said.

'I don't think he's up to anything,' said David Harris-Jones.

'I don't want to have an argument, darling,' said Prue. 'Because, as you know, we hardly ever differ.'

'Hardly ever,' echoed David. 'If then.'

'But if you do have a fault, darling, and please don't get upset, you're sometimes just too nice. You just don't see the deviousness in people. You'd take Machiavelli at his word.'

'Are you saying I'm naive?'

'No! Well, perhaps a bit. But only because you're so nice.'

'I'm with Prue,' said Elizabeth. 'I don't trust C.J. an inch. I'm going to have him watched. I'm going to have him followed.'

'Followed!' said Prue. 'Isn't that a bit drastic?'

'I don't think so,' said Elizabeth. 'I think I know C.J. better than either of you. He's never asked either of you to call him Bunny.'

The Harris-Joneses gawped in unison.

'Shouldn't you ... I mean it's really not for me to say ... well, no, I don't think I will say it,' said David Harris-Jones.

144

'Oh, come on. You must say it now,' said Elizabeth. 'Shouldn't I what?'

'Well . . . shouldn't you consult our leader?'

'Oh, my God,' said Elizabeth. 'Thank you, David. I completely forgot. Of course I should. I'll consult our leader and *then* I'll have C.J. followed.'

'He talked about squirrels nibbling their nuts? He was very nice to his cleaning lady? He said he liked the Welsh *and* the Belgians? He told Joan she was intelligent?'

'Yes.'

'Oh, my God.'

'Yes.'

'What should we do?'

'I think we should have him followed.'

'Right. Lead me to him and I'll follow him.'

'I don't think you should follow him yourself, Jimmy.'

'But I'm your leader.'

'A leader should know when to delegate.'

'But I don't do anything.'

'Well, that's the wonderful thing about leadership. You sit back and let people do things and it's a success and everybody says what a wonderful leader you are.'

'Well, yes, Sis, enjoy praise, prefer it to the other blighter, who doesn't, but I'm bored stiff sitting here in Clement Attlee sodding Mansions.'

'If you follow him, and it goes wrong, the whole thing's compromised. If somebody else follows him, and it goes wrong, we say they did it on their own initiative and disown them.'

'See your point. Good. Who?'

'It's your show, Jimmy. It's your decision. You're the leader.'

'Absolutely. Always welcome advice, though.'

'Well . . . somebody dispensable.'

'Ah. With you, Sis. David or Tom.'

145

'We might need two.'
'David *and* Tom.'

'Hand-picked you two for a vital job.'

A gust rattled the ill-fitting windows of flat twenty-two, Clement Attlee Mansions. Tom Patterson and David Harris-Jones eyed their leader warily, and tried not to feel flattered. But . . . hand-picked!

'Er . . . what job?' asked David Harris-Jones.

'Surveillance,' said Jimmy. 'Round-the-clock surveillance on a member of this organisation.'

'Oh, I'm not sure I fancy that,' said Tom. 'Spying on friends and colleagues.'

'Nor me neither,' said David Harris-Jones.

'It's C.J.,' said Jimmy.

'Oh, well, that's different,' said Tom.

'Super,' said David Harris-Jones

'Surveillance begins 16.00 hours tonight,' said Jimmy.

'Tonight!' exclaimed David Harris-Jones. 'Prue's making fish pie.'

'Did Julius Caesar say, "Cross the Rubicon? Don't know about that. Mrs Caesar's making stuffed peppers"?' said Jimmy. 'He did not. Still, Tom can go first. Somebody has to. 16.00 to 23.59 hours, Tom. 24.00 to 07.59 hours, David. 08.00 to 15.59 hours, Tom. Continue as per. Good luck, men.'

'Are we . . . er . . . are we really going to go through with this?' asked David Harris-Jones, as they drove away from Clement Attlee Mansions in some astonishment and Tom's old Peugeot.

'I think it might be fun,' said Tom.

'I . . . er . . . well, yes, Tom, but . . . I mean, it could be dangerous, I'm a married man. One does have responsibilities.'

'Are you a man or a wimp?'

'I'm a wimp.'

'Well, I'm not,' said Tom. 'Not any more. I welcome the challenge. I'm a challenge person.'

David Harris-Jones looked at Tom in amazement.

'I've done a lot of thinking lately,' said Tom. 'Linda's handed me a lifeline. I've got to grasp that lifeline. Otherwise all my headstone will say will be, "Here lies Thomas Dalrymple Patterson. He was an estate agent."'

'I'm being cremated,' said David Harris-Jones.

12 The Bald Men Who Came in From the Rhododendrons

Tom nosed his car into the rhododendrons, from which he could command a view of the entrance to the drive that led to Expansion Cottage. He was wearing a dog-collar, a false ginger beard on top of his real, grey beard and a bald wig. He had brought an exercise-cum-log book, three rounds of ham and chutney sandwiches, a large Thermos of coffee, two bananas, and a roll of toilet paper. It might be a long night.

Unbeknown to Tom, C.J. was already on his way to a very important rendezvous with a reporter from the *Daily Sludge*.

Morton Radstock had suggested meeting in a wine bar, and C.J. had chosen, out of the *Yellow Pages*, one called The Beaune to Pick With You, in Richmond, because he liked the name. They were speaking his language.

The Beaune to Pick With You turned out to be a dimly lit basement bar awash with candle grease. There were bare wooden tables and blackboards with many special offers.

Morton Radstock, so far as C.J. could see in the gloom, was an earnest young man in his mid-thirties. He was wearing dark jeans and a check shirt. His hair was short, the cut severe but stylish. He was tall and blond and needed thick glasses.

'I didn't expect you to be blond,' said C.J. 'You didn't sound blond.'

'My mother is Swedish,' said Morton Radstock. 'Shall we try a bottle of the eponymous Beaune?'

'Good idea,' said C.J. enthusiastically.

Morton Radstock ordered the wine, and they settled themselves down in the gloom.

'I'm sorry it's so dark,' said C.J. 'Will you be able to see to write?'

'Oh yes.'

'I calculated that this is almost exactly halfway between Virginia Water and Wapping.'

'But your half of the journey is much pleasanter and easier than mine,' said Morton Radstock with a wry smile.

'Well, I have what you want, so it's the law of the market-place,' said C.J. 'I didn't get where I am today without knowing the law of the market-place.'

'I imagine not,' said Morton Radstock. 'Ah. Thank you.'

Their wine had arrived, accompanied by saucers of green olives and crisps.

Morton Radstock tasted the wine.

'M'm,' he said. 'Maybe it'll get better when it breathes.'

'I could change it, sir,' said the Australian waitress.

'No, it's all right. Just a little bit anonymous as well as eponymous,' said Morton Radstock. 'It'll do.' He raised his glass to C.J. 'Cheers.'

'Cheers.'

'May I ask why you've chosen to tell your story to me?'

'I like your style. Snappy, pithy, crude, vicious.'

'You're very kind.'

'But you aren't like that when one meets you. You're civilised. You use long words. You're a decent chap.'

Morton Radstock sighed, and C.J. answered for him.

'I know,' he said. 'You have to cut your losses according to your cloth.'

'Exactly. And only use words our proprietor understands. Now, your story.' Morton Radstock got out his tape recorder. 'No problem with the dark, you see,' he said. 'Now, I hope this is going to be worth a bottle of Beaune.' He smiled slyly. 'Right. I'm ready. Shoot.'

'It'd be before your time,' said C.J., 'but have you heard of Reginald Perrin of Grot shop fame?'

'Oh yes. I bought a square hoop from a Grot shop. It was a craze.'

'I was his boss at Sunshine Desserts.'

'You were the one who drove him to leave his clothes on a beach and start a new life in disguise?'

'Well, not me personally, I hope. I think Western civilisation and the materialistic society played their part.'

'Western civilisation, the materialistic society and you! Quite a fearsome trio,' said Morton Radstock drily.

'Yes. Poor Reggie. Anyway, he's dead now, and that's where you come in.'

C.J. told Morton Radstock all about Reggie's will, and its absurd condition about absurdity, and about the plan to stage a bloodless revolution on August the twentieth.

Morton Radstock whistled shyly. He wasn't very good at whistling.

'Worth a bottle of rather moderate Beaune?' enquired C.J.

'Very much so,' said Morton Radstock. 'Why did you decide to reveal it?'

'I'm tired of it all,' said C.J. 'We've already done enough to claim our money. I want it well and truly nipped *in flagrante delicto*. I think you're the man to do it.'

'Well, thank you.'

Sly, shy, wry and dry Morton Radstock drained half a glass of wine in one gulp, pocketed his tape recorder, shook hands with C.J., walked out of the wine bar, blinking as he emerged from the murk into the glorious blossom-scented sunshine of a spring afternoon, and, seeing the story that he would write much more clearly than his immediate surroundings, stepped straight into the path of a lorry carrying deep-sea aggregates. The driver

150

needed three weeks off work to recover from the shock, Morton Radstock hovered between life and death in intensive care, his tape recorder did not survive its collision with the lorry, and, unbeknownst to C.J., his dastardly attempt to catch the blood-less revolution in the bud had failed. He arrived home triumphant at 18.03 hours. Tom noted the time in his empty logbook, and started on his third and final ham and chutney sandwich.

Promptly at midnight David Harris-Jones nosed his rusting Ford into the rhododendron bushes beside Tom's rusting Peugeot. He was wearing a green kilt, a scarlet sporran, a ginger beard and a bald wig. He had brought an exercise-cum log book, three rounds of tuna and cucumber sandwiches, a large Thermos of coffee, two oranges and a roll of toilet paper. It might be a long night.

'Anything?' he whispered.

'Came home at 18.03 hours, alone,' whispered Tom, 'but if you think you're going to be bored, forget it. The place is alive with tawny owls.'

'Super,' said David Harris-Jones, without conviction. He felt that the hooting of tawny owls would not be sufficient to keep him amused until dawn broke, and he was right. But he had to admit that dawn, when it came, was magnificent. It began with a ball of scarlet in the East, and spread to touch the mackerel sky with vermilion and orange. The clouds dispersed as the sun rose. The sky turned to lavender and then to a clear pale blue, which deepened as the day grew stronger. Wrens and tits and finches exulted. Robins scolded, woodpeckers pecked wood busily. Blackbirds and thrushes claimed their territories in song suited to a far higher purpose. Tom nosed his rusting Peugeot into the rhododendrons beside David's rusting Ford, stepped out, and farted carefully. 'Sorry about that,' he said, 'but I've been holding it in since Chertsey. I've got to spend eight hours in that car.'

Tom did indeed have to spend eight hours in his car. Of C.J. there was no sign.

By four o'clock, when David Harris-Jones nosed his car into the rhododendrons beside Tom's, the day was really quite warm for March.

Suddenly, right in the middle of the change-over, there he was, nosing smoothly out of his drive in his green Bentley, number-plate C.J.1.

David Harris-Jones's heart began to race, his pulse began to race, only his brain did not begin to race.

'Hop in mine,' said Tom. 'I'll drive.'

David Harris-Jones needed no further bidding, and they were off, a strange vicar and a strange Scotsman, both with flowing ginger beards but utterly bald, chasing an immaculate Bentley in a clapped-out elderly Peugeot.

David Harris-Jones clung on desperately as Tom abandoned the ponderous habits of a lifetime and swung the car round corners like Nigel Mansell with a grudge. At a road junction Tom turned left towards London.

'Got to risk it,' he said.

After about a mile, they saw C.J.'s car ahead. He wasn't hurrying.

'The quarry is in our sights,' said Tom excitedly.

'Yes. Super. But . . . this is awful. I feel awful. I should be driving,' said David Harris-Jones. 'You should be off-duty.'

'And miss the thrill of the chase?' said Tom. 'I think I've only just realised how boring selling houses was. I feel a new man. Don't you feel a new man?'

'Well, no, actually, I don't. I feel sick,' said David Harris-Jones. 'I used to get car-sick as a boy.'

'It's all that tuna,' said Tom. 'I just couldn't eat that stuff. I'm not a tuna person.'

'Please don't mention food,' implored David Harris-Jones desperately.

152

Tom kept his distance while keeping C.J. in his sights, but when he turned on to the A30, C.J. speeded up.

'Damn and blast,' said Tom. 'I can't keep up with him on the straight. This car just hasn't got the juice.'

'Could you stop, and I can throw up in those bushes,' said David Harris-Jones.

'I can't stop!'

'Well, we've lost him. I mean, I wouldn't have suggested it if we hadn't lost him. I'm not a complete wimp.'

'We may find him again. And in any case we have to be able to go home with our heads held high and say, "We did our best." If you really have to be sick, try to make a paper bag out of my logbook. There's bugger all in it except 09.15 ate first ham and chutney sandwich, 11.12 ate second ham and chutney sa . . .'

'Please don't mention food.'

'Sorry. I forgot. Good God!'

'What?'

'C.J.'s following us. He's just pulled out of a petrol station.'

'My God! He must have spotted us.'

'Or he has no idea who we are, doesn't know my car, and filled up with petrol.'

'He's bound to recognise us.'

'Of course he isn't. He doesn't expect to be followed, especially by the car in front of him, and what he'll see is two strange bald, bearded men. We really should have synchronised our disguises. We're going to look ludicrous if we have to follow him in anywhere.'

'Oh God. Might we?'

'David! Dig deep! Find the hero in yourself.'

Tom drove in silence. David Harris-Jones dug deep in silence. C.J., whom they were supposed to be following, followed them all the way to Egham, where he seemed to get bored by his slow progress. Suddenly he zoomed past them, the genuinely bald outpacing the falsely bald. By the time Tom could pull out, C.J. was three hundred yards ahead, and quite soon they had lost him.

'Bugger, bugger, bugger,' said Tom. 'I suppose you're pleased.'

'Well, no, actually I'm a bit disappointed. I think I must have been beginning to get into the spirit of the thing,' said David Harris-Jones.

C.J. judged that Welton Ormsby was in his mid-fifties. His dark, bloodshot eyes, constantly searching the drab bar of the Split Ratchet for better stories, told tales of nocturnal arguments and tension. His complexion gave out loud rumours of pork pies swallowed too fast on the hoof. His Old Harrovian tie supported the rumours with incontrovertible evidence of boiled eggs consumed in haste. His ballooning paunch and his thick breath collaborated to write a black comedy about his excessive drinking and smoking. There were three food stains on his ash-dandruffed suit. His wife had asked him, angrily, what they were from, but he wouldn't reveal his sauces. His breath came in short pants, and C.J. would have laid a sizeable bet that his short pants were none too clean.

'I'm sorry this pub's so drab,' said C.J., trying to hide his distaste for his contact beneath his distaste for his surroundings, 'but I calculated that Hounslow's halfway between Virginia Water and Wapping.'

'I have nothing to do with Wapping any more,' said Welton Ormsby savagely.

'What can you mean?' exclaimed C.J.

'I've been made redundant. I was told I was too old.'

'Too old!' said C.J. 'That's ridiculous. You can't be a day over fifty-five.'

'I'm forty-seven.'

'Ah!'

'I have abused my body,' said Welton Ormsby complacently.

154

'Is age the real reason?' asked C.J.

'Who knows? I don't fit in at Wapping. I'm a journalist of the old school.'

'I can see that. There's egg on your old school tie.'

'And on my face.' Welton Ormsby looked round the drab bar. The green leather upholstery on the bench seats had split in several places. 'I can't drink this beer. It's like the Thames at Wapping. Shall we have whiskies?'

'Thank you.'

'I hoped it might be thank *you*. I don't have an expense account any more.'

C.J. bought a large whisky for himself and a small one for Welton Ormsby.

'But I rang you at Wapping,' said C.J.

'I'd gone back to clear my desk. I pretended not to have time to do it during my last week. I was extending the contact. Pathetic. I am pathetic.'

'So, the first journalist I pick gets himself run over, and the second one's out of a job and just happened to be clearing his desk. Bloody hell,' said C.J.

'I fitted Fleet Street, not Wapping. I fitted low life, not high tech. That's why I still have a news sense. Those two men who've just come in, for instance, the bald vicar and the bald Scotsman, hiding their weakness under beards. What's their relationship? What's their game? Gay, of course. The beards are a smokescreen. Bent as nine-bob notes. They're meeting surreptitiously. The vicar's under suspicion in his parish. The Scotsman is playing truant from an insurance seminar. They're very uneasy. They're worried they might be being followed. They're attracted to each other because they resemble each other because they're really in love with themselves. But I expect they're very active sexually. You know what they say about bald men.'

'Do shut up about them,' said C.J. 'I didn't get where I am

155

today by caring about bald strangers. Is there any point in my telling you my story, that's what I want to know?'

'Of course. I'm a freelance now. I have contacts everywhere.'

'Right. Do you remember a man called Reginald Perrin?'

David Harris-Jones and Tom were suffering deep frustration at not being able to get close enough to C.J. and Welton Ormsby to hear what they were saying.

'I must congratulate you, David,' said Tom, as they sipped their disgusting beers. 'That was a very good bit of surveillance.'

'It's just luck that I spotted C.J.'s car in the car park.'

'You told me quickly enough for me to turn in. You sounded excited.'

'I've rather got caught up in it.'

'If they split up, I'll follow C.J.'s car. You follow the other man. He may not have a car.'

'What if he does?'

'A taxi comes along at exactly the right moment, you say, "Follow that car," and he says, "Blimey, guv, I've waited twenty-two years to hear someone say that."'

'There's never a taxi when you need one.'

'I know. Just do your best. Whatever you do, don't reveal yourself to him. Do you feel up to it?'

'Oh,yes. I'm a bit scared, but . . . I'm beginning to enjoy being scared.'

'Amazing,' said Welton Ormsby. 'Very interesting indeed.'

'Have I put the cat in the china shop?' asked C.J.

'Indubitably.'

'You can use it, then?'

'Oh, undoubtedly.'

They shook hands. Shaking hands with Welton Ormsby was like shaking hands with an exhausted, sweaty bream.

*

Welton Ormsby left the Split Ratchet, looked up and down the street, and set off towards Hounslow East underground station.

A few seconds later, a bald Scotsman with a ginger beard, wearing a green kilt and scarlet sporran, left the Split Ratchet, looked up and down the street, and set off towards Hounslow East underground station.

C.J. downed his whisky and strode out of the pub.

A bald vicar with a ginger beard downed his beer – it was almost undrinkable, but he'd paid for it – and strode out of the pub.

Welton Ormsby boarded a Piccadilly line train bound, if the indicator board was to be trusted, for Arnos Grove.

David Harris-Jones, who had been lurking just out of sight, hurried onto the platform and boarded the train two carriages away from Welton Ormsby. A frisson of satisfaction brought him out in goose-pimples. A private dick could hardly have done better.

C.J. headed towards the West. The traffic was heavy, and his Bentley had no advantage. Besides, he didn't know that he was being followed by a bald, gay vicar.

David Harris-Jones stood at the door of his carriage and peered out at every stop. At Leicester Square he saw Welton Ormsby emerge from the train. He stepped smartly on to the platform and followed his prey down the tunnels that led to the Northern line. Welton Ormsby gave no money to a music student who was playing the violin beautifully. David Harris-Jones slowed down while he found a five-pence piece.

Welton Ormsby stepped smartly on to a southbound Northern line train. The doors closed a split second before David

Harris-Jones could get on to it. He had just learnt why private detectives never have soft hearts.

The traffic was lighter now, but C.J. seemed to be in no hurry, and Tom had no difficulty in following him.

When the Bentley turned off for Climthorpe, a horrible possibility dawned on Tom. C.J. must be visiting Geraldine Hackstraw.

David Harris-Jones decided that he might as well go home, so he took the next underground train to Waterloo, where he bought a single to Goffley. He felt saddened by the unsuccessful ending to his first foray into surveillance.

Judge then of his excitement when he saw Welton Ormsby striding towards a British Rail ticket barrier.

Imagine his exultation when he discovered that Welton Ormsby was making for the train which, *en route* to more glamorous conurbations, made a brief stop at Goffley.

Tom became more and more certain that his fears were not unfounded. Why else should C.J. pull into the car park of the Climthorpe Beefeater, visit the gents' toilet, and emerge smelling, if not of roses, of things by other names that smelt just as sweet?

At each station, David Harris-Jones peered down the platform to see if Welton Ormsby had got off. The light was fading fast, and he began to worry that he might have missed him.

He hadn't missed him. Welton Ormsby got off at Goffley!

The redundant scribe walked straight across the station forecourt, and down the snicket to Schopenhauer Grove.

The reluctant spy walked straight across the station forecourt, and down the snicket to Schopenhauer Grove.

It was almost dark now, and only half the street lights were on, because the council had over-spent its budget. The gloom made David's task easier.

Nevertheless, when Welton Ormsby suddenly turned round, David Harris-Jones ducked down rapidly behind a wheelie-bin left out for the next day's privatised refuse collection.

A police car was cruising by, and David Harris-Jones had to pretend to be doing up a shoelace.

As soon as the police car had gone, he hared along to the junction of Schopenhauer Grove with Bertrand Russell Rise.

He was just in time to see Welton Ormsby turn left into Leibnitz Drive.

He ran up the gentle incline of Bertrand Russell Rise, envying the inhabitants their bright sitting rooms and cosy, drawn curtains.

By the time he reached Leibnitz Drive, Welton Ormsby was halfway along it. He had almost reached the horse chestnut in the garden of number thirty-six.

Welton Ormsby walked past number thirty-six, and turned to walk up the drive of number thirty-eight. David Harris-Jones leant against a lamppost in astonishment, as he realised that he had followed the man to the very house where he himself was living.

Prue Harris-Jones wondered if other women ironed their husbands' underpants. But David's mother always had, being obsessively tidy and deeply pessimistic, and anxious for her only son to meet his maker dressed beyond reproach when, as was almost inevitable, he was run over by a bus, and Prue had been determined not to give her mother-in-law any opportunity to criticise her.

Nevertheless, when she heard an unfamiliar fruity voice in the lounge/diner, she skipped the last two pairs and went through to find out who it was.

She found Elizabeth talking to a big, ugly man in an ill-fitting suit.

'This is Welton Ormsby, the journalist. Prue Harris-Jones, one of our members,' said Elizabeth.

Prue discovered the breamlike qualities of the Ormsby handshake.

'You may have seen me in *What the Papers Say*, where my trenchant style won me both friend and foe,' said Welton Ormsby.

'Sorry, no,' said Prue. 'I'm usually tucked up in bed by ten.'

'Very wise, dear lady. Well, I've been made redundant, a colleague of yours, known mysteriously by his initials alone, told me of your organisation, I approve of your aims, and I wish to join and help you in any way I can.'

'Isn't it marvellous, Prue?' said Elizabeth. 'Would you like some tea, Mr Ormsby?'

'I suppose you don't have such a thing as a beer, dear lady?' asked Welton Ormsby wistfully. 'Or is this an alcohol-free zone?'

'Oh no,' said Elizabeth. 'I'm sure I can rustle you up a beer.'

She hurried out of the room. There was a moment of awkward silence between Welton Ormsby and Prue Harris-Jones.

'Perhaps I should tell you that I've been followed here by some idiot of a bald Scotsman in a kilt with the boniest knees I've seen in many a long day's march,' said Welton Ormsby.

'Good Lord!' said Prue, feigning astonishment as convincingly as one could expect from someone who has made two bit-part appearances with the Haverfordwest Players.

Elizabeth returned with a bottle of beer brewed by Belgian trappist monks.

'Excuse me,' said Prue.

*

David Harris-Jones had been facing the greatest crisis of his brief new career. You are told to follow a man, but not reveal yourself to him. He goes into the house where you live. Do you wait for him to come out? Can you be sure of getting into the house and out of your disguise before he sees you?

While he pondered on his course of action, David Harris-Jones walked up and down Leibnitz Drive, trying to look as though walking up and down Leibnitz Drive wearing a green kilt with a red sporran was an absolutely normal way of spending a dark, cool March evening.

He was extremely relieved when his beloved wife came out to look for him, but less pleased to discover that the man he had followed was their first real recruit.

'Oh God,' he said. 'And I was doing so well. He hadn't the faintest idea he was being followed.'

Suddenly he felt extremely exhausted. He went into the house, changed out of his disguise, came down to the lounge/diner, and accepted the offer of a beer with enthusiasm. The Belgian beer was strong and delicious.

'I've seen you before,' said Welton Ormsby.

'You can't have,' said David Harris-Jones. 'I wasn't even there.'

'You weren't even where?' asked Welton Ornsby.

'Wherever you saw me,' said David Harris-Jones lamely.

'Is the bald vicar one of you lot as well?' asked Welton Ormsby.

'C.J. was telling Welton all about us,' said Elizabeth. 'There we were putting a tail on him, and all the time he was out there recruiting.'

'Frightfully embarrassing,' said David Harris-Jones. 'I hope he never finds out.'

'I feel so guilty,' said Elizabeth.

'I don't think you should feel too guilty, dear lady,' said Welton Ormsby. 'He wasn't recruiting. He wanted me to do a story about you. He wanted to blow your operation sky high. But why should I give good stories to those newspaper bastards?'

C.J. was sitting in the Oven D'Or, which had once been a modest café and tea shop called the Oven Door. Utterly oblivious of the storm which was about to break over his head, he was smiling pleasantly at his companion, the delectable, golden-haired Geraldine Hackstraw, senior partner of Hackstraw, Lovelace and Venison.

Also seated in the Oven D'Or was a rather strange bald vicar, who was dining on his own. For a few dreadful moments, after C.J. had picked up Geraldine and driven her out of Climthorpe, Tom had feared that he was taking her to his home in Virginia Water. Jealousy had swept through him. His relief when C.J. stopped in Botchley had been enormous.

He hadn't dared choose a table too close to C.J. and Geraldine, and in fact he was hidden from them by a low wall covered in ferns. It was just possible to catch the occasional glimpse of them through the ferns. He saw C.J. clasp Geraldine's hand, and felt another, lesser stab of jealousy. He still felt weak with desire for Ms Hackstraw. He didn't want anybody to touch her if he couldn't. He strained to hear their conversation, but he could only catch the odd word: 'face' ... 'bed' ... 'so beautiful' ... 'so juicy' ... 'dressing' ... 'want to come' ... 'After Eight mint' ... 'very hard' ... 'my place' ... 'have it off.'

He didn't like what he heard. He could imagine the rest of the conversation all too easily.

In fact, C.J.'s conversation with Ms Hackstraw was not exactly as Tom was imagining it.

'I feel I really must apologise face to face,' he said. 'It was an appalling thing to suggest that because I'd bought you seven dinners I could expect you to come to bed with me. If I bought

162

you fifteen dinners, twenty dinners, I still wouldn't have that right.'

'No.'

'Oh God, Geraldine, why are you so beautiful?'

'How's your melon and bayonne ham?'

'Don't change the subject. Wonderful, actually. The melon's so juicy. The ham is perfect.'

'Good.'

'How's your warm salad?'

'Very good. The dressing's exquisite.'

'No, but, if we did have fifteen, twenty dinners together, I'd like to think that you'd *want* to come to bed with me. And if after twenty, why not after eight? Oh, Geraldine, I feel so good tonight. I feel in mint condition.'

'After twenty dinners, Bunny, who knows? After eight, mint condition or not, I'm afraid you have no chance,' said Geraldine Hackstraw.

'You're a very hard woman, Geraldine,' said C.J.

'Bunny! You promised. No strings.'

'Oh, I'm not insisting. Just . . . persuading.'

'Attempting to persuade. Now stop tormenting yourself, and try to think about the food.'

'Easier said than done,' said C.J.

But when the waiter came to clear away their plates after the starters, C.J. showed that he had been thinking about the food.

'I've changed my mind about my plaice,' he said. 'I think I will have it off the bone.'

It was at this point that Tom stopped trying to listen. What he heard was upsetting him too much. He concentrated on enjoying his cassoulet, which was rich and succulent. Food, not sex. Linda, not Geraldine. Lovely rich duck. Beautiful Toulouse sausage. Gloriously unwise beans. Food, not sex. Linda, not Geraldine. Wonder how David's got on. On duty at twelve. Hope C.J. doesn't bring Geraldine back. No, I don't mind if he does. It's not my problem. Linda, not Geraldine. Chomp, chomp. Never need to see Geraldine again after tonight. Linda, not Geraldine. All night in a car, then call on Linda.

About half an hour later, Tom saw C.J. lean across and put his hand gently on Geraldine's. The restaurant was full now, and he couldn't hear a word of what C.J. was saying. He told himself that he didn't care, and he almost believed himself.

'I really think, Geraldine,' C.J. was saying, 'that I can't go through any more dinners like this. I thought I could, but I can't. I get the most dreadful pain in . . . in a place where no man likes to get a dreadful pain. I have never believed in banging one's head against the pricks. I simply can't take it, Geraldine, so . . . I really do think that unless you can see your way to . . . to something more . . . I really do believe, regretfully, that we oughtn't to see each other again.'

'That won't be too easy,' said Geraldine Hackstraw. 'Mrs Perrin has invited me down to monitor your progress towards absurdity tomorrow.'

C.J. closed his eyes and groaned.

13 Ms Hackstraw Sees for Herself

It came as a shock to Elizabeth to realise how much time had passed since the day when they had all gathered to hear Reggie's will.

'Is it really ten weeks?' she had asked Ms Hackstraw, who had telephoned her at just about the time that Tom and David were setting off in pursuit of C.J.

'It will be tomorrow. I think it's about time I checked on your progress. Shall we fix an appointment?'

It had seemed natural to say, 'Why don't you come to us? We're having a meeting tomorrow morning to review our progress. Why don't you sit in?'

'I suppose I could,' Ms Hackstraw had said. 'I suppose I could put Mr Linklater off.'

Poor Mr Linklater. He might have been interesting, but we will never know. The nearest he will come to the centre of our narrative will be to be put off by Ms Hackstraw. Compulsive worriers among you, and those of you with extremely caring natures, will be delighted to learn that Ms Hackstraw's secretary was able to arrange an appointment with him for eleven thirty the following Tuesday.

By nine thirty that morning, they were all settled in their usual seats, except for Tom.

Elizabeth rose from her self-sacrificial pouffe to address them. She was wearing a very smart red suit which set off her silvery hair to perfection. She didn't intend to be outdone by Ms Hackstraw.

'Ladies and gentlemen,' she said. 'I have acted unilaterally and perhaps out of order.'

'Shame!' said Jimmy, who wasn't finding it easy, squashed into the middle of the settee by two randy old men, to feel like a leader. 'Joke!' he added.

'Today is ten weeks since the reading of Reggie's well,' continued Elizabeth.

'Incredible how tempus fooges. Fooge, fooge, fooge. Remorseless,' said Jimmy.

'Ms Hackstraw rang yesterday,' said Elizabeth. 'I invited her to sit in this morning.'

Doc Morrissey's wizened old face twisted strangely, and he shifted uneasily in his seat.

'I phoned Jimmy last night to tell him,' said Elizabeth.

'I said, "Well done, that woman. You have my permission posthumously",' said Jimmy.

'I think you mean "retrospectively",' said Elizabeth. '"Posthumously" would mean you're dead.'

'Ah. Not quite yet, except perhaps from the neck up,' said Jimmy. 'Joke. No, awkward wallahs, words. Don't always get the hang of the blighters. Sorry. Talking too much. Carry on.'

'I haven't had a chance to tell the rest of you yet.'

'I knew anyway,' said C.J. 'A little bird told me last night.'

'Oh, it bloody did, did it?' scowled Doc Morrissey.

C.J. was having great difficulty in hiding his feeling of smugness. Welton Ormsby would even now be tapping away at his word processor, lighting a fire under this little lot.

Elizabeth was having great difficulty in hiding her fury with C.J. But she had to. She couldn't raise such an important matter before Tom arrived. He'd be hurt.

Besides, she wanted to see C.J.'s face when Welton Ormsby walked in.

If Welton Ormsby walked in. Supposing he had only been checking on C.J.'s story? Elizabeth had wrestled with that possibility during the long reaches of the night.

A white BMW nosed to a halt in Leibnitz Drive.

'I think this is Ms Hackstraw now,' said Elizabeth.

Doc Morrissey sighed and closed his eyes.

C.J. stared at the ceiling.

The doorbell rang, and Elizabeth went to let Ms Hackstraw in.

'Good morning, everyone,' said Geraldine Hackstraw, smiling as she entered the room.

She was wearing a no-nonsense black suit but still managed to look ravishing. Her grey eyes were as clear as a mountain stream, and her full lips were a deep red.

Jimmy turned to C.J., who was crossing his legs and grimacing.

'Stunner, isn't she?' he whispered pleasantly.

C.J. groaned.

Jimmy turned to Doc Morrissey.

'Damned handsome woman, isn't she?' he whispered pleasantly.

Doc Morrissey sighed.

Jimmy frowned, puzzled by this reception of his innocent remarks.

'Welcome to Leibnitz Drive, Ms Hackstraw,' said Elizabeth, who had followed her in.

'Thank you, Mrs Perrin.' Geraldine Hackstraw gave a regal smile. She indicated Tom's rocking chair. 'Shall I sit here?'

'That's actually Tom's seat,' said Elizabeth. 'He's late.' She could imagine how hurt he'd be if his seat was taken.

'Seat here,' said Jimmy, leaping to his feet. 'Kitchen chair for me. No. Insist.'

'Well, thank you.' With another regal smile, Ms Hackstraw sat between C.J. and Doc Morrissey. She crossed her legs,

167

drawing their attention to her long, elegant calves. She turned a radiant smile on C.J. and on Doc Morrissey. 'All pals together.'

Doc Morrissey emitted a low moan. C.J. tried to smile, but his lips stuck. He ran his hand over his bald pate.

Joan nudged Hank, and he hurried into the kitchen, and returned with a kitchen chair.

'Thanks, Hank,' said Jimmy. 'Much appreciated.'

Although the chair was hard and modest, Jimmy felt more like a leader than he had in the middle of the settee.

'Where *is* Tom?' said Linda.

'Oh my God!' said David Harris-Jones.

Everyone turned to look at him.

'What?' asked Linda anxiously.

'Oh, nothing to be alarmed about,' said David Harris-Jones, looking thoroughly alarmed. 'It's just . . . I wondered if he's gone back to keep watch. He wouldn't have, would he? I never thought. I mean, I realise now, I should have realised last night, but . . .' He couldn't help giving Prue a coy little smile. Whether it was the testosterone, or the prayer, or the feeling of being a man of action, there hadn't been a night like last night for quite a while. '. . . but . . . er . . . he doesn't know that we know about . . .' He realised that it wasn't for him to reveal to C.J. that they knew about his treachery. '. . . what we know and he doesn't,' he finished lamely.

Ms Hackstraw stared at David Harris-Jones in amazement.

'What's the oaf on about?' asked C.J.

'Oh, I'm an oaf, am I?' said David Harris-Jones, man of action. 'Well, in that case let me tell you . . .'

'Let Jimmy tell him,' said Elizabeth.

'Ah. Thanks,' said Jimmy. 'David and Tom had you under surveillance, C.J. Followed you to . . .'

'The Split Ratchet,' said David Harris-Jones.

'Wixton Ambleby turned up here last night,' said Jimmy, thoroughly enjoying himself. 'Didn't do your bidding. Joined

168

us. Tricky coves, journalists. How does it feel knowing everybody knows what a bastard you are, you bastard?'

'Jimmy! Can you keep it . . . er . . .' began Elizabeth.

'Oh. Right. With you. Keep it polite.' Jimmy sighed. 'Not a very nice thing to do, C.J., was it?'

'All right,' said C.J. 'It seems that the pigeons are well and truly out of the bag. Yes, I betrayed you.'

'Why?' asked Elizabeth gently.

'I'm fed up with it,' said C.J. 'I feel we've been absurd enough for long enough. I want my million pounds. Come on, Geraldine old girl, hand it over.'

'Geraldine old girl!' muttered Doc Morrissey bitterly.

'We've done enough, haven't we?' asked C.J.

'I haven't a clue what you've done,' said Ms Hackstraw coolly. 'Nobody's told me. I thought that was the point of this meeting.'

'Well, yes,' said Elizabeth. 'But things have got a bit complicated.'

'If Welton Ormsby's joined you, where is he?' asked C.J. 'He hasn't joined you! He was checking my story, that's all. A journalist never changes his spots.'

Elizabeth smiled uneasily.

'Ha!' said C.J. 'You're worried.'

'Yes,' admitted Elizabeth, 'but so are you.'

The garden gate creaked, and everyone turned to look out of the front window. Welton Ormsby was showing immaculate timing for the first time in his life.

The redundant journalist didn't look his best in the mornings. He didn't feel at his best either. Not that he had looked or felt at his best in the afternoons or evenings either for several years now. Hank went to fetch another kitchen chair – 'I know my place' – and Welton Ormsby subsided on to it with a sigh of relief. He was sweating along his hairline, and a tiny piece of cotton wool was covering a cut under his chin.

'You bastard!' said C.J.

'Often,' admitted Welton Ormsby complacently. 'Usually even. Not today. I don't want to give this story to "the press". I owe those bastards nothing. I'm going to live for this one, C.J.'

'You mean . . . you think there's something in it?' C.J. shook his head in astonishment.

'Brilliant idea,' said Welton Ormsby.

'Where is Tom? I'm worried,' said Linda.

'He must be . . . Oh, God, I hope he isn't . . . but he must be . . . but if he is, why didn't he follow C.J.?' said David Harris-Jones.

'Can you explain that?' asked Jimmy.

'Certainly,' said Prue. 'David's thinking that Tom must be in the rhododendron bushes opposite C.J.'s, keeping watch, but in that case why didn't he follow C.J. when he saw him leave?'

'Or didn't you go home last night, C.J.?' suggested Joan.

Doc Morrissey drew in his breath sharply.

'Never mind drawing in your breath sharply, you clapped-out old roué,' said C.J. to Doc Morrissey across Ms Hackstraw. 'I was at home and *on my own*. We aren't all randy old goats.'

'Shouldn't we go and find Tom?' wailed Linda.

'I'll go,' said David Harris-Jones. 'Oh, God. I can't. I left my car there.'

'Hank'll volunteer,' said Joan. 'Won't you, darling? It'll keep you awake.'

So Hank drove David Harris-Jones and Linda to Virginia Water, where they found Tom fast asleep in his car.

Linda shook his shoulder gently, he woke up, stared blearily around him, and said, 'Oh, my God, I fell asleep. What time is it?'

'Nearly eleven.'

'Oh, my God. I've been asleep for hours. Oh, Lord. I think that's the first time I've ever fallen asleep on the job.'

170

Hank met Linda's eyes and challenged her to say something. She resisted.

'Eleven o'clock!' said Tom. 'Where's C.J.?'

'Over at Leibnitz Drive,' said Hank.

'Oh, thank God. Lucky he went there, that's all I . . .' Another thought struck Tom. 'Why didn't you relieve me, David? I know your car's here, but somebody could have brought you. I mean, I've been on duty for twenty-eight hours.'

'I'm awfully sorry, Tom,' said David Harris-Jones. 'But . . . the surveillance ended last night. I forgot about you, to be honest. You see, we found out what we needed to know.' He told Tom all about Welton Ormsby.

'Well, thank you for not telling me. I'd have been devastated to have missed another night among the tawny owls,' grumbled Tom.

'I'm sorry.'

'Don't be cross, darling,' said Linda. 'David was incredibly stupid, but what do you expect? And I love you.' She hugged Tom.

'I love you too,' he said.

'Oh, Tom!'

'Enough of the Mills and Boon,' said Hank. 'There's a meeting in progress. We must get back.'

Hank and David drove back on their own, and Linda drove Tom.

'Did you mean it when you said you loved me?' she asked.

'I don't say things I don't mean,' said Tom.

'You said it once before.'

'I'm older now.'

'That's true.'

'Will you marry me?'

'Are you absolutely sure of this?'

'Absolutely.'

'Oh, Tom.'

*

'Oh, my God. There's another bloody molehill,' said Jimmy, peering out through the French windows. 'Sentimental bastard, Kenneth Williams.'

'Kenneth Williams?' repeated Prue, puzzled. 'Where does he come in?'

'*Wind in the Willows*. Moles and rats, all that caper. The cove wrote it.'

'That was Kenneth Grahame,' said Ms Hackstraw.

'Ah. Well, he was a sentimental bastard, whoever he was. "Moley"! Never heard such nonsense. Bit of a cock-up on the anthropowhatsitical front.'

Silence returned after Jimmy's conversational effort. Ms Hackstraw glanced at her watch for the fourth time.

At last the cars arrived. Tom's heart beat fast and sank to his boots at the sight of Geraldine. He was very conscious of the greyness of his beard, now that the ginger one had gone. He sat down hurriedly. It's unwise to remain standing when your heart is beating fast in your boots.

'I'm sorry, Ms Hackstraw,' he said, rocking gently in his chair in the hope that this would calm him. 'I didn't realise you'd be here, and I haven't washed or anything.'

'Why should you?' said Ms Hackstraw sweetly. I'm sure you're as fragrant as ever.'

Welton Ormsby, who had never been described as fragrant in his life, sighed loudly.

'Are you all right, Tom?' Linda enquired, giving him a searching look.

Tom was not all right. 'Absolutely,' he lied. 'I'm fine.' He prayed silently. Oh God, if you exist, forgive me for forgetting you, and, now that I've remembered you, please make me free of desire for Ms Hackstraw. He could feel Linda's hand touching him. He was so tired. It was so hard to fight. He clasped Linda's hand fiercely. He couldn't look at Ms Hackstraw. He couldn't breathe. And she knew it. Say something, Tom. 'Yes, I'm fine. I like nothing better than listening to tawny owls all night. I even heard a barn owl, and I think there may have been a long-eared owl over towards Sunningdale, so it was quite a privilege to be totally forgotten by everybody.'

'Can I have my hand back, Tom?' requested Linda.

'Oh. Sorry. Was I hurting?'

Linda gave him another searching look.

'Tom doesn't know his own strength, do you, Tom?' said Geraldine Hackstraw.

Tom felt himself blushing and knew that he was sweating.

'Tom and I have a bit of news, don't we?' said Linda.

'Yes, we do. We have a bit of news,' said Tom. He hesitated. It was terrible to find that, after enjoying all the thrill of the chase, he was as frightened of women as ever. 'Yes, we do. Linda and I are engaged.'

'Oh, that's wondeful,' said Elizabeth.

'Yes, that's wonderful news. Congratulations,' said Ms Hackstraw. 'But my time is limited. Do you think we could get on with the meeting?'

Tom looked her straight in the eyes, and held the look until she was forced to look away. Jimmy had begun to speak, but neither Tom nor Ms Hackstraw were aware of what he was saying. It was Tom's turn to give a deep sigh, but it was an expression of achievement, of resolution of a problem. He believed that it just might be possible to live without Ms Hackstraw. Linda reached out for his hand again, and he squeezed her hand and smiled. Now at last it was possible to listen to their leader.

Jimmy was just finishing saying that Ms Hackstraw's presence must make no difference. C.J. and Doc Morrissey smiled wryly. 'Now, the purpose of this meeting . . .'

'Excuse me,' interrupted David Harris-Jones. 'I . . . er . . . I think we have one other thing to discuss first.'

'Really?' said Jimmy, distinctly put out. 'What?'

Ms Hackstraw looked at her watch again.

'Is this necessary, David?' asked Elizabeth.

'I think so. I'd like to ask Mr Ormsby to . . . er . . . to leave the room for a moment.'

Prue looked at her husband in astonishment.

'Oh!' said Welton Ormsby. 'Am I not trusted? Right.'

He went off to the kitchen with bad grace, slamming the door petulantly.

'The question I want to ask is, "Can Welton Ormsby be trusted?"' said David Harris-Jones. 'I mean, we are about to reveal our secrets.'

'Probably listening at keyhole,' warned Jimmy. 'Unscrupulous blighters, journalists.'

'I'll go and get a glass of water for Tom and see what's happening without his realising what I'm doing,' said Joan.

She went into the kitchen, where Welton Ormsby, a compulsive reader of unimportant matters, was studying the operating instructions for the electric hob.

'Glass of water for Tom,' said Joan.

'I'm not listening at the keyhole,' said Welton Ormsby.

Joan returned with a glass of water and the news that Welton Ormsby wasn't listening at the keyhole.

'But can he be trusted?' said Tom. 'I risked life and limb chasing C.J.'

'He did,' said David Harris-Jones. 'He drove like Nigel Mansell. It was fantastic. Very exciting!'

Linda and Prue looked at their men in astonishment.

'We have to trust him,' said Joan as she sank back into her floral armchair. 'Like you trusted Hank. Otherwise we may as well admit that we can't trust anybody, and that means we'll never be able to tell anybody, and that means there'll only ever be eleven of us, and that means our chances of overpowering the government, police and armed forces are pretty slim, and that'll be no sort of memorial for Reggie.' Her voice cracked with emotion and she blew her nose angrily.

'Wicked,' said Hank.

'Super,' said David Harris-Jones.

'Yes, well,' said Elizabeth, and she gave Joan an intense look, 'any further comments?'

'Put it in a nutshell. Well done, that former secretary with legs that seem to go on for ever,' said Jimmy. 'Call him in.'

Prue fetched Welton Ormsby.

'Procedural matter,' explained Jimmy. 'Not a question of not trusting you.'

'Well, I should hope not,' said Welton Ormsby, 'because if you aren't going to trust me, what chance have you got of trusting C.J., alias Conniving Judas?'

'Conniving Judas! That's rather good,' said Doc Morrissey.

'Well, you have a point there,' said Elizabeth. 'How do we trust you, C.J.?'

'A leopard never changes his spots twice in the same place,' said C.J.

'You can trust C.J.,' said Geraldine Hackstraw. 'I can vouch for him.'

'Vouch for that power-mad lounge lizard?' said Doc Morrissey. 'How?'

'Simple,' said Geraldine Hackstraw. 'If what you're doing is absurd, to nip it in the bud must be very sensible, and if C.J. is being sensible he does not qualify for a million pounds.'

'What's all this about a million pounds?' said Welton Ormsby, and everbody's hearts sank. Now this would have to be explained.

'You've opened a whole new can of pots calling the kettle by any other name there,' said C.J.

They told Welton Ormsby about the money.

'So you're all going to be rich except me?' said Welton Ormsby.

'If you prove useful to us,' said Elizabeth, 'we'll be prepared to do the decent thing.'

'Absolutely. Well said, that . . . what is the decent thing?' said Jimmy.

'A small levy on our legacies,' said Elizabeth. 'Even one per cent would be ten thousand pounds each.'

Elizabeth's comment was received with less than a roar of approbation, but at last Jimmy said, "Spose it's only fair. *If* he proves useful.'

'I could be your press officer,' said Welton Ormsby.

'Good thinking,' said Jimmy.

'Super,' said David Harris-Jones.

'Wait a minute,' said Joan. 'We're operating a total security blanket. We don't want press coverage.'

'Then I'm the ideal man,' said Welton Ormsby bitterly. 'Nobody's as good at not getting things in the papers as I am.'

'Splendid!' said Jimmy. 'That's perfect, then.'

'Wicked,' said Hank.

'Employing an incompetent press officer so as to retain total security, I'm sure Ms Hackstraw will agree that that's absurd,' said Elizabeth.

'Now we *must* move on,' said Jimmy. 'Ms Hackstraw keeps looking at her watch. Not admiring her delicate wrist, much as she might . . .'

Doc Morrissey and C.J. glared at Jimmy.

'. . . but looking at blasted tempus still fooging away like billy-ho. Right. Procedure's this. Think Tank report. Policy Research Unit report. Then I report.'

'Sorry . . . er . . . what do you report on?' asked Prue.

'I report on what I think of Think Tank report. I report on what I think of Policy Research Unit report. In other words, being leader, I lead.'

Elizabeth explained all the ideas about face drops and age hostels and young age pensions that the Think Tank had put forward. Joan explained the policies for employment and age-friendly supermarkets that the Policy Research Unit had come up with.

Finally, their leader stood up, and gave his report on their reports.

'Top-hole,' he said. 'Absolutely A1. Brilliant stuff. Amazing start, and plenty more where that came from.'

He sat down, so that people would realise that he had finished his report.

The meeting drew to a close. Jimmy escorted Geraldine Hackstraw to her car.

'How do you . . . er . . . how do you think we're doing?' he asked.

'Let's put it this way,' said Geraldine Hackstraw. 'It's been a pretty absurd morning.'

'Good,' said Jimmy, attempting a smile. 'Good.' He became grave. 'Geraldine?' he said hoarsely. He was staring at her fiercely, and his battered old face twitched with tension.

'Yes?'

'No. Nothing.'

14 *Jimmy Has a Brainwave and Opens a Cardboard Box*

March gave way to April, as it does on all the best calendars. The lawns of the retirement homes were lush and green after the winter's rains. Rustic garden furniture appeared in the sheltered gardens of sheltered flats. The fattening heads of the tulips gave promise of astounding colours to come. Wardens sang tunelessly. Caretakers whistled through the gaps in their teeth. Nurses smiled. Jimmy, Elizabeth, C.J., Tom, Linda, David, Prue, Joan, Hank, Doc Morrissey and Welton Ormsby scoured the land for new recruits.

In retirement homes from Penzance to Wick they persuaded people away from their television sets and talked to them about honour and respect for age and maturity. They told overworked young executives that the fear of redundancy would be banished for ever. They promised repressed, depressed psychologists a world in which they would be able to work long into old age. They sat in outpatients' waiting rooms and talked to people swathed in bandages and shock about a world where the elderly would no longer need to walk the streets in fear. They loitered outside the clinics of arthritis specialists to bring news of a future in which jars of marmalade and Bovril would be easy to open.

And they made their first converts. In the first week they recruited a neurotic stock controller, the mugged widow of a fishmonger, a rheumatic retired headmistress, a bored eighty-seven-year-old retired film critic, a recently sacked recruitment manager, and an undertaker with a deep fear of death. It wasn't dramatic, but it was a start. They impressed on these people the need for secrecy. They asked them to spread the word, and to impress the need for secrecy on those to whom they spoke.

Jimmy wasn't really in his element. 'Awkward blighter, persuasion. Can't order people around,' was one comment he made.

One bright, breezy, showery afternoon, when soft-soaping people was making him feel claustrophobic, an urge of almost irresistible intensity swept over his starved loins, and he visited a house of ill-repute in Fulham, where a girl called Ivy Belper helped him forget all about the revolution for an hour. Twice, in the warmth of the late afternoon, he attempted to telephone Ms Hackstraw, but on each occasion his courage failed him. 'Black mark, Jimmy,' he told himself. 'Wat Tyler would have phoned – if they'd had phones in his day, of course.'

Elizabeth found, in the service of the revolution, in the creation of a suitable memorial for Reggie, a sense of purpose which enabled her to overcome his absence and to feel an almost mystical sense of his presence. She wondered how the essence of Reggie would cope with her invitation to C.J. to dinner, chaperoned though she was by David and Prue Harris-Jones. She wondered how the essence of Reggie would cope if it had heard her, on the doorstep of number thirty-eight, Leibnitz Drive, on a clear starry evening ideal for essences floating in the ether, saying, 'It's been lovely having you, Bunny.' When C.J. had driven off, she had looked up at the light of an aeroplane, passing slowly across the mellow suburban sky, and she had imagined it to be the essence of Reggie, watching over her. 'I'm being nice to him for the cause, Reggie,' she whispered. 'I still don't entirely trust him, despite Ms Hackstraw's assurance.' The light winked, and winked, and winked, and she felt certain that it was Reggie. She stood for several moments, then returned reluctantly to her Reggie-less kitchen.

C.J. had seen the force of Ms Hackstraw's remark concerning the million pounds. He thought about the money almost all day and often for much of the night. He threw himself into the project, having accepted that he had no alternative. He was surprised to find that, occasionally, he actually managed to recruit somebody, but he just thought that there were some very odd people around, and some very gullible people around, and some very unhappy people around. It never crossed his mind that there might be any real merit in the venture, or even the remotest chance of eventual success.

He had decided to play a waiting game with Ms Hackstraw. How long would it take her to get desperate if she didn't see him? He didn't want to be conceited. Two weeks, perhaps, possibly even three.

The invitation from Elizabeth had been a surprise. He had flirted with her once, in Godalming, and he had arrived for dinner in Leibnitz Drive in moderately stimulated mood, prepared to flirt again. But those Harris-Joneses had been there, in pink sweaters, and flirtatiousness had been strangled at birth. And then, on the doorstep, she had called him Bunny. She hadn't called him Bunny since Godalming. He wondered if he could possibly play her off against Ms Hackstraw.

Tom and Linda had fixed a date for their wedding. They slept together twice a week, once at his flat, and once at hers. This was a new Tom, still easily hurt, still pompous, still often looking like a walrus that has heard bad news, but in the inner recesses of his Tommishness there lay a romantic and passionate and . . . whisper it around the Surrey hills . . . a sexy man. Tom found the job of recruiting supporters for the revolution surprisingly satisfying. Sometimes he could pass a whole morning without estimating the measurements of the rooms he visited. He astounded Linda, rolling over after a satisfactory climax, by saying, 'I think, when this show's over, when we've got two million pounds, I might set myself up as a private dick. Move over, Philip Marlowe.'

He didn't think about Ms Hackstraw at all.

And Linda? She had supported the revolution only out of love for her mother. But, as the days passed, she began to feel real hopes for this absurd and fragile cause. There were whole days when she didn't think of Harrods or Harvey Nichols at all. She regained something of the idealism which she and Tom had shared in the early days of their marriage, before mail-order catalogues had become her main reading. And over all her new enthusiasm, dusting it with the fine perfume of sex, was the enchantment she felt in her new, improved more-than-twenty-per-cent-better Tom, who was on special offer to her and her alone.

David and Prue Harris-Jones had never been happier, although the fact that they never spoke about their errant son was like a curtain drawn between them. David's foray into tailing C.J. hadn't given him, as it had given Tom, a burning desire to become a man of action. He wouldn't roll over, after a satisfactory climax, and say, 'I might set myself up as a private dick.' There were, however, occasional satisfying climaxes, and, if all that he said after them was 'super', well, Prue was happy with that and in full agreement with his choice of adjective. Living at number twenty-eight with Elizabeth was more exciting than Haverfordwest, and they soon developed a real sense of commitment to the unlikely cause. But, and this is where I have been remiss, gentle reader, but I didn't want to worry you unnecessarily – for all I know life may be pretty hard for you these days – so I didn't tell you something which I will have to tell you now if the syntax of this sentence is not to become irretrievably complicated, which is that a moth had got into David and Prue's sweaters in their little house on the outskirts of Haverfordwest, but (and now at last we are back at the 'but' which began this sentence) but perhaps the most important ingredient of all in the cocktail of events which created David and Prue's happiness was their gradual realisation that the moth had not accompanied them from Haverfordwest to Goffley, and there was therefore no reason to expect any further damage to their identical sweaters.

Joan and Hank had also fixed a date for their wedding, and, very slowly, Hank's energy level began to grow. This was a different energy, not the frenzied excitement that had coursed through his veins during those years in the City. Hank, who had worked with people whose jobs made them so strung up that a football riot was their idea of a quiet weekend, had become cosy and cuddly, and, in time, a truer, less selfish sexuality might emerge. Slightly to her surprise, Joan found that she preferred this slower, gentler version of her white-haired, lined, baggy, lived-in man.

Both found pleasure in the cause. For Joan it was a way of acknowledging to herself that she had loved Reggie without causing any problems to her relationship with Hank. For Hank there was wry pleasure in attempting to overturn the world he had once thought it so important to build that he hadn't minded losing his health in the process.

Doc Morrissey felt, in his heart of hearts, that Ms Hackstraw would never lie in his bed, nor he in hers. He felt that, after the revolution, he would be happy giving away large sums of money while also keeping large sums of money, and that he would die happy, amidst affection and garam masala. He was happy to serve the revolution, in which he had begun to feel he had a personal investment ever since his idea of young age pensions had become such an important plank of policy. But he had a problem. This mild, gentle old man, who loved quiet philosophy and spicy cooking, who enjoyed seeing people happy and didn't even resent Hank's refusal to let him examine Joan's chest, was possessed of a violent hatred for C.J. If C.J. wasn't seeing Ms Hackstraw, he no longer needed to see her. If C.J. was, he must.

But was C.J. seeing her, and how could he find out?

Welton Ormsby threw himself into the cause like a drowning man, which Elizabeth thought was probably what he was. He didn't talk at all about his wife and children, and it seemed clear, from his state in the mornings, that he spent a large part of each evening in the pub. Elizabeth suspected that he no longer went home to them at all.

He had a slight problem with recruitment. People didn't take to him. Insects took to him, perhaps for the alcohol in his blood, and so he was rarely free from unsightly red lumps, which developed white heads when he scratched them. Pollen took to him, so that he was greatly given to violent bursts of loud sneezing during that spring and early summer. Germs took to him, so that he would usually have some minor ailment, like conjunctivitis, or dyspepsia, or cold sores, or a boil in his ear. People, on the whole, didn't take to him. Luckily, he made no attempt, during those months leading up to the revolution, to press his sexual suit (or indeed any other suit) on any of his colleagues, of either sex. It seemed that he had accepted that nobody could possibly find him attractive, and that, Elizabeth felt, was his saving grace.

An impressive team of recruiting officers, I hear you exclaim. No doubt the slow trickle of recruits swelled into a fierce stream, you justifiably predict.

Wrong! Very much the reverse. For it was at this juncture that Jimmy had his brainwave.

'Coaches,' said Jimmy excitedly.

'What?' asked his puzzled sister.

'Coaches.'

'Coaches of what? Tennis? Dialogue?'

'Not coaches *of* anything. Coaches as in buses.'

'Ah.'

They were sitting in the garden of number thirty-eight, Leibnitz Drive, on a warm early April evening. Fingers of high cloud reaching towards them from the South-West suggested that the weather might soon break.

Jimmy had telephoned Elizabeth in some excitement. He had something to show her, he said, and something to suggest.

He had a glass of Belgian trappist beer. She had a gin and tonic. Mr Potter at number forty was mowing his lawn. At number thirty-six the Meakers had the sprinklers going. The scene was – Elizabeth hardly dared use the word even to herself – Perrinesque.

'That's your suggestion, is it, Jimmy? Coaches.'

'Yes. Fantastic things. Not as good as buses, of course, but buses have routes and schedules, so we can hardly have them.'

Elizabeth recalled how Jimmy's enthusiasm for buses had surfaced after his honeymoon in Malta with Lettuce. Had it lain dormant since then, or had it smouldered undetected?

A heron flapped lazily westwards, hunting for ponds.

'So, what do you think of my idea?'

'To tell you the truth, Jimmy, I don't think I've grasped the full implications.'

Ponsonby the Third trotted between the molehills and jumped on to Elizabeth's lap.

'Oh. Well, it's simple. Suggesting we hire every coach in Britain.'

'What for?'

'For August the twentieth. To transport the old people to Whitehall.'

'Jimmy! Do you expect so many?'

'Got to have faith. Wat Tyler didn't say, "I don't expect many peasants'll turn up," Anyway, better too many than too few. Too many coaches, run half-empty, no crisis. Too few, can't transport the rebels, crisis. Nice beer. Too strong, but tasty.'

'Another?'

'I'm driving. Yes, please.'

Ponsonby the Third yowled with displeasure as Elizabeth stood up.

'Man wants beer, cat loses lap, story of life,' said Jimmy, in rare philosophical bent.

Elizabeth fetched his replenishment, and sat down again, but the cat no longer trusted her and stalked off stiffly, pausing only to pee all over the parsley.

'Won't it alert suspicion somewhat if we book every coach in the country to go to Whitehall?' she asked gently.

'Thought of that,' said Jimmy proudly. 'Book them through old people's homes, charities, what have you, destination seaside, lakes, etcetera. Come the great day, hijack them. Drive to London, or else.'

'Hijack every coach in England?'

'Yes. And Scotland and Wales. Mad?'

'Yes. I think Reggie would be proud of you.'

Jimmy smiled, a slow long smile of pure pleasure. It was a smile that took the care and failure out of his face. He still had a good head of hair, and when he smiled Elizabeth saw, for just a moment, the hopeful handsome young man he had once been.

'Think that's the nicest thing you've ever said to me,' he said. 'What a prospect. Snakes of coaches closing in on London along every road, full of rebellious senior citizens. Even Wat Tyler couldn't boast of that.'

'Now,' said Elizabeth, 'what have you got to show me?'

'Security,' said Jimmy. 'Wait till first owl fart.'

'Do you mean dusk?'

'Got it in one.'

They reminisced as daylight faded. It was getting much too cold to sit out, but they didn't notice.

At last it was dark enough. They heard an owl hoot. David and Prue Harris-Jones joined them, and Jimmy led them to his jeep. He opened the rear door, and shone a torch into the interior. It was full of boxes. He lifted the lid off one of the boxes.

It was full of automatic rifles, gleaming, immaculate, virile, awful, deadly.

'Only the tip of the iceberg,' said Jimmy.

There was a stunned silence.

'Wondering where I got them,' said Jimmy. 'Can't tell you. No names, no packdrill.'

'No, it's just that . . . I mean I . . . I mean, I thought the . . . er . . . the revolution was supposed to be . . . er . . . and so I suppose I . . . I didn't think we'd . . . and I'm not sure if we . . . er . . . and I don't feel I . . . so . . . well . . .' said David Harris-Jones.

'I have to say I agree with every word David said,' said his adoring wife Prue.

'It's to be a *bloodless* revolution, Jimmy,' Elizabeth pointed out.

'Oh, absolutely, with you all the way,' said Jimmy. 'Need a threat, though, in order not to use it. Whole principle of nuclear debate in nutshell. Have them, so as not to use them. Don't have them, find you have to use them, haven't got them, up shit creek without a paddle, excuse my French.'

'We can't give our supporters guns, Jimmy,' said Elizabeth. 'They'd go off by mistake. People with the shakes and St Vitus's dance would be a liability. People with poor sight would be a

186

liability. Nervous people would be a liability. Bad people, sad people and mad people would be a liability. People suffering from paranoia might shoot the police. It'd be a bloodbath.'

There was a long silence. Jimmy looked crestfallen.

'People suffering from anoraksia nervosa might shoot everbody wearing anoraks,' said Elizabeth, in an attempt to lighten the atmosphere. There was another long silence.

'No guns, that what you're driving at?' asked Jimmy.

'No guns.'

'No guns at all?'

'No guns at all.'

'Took a lot of whistling and not a little prayer to get these. Better get home and start taking them back, I suppose.'

'Yes. I'm sorry, Jimmy.'

'It really is best, Jimmy,' said Prue.

'Super,' said David Harris-Jones.

Jimmy shut the box, took a last regretful look at the boxes, closed the back doors of the jeep, and walked slowly towards the house.

'Another beer, Jimmy,' offered Elizabeth.

'Have to admit, very upset,' said Jimmy. 'Take your point, but very upset. When upset, when depressed, try to drown your sorrows in drink, fiasco, end up more upset, more depressed. Yes, please, be lovely.'

Jimmy sat in the rocking chair, and rocked gently, cradling his glass of beer like a sick child clutching a doll.

David and Prue Harris-Jones went off to bed, with a mixture of tactfulness and hope.

'You liked my idea about the coaches, though, didn't you, Sis?' he said.

'Very much, Bro,' said Elizabeth.

15 The Wedding Breakfast

Tom Patterson sat in front of the Registrar's desk, in his best suit and an increasing state of nerves. He pulled nervously at his beard, trimmed, like his hair, by Pierre of Goffley, so that he might almost have looked spruce, but for his moderate paunch. He glanced at his watch. It was already 3.33. There had been so many scenes, in books and plays and films, of people being left at the altar that it was barely conceivable that any groom or bride could be unaware of the possibility.

Behind Tom sat Jimmy in his major's uniform, though he had no idea whether he was still permitted to wear it; Elizabeth in tactfully reticent beige; Joan in virginal white; Hank in a light green Cerutti suit; David and Prue Harris-Jones in blue suits; Doc Morrissey in a sports jacket; Welton Ormsby in a suit that was the right size on average, but only because the trousers were two sizes too big for him and the jacket was two sizes too small; Ms Hackstraw in a low-cut, off-the-shoulder turquoise dress which revealed as much of her fine, firm breasts as it was possible for a guest to do without committing a major social solecism; Tom and Linda's son Adam, from the BBC, a good-looking young man of twenty-eight with just a touch of his father's pomposity in his look, and his girl friend Angie, who was blonde and beautiful and distantly related to Jeremy Paxman, and was wearing a long dress that looked as if it had set out to be a sari but had lost the courage of its convictions on the way; and their twenty-seven-year-old daughter Jocasta, who had also been invited to bring her boyfriend, and had replied, 'It's actually a girlfriend, sorry,' to which Tom, after a pause, had said, 'Do you mean girlfriend girlfriend or friend who's a girl?' and Jocasta had said, 'Girlfriend girlfriend, she's called Helga and she's German and she's very nice and she cries if anyone mentions the concentration camps,' and Tom had said, 'Fine. Terrific. We look forward to meeting her very much, darling. She sounds fun,' and now here they were, in black trouser suits, like lesbian Harris-Joneses.

Among the other guests were Alan Maseby-Smythe, the only estate agent with whom Tom was still on speaking terms, and his lovely lady Sonia; Dinky Follifoot, a friend from Tom's schooldays, with his third wife Clarissa, whom Tom had not yet met; and Madge Grizell and Lucy Middleham, two schoolfriends of Linda, neither of whom had ever married.

All the guests began to share Tom's worry. Then at last, at 3.39, Linda entered, smiling broadly, and enjoying her moment to the hilt, on the arm of Charles Manton, the widower of another schoolfriend of Linda's, who had been chosen because Linda could hardly be given away by Jimmy, under the circumstances. She was wearing a mid-calf peach skirt with matching soft draped jacket, very high-heeled black shoes and a wide-brimmed black hat trimmed with peach.

The ceremony went smoothly. Tom was so determined not to seem nervous that he boomed out his response in the cheery little flower-bedecked register office. Linda's voice was charmingly shaky.

After the register had been signed, several of the guests filed out, but Elizabeth, Jimmy, C.J., Doc Morrissey, Joan, Hank, David and Prue Harris-Jones, Welton Ormsby and Ms Hackstraw remained, and Tom and Linda's first walk of their second married life was a short one, for they sat down among the guests.

'The ceremony's over,' said the puzzled registrar. 'It's the next wedding now on our assembly line of joy.'

'We *are* the next wedding,' said Joan.

Linda removed her hat, so as not to overshadow the bride.

Joan stepped forward, magnificent if somewhat less than truthful in virginal white. Hank stood behind her, smiling shyly, a gentle giant with fading bags under his eyes.

More guests filed in. They included Joan's old schoolfriend Sarah Treacy and her balding car-dealer husband Mike; Tim Ripley, a friend of Tony Webster who had supported Joan when Tony deserted her for a lady osteopath from Auckland; two schoolfriends of Hank, Eamonn Cohen, an Irish Jew and Dennis Trestle, manager of a market garden near Newark, who was accompanied by his live-in lover, Melanie Twist, a florist of some renown; and three of Hank's City colleagues, Dan Peters, Rick Holdsworth and Barry Kelsgrove, who were accompanied by their wives, who were called, respectively, Nicky, Nicci and Niki.

After the meal, the tables were moved to make space in the centre of the room, and there was dancing to the music of Jed Musselburgh and the Marshmallows.

Elizabeth had felt that the idea of a joint wedding breakfast was a risky one, but it had all gone terribly well. She had wondered whether the Hildon Hall Country House Hotel would be too grand. After all, it was a magnificent Grade I listed Queen Anne mansion with a long drive, impressive wooded gardens with a notable cedar of Lebanon in front of the house, elegant moulded ceilings, notable chandeliers made of Venetian glass, and a chef who had once spent two days washing up for Marco Pierre White. But the Wellington Suite had proved just the right size, and the event had gone with a swing from the start.

Much of the credit for that must go to Tom's elderflower champage. His suggestion that he provide his home-made champagne had delighted Ms Hackstraw, who was paying for half the reception by releasing funds on the promise of absurdity

190

to come, and it had delighted Hank's father, who was paying for the other half and had chivalrously given the money to Joan's mother in secret, so that she need not feel ashamed of her poverty. It had not delighted Elizabeth, C.J., Doc Morrissey, David and Prue Harris-Jones, Jimmy or Joan, who all had experience of Tom's home-made wines. But, like Linda before them, they had been astounded by its delicate mixture of fruitiness and dryness, its surprisingly complex depth and its long nose.

Credit must also go to the chef, who also, coincidentally, had a long nose. Something must have rubbed off during his two days of washing up in the vicinity of genius. The meal of game terrine with cranberry and juniper berry coulis, poached sea trout with saffron and lime coulis, and brandy-snap baskets with pistachio ice-cream and strawberry and kirsch coulis seemed to have pleased everybody.

The speeches also had been models of their kind, reasonably witty, very sincere, and, above all, extremely short.

And now the music of Jed Musselburgh and the Marshmallows was also perfectly judged, not too loud for conversation, but lively enough to get people on to the little dance floor, and traditional enough to give opportunities to those who knew how to do ballroom dancing.

So why wasn't Elizabeth happier?

C.J. was also not as happy as he should be. He felt a pressing need to confide in someone. But who?

Prue. In her matching blue suit and sensible hat, Prue looked . . . sensible. He would confide in her.

He approached her, magnificent but absurd in his morning dress, and plonked himself into an empty chair beside her at her round table.

'Lovely weddings,' he said.

'Lovely.'

'Yet I feel like a fish out of water but you can't make him drink.'

'Oh dear.'

'I don't like it. I didn't get where I am today by feeling like a fish out of water but you can't make him drink.'

'I imagine not, C.J.,' said Prue, smiling ruefully to herself, acknowledging how often, in conversation with C.J., one found oneself saying, 'I imagine not, C.J.'

'Nice music. Suitable.'

'Very. Er . . . is there any . . . er . . . any reason why you feel like a fish out of water but you can't make him drink?'

'Yes. Yes, there is. Ms Hackstraw.'

'Ah.'

'We have had dinners together. I have invited her back to Expansion Cottage. She has hitherto refused. I didn't like that. I didn't get where I am today by having women refuse me.'

'I imagine not, C.J.'

'I'm ignoring her, and waiting for her to crack.'

'I see.'

'She hasn't cracked yet.'

'Ah.'

'You're a woman, Prue. You'll understand about female psychology.'

'Do you understand everything about all men, C.J., just because you're a man?'

'Well, no, obviously not.'

'Well, I don't understand everything about a woman like Ms Hackstraw, just because I'm a woman.'

'No, of course not.'

'I do think one thing, C.J. Now that you've started waiting for her to crack, you'll have to go on waiting. You can't change horses in mid-stream while leading them to the water.'

'True,' said C.J. glumly. 'That's very true, Prue. Well, thank you.'

192

'I don't think I've been much help.'

'You've been a great help,' lied C.J. glumly.

'Let's dance, Alan,' said Alan Maseby-Smythe's lovely lady Sonia.

'In a minute, dear,' said Alan Maseby-Smythe hastily. 'I want to nobble Tom while he's had a few drinks but before he's had too many.'

Alan Maseby-Smythe strode past the dance floor, where Joan's mother was dancing beautifully with Hank's father, and Jocasta was clinging unashamedly to Helga. He was making a beeline for Tom, although it was more of a zigzag than a beeline, because he didn't want it to look as if he was making a beeline. He had a proposition to put, but he wanted it to look as if it were just a casual suggestion.

'Tom!' he said, as if surprised to find himself face to face with him. 'Missing the world of property are you?' Characteristically, he gave Tom no time to reply. 'Well, I've been thinking. How would you like to come into partnership with me? How does "Maseby-Smythe and Patterson" grab you? Has a good ring, doesn't it?'

'No.'

'Good. Well . . . what?'

'No.'

'Oh. Oh, I see, Well, all right, then. "Patterson and Maseby-Smythe." It doesn't have quite the same ring, words have a natural order according to their sounds, don't they, but all right, I'm not a petty man. "Patterson and Maseby-Smythe." So be it.'

'It's got nothing to do with that,' said Tom. 'It's very kind of you to offer, Alan, and I do appreciate it, but I'm involved in something far more exciting than being an estate agent.'

'Good God,' said Alan Maseby-Smythe, as if it were almost beyond his powers of imagination to conceive of anything more exciting than being an estate agent. 'Good God! What?'

'I can't tell you,' said Tom, touching the side of his nose. 'Security.'

As he walked away, Tom looked round to see Alan Maseby-Smythe staring at him open-mouthed. He felt a slow exultation swelling within him. 'I truly do believe,' he told himself, as he sipped his own elderflower champagne and smiled benevolently at his guests, 'that this is the happiest day of my life.'

Three of the guests favoured by Tom's benevolent smile were David Harris-Jones, Hank Millbeck and Tim Ripley, Tony Webster's friend. They were standing close to the bar counter, as far as possible from Jed Musselburgh and the Marshmallows.

'What was Tony Webster really like?' asked Hank.

'Put it this way,' said Tim. 'You've nothing to worry about. He had this sort of infuriating habit of sort of saying "great" all the time. It drove me up the wall, know what I mean, but now he's gone I kind of miss it.'

'Super,' said David Harris-Jones.

'Wicked,' said Hank.

'How's he liking New Zealand?' asked David Harris-Jones.

'He says it's great,' said Tim Ripley.

'Super,' said David Harris-Jones.

'Wicked,' said Hank Millbeck.

Doc Morrissey made a rather tortuous beeline for Prue. The reason in his case was drink, not deception.

'May I sit here?' he asked, indicating the empty seat beside her at a table from which everyone had gone to join the dancing.

'Please do. Nobody seems to want to talk to me. I'm not a social success,' said Prue.

'Nonsense. I'd ask you to dance with me if I hadn't got a rather peculiar pain.'

194

'Oh, dear. It's nothing serious, I hope.'

'So do I. Talking of . . . er . . . peculiar pains, I saw you chatting to C.J. earlier.'

'Yes,' said Prue cautiously.

'Not being inquisitive, but may I ask what you were discussing?'

'No, I don't think you may, Doc. It was confidential.'

'I thought as much. Is he seeing her at the moment?'

'Doc!'

'No. Quite. Can't expect you to tell me. Do you mind if I . . . er . . . I just need to talk to somebody.'

'No, I'd be delighted to talk.'

'Good. You're a splendid woman. Does David realise how lucky he is?'

'Oh yes. I keep telling him.'

'Good girl.' Doc Morrissey laughed. 'It's Ms Hackstraw.'

'Ah.'

'We've had dinners together. I've invited her back to my little den in Southall. She has consistently refused. I led a happy life before I met her. She made me miserable. I gave her up as a bad job.'

'I don't see the problem.'

'You were talking to it earlier. I'm congenitally incapable of leaving the field clear for that conceited, pompous bastard. I kid myself it's for Ms Hackstraw's sake, but it's probably for my own.'

'I can't tell you what C.J. and I discussed,' said Prue, 'but I can tell you this. If you do leave the field clear, I don't think there's much chance of C.J. leading a horse through it, and no chance at all of his making it drink.'

'Thank you, Prue,' said Doc Morrissey. 'You've been a great help.'

Unlike C.J., he meant it.

*

Jimmy was trying hard not to feel sorry that Linda had married Tom again and that further incest was even more out of the question than before.

He was trying hard not to think of Ms Hackstraw.

He was trying hard to get a chance to do a bit of tactful sounding-out of Dan Peters, Rick Holdsworth and Barry Kelsgrove, and at last he saw his chance. They had been dancing, frenetically, adrenalin-pumpingly, with each other's wives, namely, respectively, Niki, Nicky and Nicci. As the six of them returned, exhausted but laughing, to their table, Jimmy pounced.

'Mind if I join you?' he asked. 'Can't very well say "no", can you?'

He plonked himself down, raised his glass, and said, 'Cheers.'

'Cheers,' they responded, cautiously.

'Not a dancing man,' said Jimmy. 'Awkward wallahs, dances. Never quite got the hang of the coves.' He lowered his voice. 'Hank burnt out, discarded like used condom pardon my French. Bad show. Any of you frightened of the same fate?'

They looked at him in astonishment, and he sensed that uneasy glances passed between the men and their wives.

'No need to say anything,' said Jimmy. 'Leave it at that, eh? Just like to say, ever you do feel . . . the way you might feel, we have certain plans, can't say more, security, sure you understand. All you need to do, give us a ring, come and see us, be most welcome. Think carefully about it. Said enough, possibly too much.' He stood up. 'Nice to have had this little chinwag.'

He walked away, leaving six astounded people in his slightly unsteady wake.

He weaved his way over to Elizabeth's table and asked, 'How are you doing, Big Sis? Just chatted to Hank's friends, put them in the picture, well, not entirely in the picture, security, eh? Fancy I struck a chord. Fancy the three men were interested.

196

Fancy Nicky and Niki saw my point of view. Not so sure about Nicci. I say, old girl? Anything wrong?'

Elizabeth burst into tears.

'I miss Reggie so much,' she wailed.

'Course you do,' said Jimmy. 'Course you do. Forced to. I miss Lettuce. Tricky little customers, weddings. Set the emotions astir. Here, have my hanky, haven't used it, have a good blow, always helps to have a good blow.'

He sat down beside her. She had a good blow and tried to smile. He patted her hand, and just for a moment he wondered if there could ever be anything between them. No. Out of the question. Be drummed out of the regiment of respectable life. And she'd never wear it. Good old stick, Elizabeth. Ask her to dance.

'No great shakes on the dance floor,' he said. 'Fancy tripping the light fantastic with your poor old Bro, though?'

'Lovely,' said Elizabeth.

So Jimmy and Elizabeth stepped on to the floor, which by now was quite crowded. Dan Peters, Rick Holdsworth and Barry Kelsgrove were back there, dancing with Nicci, Niki and Nicky in the third possible combination of partners. Tom was dancing with Linda. Hank was almost asleep on Joan's shoulder, Joan's mother was leaning on Hank's father's shoulder, David and Prue Harris-Jones were circling carefully, Alan Maseby-Smythe's lovely lady Sonia had finally dragged him on to the floor, and Welton Ormsby was dancing with himself.

Jimmy trod on Elizabeth's toes.

'Sorry,' he said. 'Bit of a cock-up on the footwork front.'

'It's all right,' she said resignedly.

'Cheer up, old girl,' he said, steering her carefully and arthritically through the throng of dancers. 'Lovely woman like you, soon find somebody else.'

Elizabeth burst into tears again.

*

Jed Musselburgh and the Marshmallows embarked upon a rhumba.

'Shall we sit down?' said Tom to his bride of four hours. 'I'm not a rhumba person.'

They sat down, in a far corner of the room, at a table that had been temporarily abandoned.

'I've something to confess,' said Tom earnestly, as his wedding swirled about him.

'Oh, God.'

'Oh, nothing to worry about. It happened before we were reconciled. I fell madly in love for the first . . .' He realised his appalling *faux pas* almost in time. '. . . time in my life apart from you.'

'I see. If it was before our reconciliation, do you have to tell me?'

'I want to set the record straight. It was with Ms Hackstraw.'

'What??'

'Yes, I know, but she is very attractive. I was utterly and totally obsessed by her. I'd never ever felt . . . apart from with you, of course . . . anything remotely like it. It was earth-shattering. Terrifying. I was on fire.'

'Well, terrific. Funny you've never been earth-shatteringly on fire with me.'

'I have. Often. I've been blazing. I've been a furnace. I just didn't show it. I'm not a showing-things person.'

'I wish you hadn't told me this.'

'I had to, Lindyplops. This is the most important day of my life, and I want to start with a clean slate.'

'You're a clean-slate person, are you?'

'Yes, I think I probably am. Nothing happened, Lindysquids.'

'No, because she wouldn't let it, or you wouldn't be here now. I thought you were a changed man. I even thought you meant it when you said you wanted to be a spotted dick.'

'Private dick, not spotted. A spotted dick's a pudding.'

198

'Well, that's what you are. A great pudding, and I'd love to pour custard over your spotted dick. You've ruined my wedding night.'

'Lindypoohs.'

'I am not your Lindypoohs.'

Linda stormed out of the reception. Tom followed. Joan, about to wake Hank up, saw them and thought, Maybe falling asleep isn't so serious after all. I'll let him rest.

'Is anybody sitting there?' asked Ms Hackstraw.

Prue Harris-Jones shook her head.

'No,' she said. 'Nobody wants to sit beside me. I'm a bore.'

'Rubbish,' said Ms Hackstraw. 'I've seen streams of men sitting beside you, chatting you up, telling you how exciting they find you.'

'They haven't been saying that at all.'

'I find that hard to believe. They've been so intent, so close to you, so . . . secretive.'

'They've been telling me their troubles and asking my advice.'

'Would it have been about me, by any chance?'

'That's a leading question.'

'We aren't in court now.'

'Aren't we? I feel I'm being cross-examined.'

'You aren't a bore. You're very intelligent.'

'One can be intelligent and a bore.'

'So C.J. and Doc Morrissey were both asking your advice about me. Ironic.' Geraldine Hackstraw changed gear almost visibly from lawyer to woman. 'Because I want to ask your advice about them. You're so . . .'

'If you say "sensible" I'll scream the place down,' said Prue.

'You're so . . . happy with David that I don't know if you'll be able to empathise with my problem,' improvised Geraldine Hackstraw swiftly. 'Everyone knows that I had an unhappy marriage. Everybody knows that I'm beautiful. Well, I'm sorry, but there's no point in my pretending I'm not.'

'I wasn't going to.'

'You don't know what a problem it is being beautiful.'

'Thank you.'

'Oh, Prue, I didn't mean . . . I thought . . . I mean, you are pretty, and sexy, and *very* attractive, which is much more exciting than being beautiful. Men find me daunting, they expect me to have a lover, and, when they find I don't, they wonder if there's something wrong with me, when the reason I don't is because I meet very few men and most of those are so dull I wouldn't spend five minutes with them, let alone the rest of my life, and then I met C.J. and Doc, interesting men, who gave me nice dinners, and want more, which I don't want to give them, and now they ignore me. Time is passing, Prue. I won't be immune from its effects for ever. How do I get what you've got?'

Prue looked puzzled.

'What have I got?' she asked.

'A man you can wear identical sweaters with for the rest of your life. How do I find a man for the rest of my life?'

Prue shook her head in a mixture of disbelief at what she was hearing and of inability to give a satisfactory answer.

'It's luck,' she said. 'It doesn't matter what you do or who you are. In the end it's all luck.'

It had gradually dawned on C.J. that Geraldine was never going to crack. It was a huge blow to his self-esteem, but his sense of realism forced him to admit it to himself, if not to anybody else.

He had no difficulty in admitting to himself that Geraldine Hackstraw was not the only pebble in the sea. He had been eyeing with some favour a lady who was in fact Melanie Twist, a florist of some renown. His request for a dance was met in the affirmative. A waltz was in progress. C.J. danced stiffly but correctly, holding his body unnaturally erect. Melanie Twist swirled and cavorted, being both musical and drunk. Her live-in lover, Dennis Trestle, returning from the Gents, watched sourly, being neither musical nor drunk. For years he'd been led a few merry dances, but few merrier than this. He had sown his seeds dutifully in his market garden, while Melanie had sown her wild oats with the most eligible men in Newark, Retford and Gainsborough. She referred to this area as her stomping ground. Dennis Trestle expressed it differently.

C.J.'s misfortune was to be in the wrong place at the wrong time. The place was at the end of Dennis Trestle's fist. The time was 10.46. C.J. fell to the floor; Dennis Trestle pulled Melanie Twist from the room, while she shouted obscenities at him; Jed Musselburgh and the Marshmallows switched to the hokey-cokey forty-seven minutes earlier than scheduled; Doc Morrissey ricked his neck laughing; Tom and Linda re-entered in happy reconciliation and stared at the prone figure of C.J. in deep alarm; and Jimmy summed up the general sentiment in the pithy phrase, 'Awkward wallahs, weddings.'

C.J. was helped to a nearby table, a large brandy was summoned, and he began to recover his poise. As soon as they were sure that it wasn't his heart, Tom and Linda re-joined the dancers with enthusiasm if not style.

Joan and Hank also took to the floor, and Hank astounded Joan by thowing himself into the dance with something that could, with only marginal exaggeration, be described as energy.

After the dance he led Joan back to their table, and said, 'You loved Reggie, didn't you?'

'Yes. Yes, I think I did.'

'Elizabeth knew you loved him, didn't she?'

'Yes. Yes, I think she did.'

'Did you love Tony Webster?'

'At first.'

'Do you love me?'

'Yes.'

'One day, will you answer that you loved me "at first"?'

'No. I'll love you for ever.'

'Let's dance.'

'Again??'

'I think my energy's coming back,' said Hank Millbeck. 'I can't wait to get you to bed.'

'Wicked,' said Joan.

Drink was running freely in C.J.'s blood. His dander was up. He had no idea that he cut a rather absurd figure in his morning dress and with the beginnings of a right royal black eye. He weaved his way towards Elizabeth, across a room that was swaying slightly, to his surprise, as earthquakes were rare in Surrey.

He made a slight detour to pass close to Ms Hackstraw, who began to smile at him, albeit uncertainly. He weaved straight past her, trying not to look smug, and collapsed in a heap in the chair beside Elizabeth.

'You called me Bunny in Godalming,' he said.

'I did indeed, C.J.,' admitted Elizabeth cautiously.

'A lot of water's passed under the burning bridges since then.'

'A lot of water.'

'Too much water.'

'Much too much water, C.J.'

'You called me Bunny again the other night.'

'I did indeed, C.J.'

'You aren't calling me Bunny tonight.'

'I haven't heard from you since I called you Bunny last time. You can't call people Bunny if they never behave Bunnyishly.'

'Oh. Right. I'd better behave Bunnyishly, then.'

'I think you had, C.J.'

'Will you come out to dinner, Elizabeth, so that I can behave Bunnyishly?'

'That would be delightful, Bunny.'

Geraldine Hackstraw, like Queen Victoria, was not amused.

And she likened herself to Queen Victoria in more ways than that.

People were over-awed by royalty, and they seemed over-awed by her.

She'd seen Jimmy casting her glances. She knew that he was frightened of her.

She wondered if he would ever pluck up the courage to speak to her.

She couldn't risk it. She would go and speak to him.

Well, she had to speak to some man. It had not been a good evening for her, with C.J. and Doc Morrissey pointedly ignoring her, Tom marrying Linda, and all the other men being spoken for or smelly or ugly or both or finding her as unapproachable as Queen Victoria.

She walked resolutely over to the old soldier, who was standing at the edge of the dance floor, watching the dancers enviously. Her carriage was as erect as any soldier's and as graceful as any dancer's.

Jimmy almost leapt out of his leathery skin when she came up beside him and said, 'Aren't you ever going to ask me out to dinner, Jimmy?'

'What did you say?' he gasped.

She repeated the question.

'Well, blow me over with a pickled gherkin,' he said. 'Was trying to pluck up courage to ask you that.'

'Am I so very fearsome?'

'No. Not at all. It's just . . . man of action not words. Don't expect Monty was good at asking women out to dinner. Attila the Hun probably never asked a woman out in his life.'

'Well, he'd just have grabbed them.'

'Absolutely. Not his fault, lived in the dark ages. We don't. You'd be livid if I just grabbed you. Quite right too.'

They watched the dancing in silence for a few moments.

'You haven't answered my question,' said Geraldine Hackstraw gently.

'Answer's "yes".'

'When?'

'Now. Geraldine, will you come out to dinner with me?'

'I'd love to. When?'

'How about . . . haven't got my diary on me, but I'm sure I'm free . . . Tuesday?'

'Tuesday it is.'

'Jolly good. Fancy a quick turn on the floor? Fancy footwork not my forte, but do my best.'

C.J. and Doc Morrissey smiled to themselves as they saw Jimmy take the floor with Ms Hackstraw.

There's one born every minute, their secret smiles asserted.

Their secret smiles froze somewhat as they saw how beautifully Geraldine Hackstraw danced. She avoided Jimmy's clumsy feet so deftly and so gracefully that she might have been dancing with Nureyev in his prime.

Everyone knew that the happy couples weren't going on proper honeymoons until after the revolution, but it had still been planned that they would be seen off for their one-night breaks in traditional style. They had been expected to leave much earlier, but now at last they did.

The guests assembled outside the hotel and scattered confetti over the two Rolls Royces. In the vast sky, many more stars than anyone could remember were twinkling. It was a magnificent, velvet night, a summer's night in spring, a night when thoughts turned to sex, and infinity, and global warming.

Tom and Linda waved and smiled, Joan and Hank waved and

smiled, and the cars sped off, silent save for the ticking of their clocks, the beating of lovers' hearts, and the crunching of old boots and cans upon the gravel.

As soon as the guests had all gone back in to the reception, the two cars returned up the drive, and went round to the back of the hotel, where the duty manager was waiting to escort the two couples to the bridal suites.

Slowly, the guests began to disperse, some eagerly, some reluctantly. Jed Musselburgh and the Marshmallows began to play the last waltz. On the crowded dance floor, couples mooched and smooched and dreamt.

At a table near the bar, a very drunk David Harris-Jones was talking earnestly to a fairly drunk Adam and a very drunk Angie. He told them the name of the revolution and its acronym. He told them its aims and policies. He told them the complete story of its foundation and development. He even told them its date.

Prue collected him and led him to the door with loving exasperation.

'I'm sorry,' she said to Adam and Angie. 'Has he been boring you?'

'No,' said Adam. 'He told us all about the revolution. I wouldn't have missed it for anything.'

The last guests left. The hotel staff cleared away the perishable food and then locked the door on the chaos of the Wellington Suite.

Under the makeshift bar, stretched across the carpet, with a half-smoked, unlit cigar in his mouth, Welton Ormsby slept.

16   *Coaches, Chaos and C.J.*

On the day after the weddings, the leaders of the Bloodless Revolution of Senior Citizens and the Occupationally Rejected were in very diverse moods.

The four middle-aged newly-weds were in romantic vein as they enjoyed their one-day honeymoons.

Doc Morrissey was enveloped in peace. His elderly limbs were pleasantly lethargic. His dressing gown was red and blue, and allowed pleasant breezes to waft around his body. His spice cupboard was overflowing. His coffee pot was full. His two eggs were boiled to perfection. His Sunday newspaper was rich in advice on how to invest a million pounds and how to spend a million pounds. Later, he would cook. Before that, he would have a long, hot, lazy bath, soaking his limbs in the joy of his release from tension. He was free from sexual yearnings, and there was no need for jealousy.

C.J. was excited. He roamed through Expansion Cottage like a herd of buffalo, seeing it with Elizabeth's eyes, making a list of things that would need to be bought – flowers, candles, pot-pourri. Gentle things for a lady who would call him Bunny. He was quite surprised, when he caught sight of himself in a mirror, to see that he was bald and slightly frail.

Major James Anderson was almost frisky as he planned the booking of coaches for the great day. There was a slow-burning vitality in his loins as the clock ticked slowly on, bringing dinner with Ms Hackstraw ever closer. There was life in the old dog yet. He could even begin to think it amusing, rather than shameful, that his flat was in a block called Clement Attlee Mansions.

Welton Ormsby was in a nightmare land where there wasn't even a word for friskiness. Steam hammers beat in forehead and temples. A large brick had lodged in his throat. He felt extremely sick, and a gale was rumbling through his innards, causing crevices to bulge, ribs to swell, stomach wall to contract violently before its force. If he survived – and he rather hoped he wouldn't – he would never drink again.

But the condition of David Harris-Jones was the worst of all. His physical state was very similar to that of Welton Ormsby with, did he but know it, rather less of a gale running through his more placid insides. But his mental condition was far worse.

'He said what?' he asked Prue again.

'I asked if you'd been boring them.'

'Charming. I'm a bore, am I?'

'Of course not.'

'So why ask them if I'd been boring them? Why assume that I must have been?'

'Because you were pissed out of your mind and everyone's boring when they're pissed out of their minds.'

'Right. Sorry. So . . . what *exactly* did he say?'

'He said, I'm sure of the actual words, I was so appalled, he said, "No. He told us all about the revolution. I wouldn't have missed it for anything."'

'I bet he wouldn't. What a gift of a story for a BBC man.'

At twenty past eleven, David felt well enough to believe that he had a realistic chance of making it down to the kitchen without being ill on the stairs. Prue helped him. He looked wan and frail in his Ralph Vaughan-Williams limited edition bath robe, which had been a present from his dear mam. There were moments when he wished that the Welsh weren't such a musical nation.

207

He made it safely to the kitchen, collapsed into a chair, accepted a jug of water and three paracetamol, and told Elizabeth what he had done. In his mood of self-disgust, there was an element of perverse pleasure in the admission of his guilt.

'He's a lovely boy,' said Elizabeth. 'He may not tell.'

'Angie's distantly related to Jeremy Paxman,' said Prue.

'It doesn't look good,' said Elizabeth. 'But there's no point in despairing till it happens.'

But David Harris-Jones did despair. It seemed highly unlikely to him that Adam would not use his information. If his drunken indiscretion had betrayed the revolution, he would never forgive himself, and Prue, though she would always stand by him, would never forgive him either.

The next day, at the usual Monday morning planning meeting in their usual chairs in the lounge/diner, David Harris-Jones admitted his sin to the whole group and felt again that disturbing element of pleasure mixed in with the pain of disgrace.

'I must say that I'm disappointed in you, David, both as a friend and as a colleague,' said Tom. 'We went through such times together, during our surveillance period. I felt a sense of kinship. I don't want to sound pompous, I'm not a pomposity person, but I feel let down.'

'The man's a dolt,' said C.J. 'Always was, always will be. I should never have employed him.'

'I must say Reggie deserved better,' said Joan.

'The lesson is, if you can't hold your drink, don't drink,' contributed Welton Ormsby.

'Can't believe what I'm hearing,' said Jimmy almost cheerfully, his new friskiness proving difficult to subdue. 'All right, bit of a cock-up on the security front, telling young people involved with the BBC. But no news is good news and nothing's happened yet. Adam is family, a decent boy, he may keep quiet. All right, Angie's distantly related to that blighter who asks

208

aggressive questions, but she loves Adam. We assume that all is not lost. We press on as per regardless. Last Monday I put before you my plan to book every coach in Britain. We have made significant progress. How do we stand as of now, Hank?'

'Coaches ordered – three hundred and three,' said Hank. 'Supporters recruited so far – four hundred and thirty-eight.'

'Excellent,' said their leader. 'Main objective this week – book more coaches.'

'This is ridiculous,' grumbled C.J. 'I didn't get where I am today by booking more coaches.'

'We do actually have less than one and a half people per coach,' pointed out Hank.

'Maths not my strong suit,' said Jimmy. 'Take your word for it, though.'

'Hank had to be good at maths on the futures desk,' said Joan.

Hank sighed, just at the thought of all that frenzy. A few weeks ago he had seen a programme by Clive James about Bombay. They had shown its frenetic stock exchange. Madness, destroying Asian philosophy at a stroke. Madness. He sighed again.

'Sorry,' said Joan. 'I shouldn't have mentioned the futures desk. Hank's trying to forget the past.'

Hank sighed again.

'The ratio of coaches to people does seem . . . er . . . well, not that I want to . . . especially when I've just . . . but it does, doesn't it?' said David Harris-Jones.

'All a question of a cove called Faith,' said Jimmy. 'Our supporters will themselves recruit other supporters. Like compound interest.' He couldn't hide a flash of self-satisfaction at his simile. 'If we don't book coaches soon, all coaches booked, no coaches left. When all coaches booked, when no coaches left, recruitment becomes our sole aim. Next two weeks, coaches. After that, still got all summer to find the buggers to fill the coaches. Useful wallah, faith. Thoroughly recommend the cove.'

'Shouldn't we decide democratically?' pleaded Elizabeth.

'Been through all that, Sis,' said Jimmy. 'Sod democracy. This is war. Well, not war.' He sighed regretfully. 'Coaches first, supporters second, or I resign.'

There was a long silence. Jimmy stared at them, and they stared at him.

'Good,' said Jimmy. 'That's settled then.'

'How do we pay for all these coaches, though?' asked C.J. 'Presumably we have to put down deposits.'

'Good question,' said Jimmy. 'Glad you asked it.' He hesitated, trying to summon the right words in the right order. It wouldn't be easy.

'Well, answer it, then,' said C.J.

'Going to. Thinking it through. Difficult trying to part a blighter from his lolly, specially when the blighter's notoriously mean. Sorry. Mustn't alienate those you're wooing. Bad tactics. Slur withdrawn. Er . . .' He paused again, thinking hard, hurting his sluggish brain. 'C.J., you are the only person here with lots of lolly. Lend us money, lots of coaches, lots of people, great success, money paid back plus interest plus inheritance. Result, one very rich C.J. Sometimes need to spend lolly to earn lolly. That's why rich people become very rich and poor people don't even become slightly rich.'

There was a pregnant pause.

'Quite right,' said C.J. 'I'm amazed at your grasp of economics, frankly.' He got out his cheque-book. 'I didn't get where I am today without spending lolly to earn lolly,' he said, and, to general astonishment, he wrote out a cheque for twenty thousand pounds, payable to Elizabeth.

Afterwards, everyone agreed that it had been Jimmy's finest hour.

*

210

They monitored every BBC news bulletin, but the news didn't break. Every telephone call caused hearts to flutter, but none of them were from journalists.

Just before six that Tuesday evening, at the exact moment when a sexually excited Jimmy was slipping into his stained old bath in Clement Attlee Mansions at the beginning of his pre-Geraldine ablutions, Adam and Angie walked up the garden path of number thirty-eight, Leibnitz Drive.

David Harris-Jones was watching *Neighbours* with the sound turned down, while waiting anxiously for the six o'clock *News*. Prue was chopping onions and using the opportunity to have a real cry undetected. Elizabeth was browning chunks of beef. The doorbell sounded ominously loud.

David Harris-Jones went pale when he saw who it was. He invited them in, and went into the kitchen.

'It's Adam and Angie,' he said.

'Oh God,' said Prue. 'The moment of truth.'

David Harris-Jones returned to the lounge/diner and offered Adam and Angie a drink. Angie accepted an orange juice and Adam a beer. They were both wearing jeans and tee-shirts but Angie also had a striking patterned waistcoat. They seemed friendly and relaxed. David Harris-Jones was anything but relaxed and felt dreary and stuffy in his fawn sweater. His heart was thumping.

'Elizabeth and Prue are cooking,' explained David Harris-Jones as he got the drinks. 'Prue's chopping onions. They'll be in when they've washed their hands.' He could hear the tension in his voice.

'Onions are awful to get off hands,' said Angie.

'Awful,' agreed David Harris-Jones.

'I once chopped some chillies and then touched my willy,' reminisced Adam. 'It was absolute agony. Ruined our Saturday night, right?'

'No sex, please, we're preparing a curry,' said Angie.

211

They all laughed. Was this the sort of conversation people had before the balloon went up? David Harris-Jones hardly dared hope that it wasn't.

At last Elizabeth and Prue entered.

'I must say that was a lovely wedding,' said Adam.

'Or rather those were lovely weddings,' said Angie.

'Right, Ange. Mustn't forget Joan,' said Adam, 'but I was really thrilled to see Mum and Dad getting it together again, right? They both have really improved enormously as people.' He seemed utterly unaware that he might be sounding a trifle condescending. 'I thought they'd be devastated that Jocasta's lesbian. Took it in their stride. I was proud of them.'

'It was a very nice evening. Thank you,' said Angie.

'I'm so glad you enjoyed it,' said Elizabeth, feeling as stiff as the Queen at a Bedouin banquet.

'Anyway, we didn't come to discuss that,' said Adam, introducing the conversational equivalent of sheep's eyes. 'We came to discuss the revolution, right, Ange?'

'Right,' said Angie.

Adam handed Elizabeth a list of names.

'There are twenty-seven names there,' he said, 'and that's only in two days.'

'Sorry,' said Elizabeth, 'what are these names?'

'Supporters,' said Angie, as if it was obvious. 'They all want to join.'

David Harris-Jones felt faint. He felt that he was going to faint. He must speak.

'Join?' he said, sounding unnatural, his tongue sticking to the roof of his mouth.

'Join the revolution,' said Adam. 'It's a fantastic idea. Look what it's done for Mum and Dad.'

'But it's for old people,' said Prue.

'We disagree,' said Angie. 'We think that's exactly the kind of ageist attitude you ought to be trying to fight, right?'

212

'I'm twenty-eight,' said Adam. 'In the youth culture that means I'm well and truly past it already.'

'We've been through seven completely different sets of musical tastes already as we find we're too old for the last one, right?' said Angie.

'Fashion, same story,' said Adam. 'It's incredibly expensive and the pressure's terrible. Everything you buy, you think, "Oh God, am I going to look as if I'm no longer young?" I mean till you're eighteen you're happy to be growing older, right, cos you're getting grown up. After that it's downhill all the way, right? Well, that's ridiculous, right?'

'Right,' said David Harris-Jones.

'We'll end up with nine-year-old murderers and rapists. Well, more like seven-year-old. There'll be almost no childhood at all, and that's because of youth culture, which is a bit ironic, right?' said Adam. 'And then you start work and your youth's over overnight. I've got friends in business, twenty-four, twenty-five, drink orange juice all night so clients don't smell booze on their breath the next day. Well, it's not right, right?'

'Right,' said Angie. 'That's why young age pensions is such a fantastic idea.'

'I mean, I don't know how you guarantee universal employment at twenty-eight, but I suppose that's something you've worked out, right?'

'Right,' lied Prue.

'Take the arts,' said Adam. 'Plays, books, painting, music. If you're young, you have to chuck out all meaning, all shape, all form, all plot, all story. Otherwise they say you've copped out, you're old-fashioned, your friends say seriously insulting things like, "Here comes Terence Rattigan." So now it's all chaos, right? You've heard of chaos theory. Well I have my own chaos theory. In the past, long ago, like between the wars, before society broke down, smug world, solid bourgeois values, nuclear family but no nuclear weapons, job of the arts, smash it

213

into chaos, right? Now we've got a chaotic world, family breakdown, law and order breakdown, chaos. So I reckon artists ought to be imposing order on chaos. The point is, I want to write, and I want to feel that what I think about writing is right, right, before I write, right, because I'm young and I could be wrong, right?'

'Right,' said Angie.

'Ten years on a pension, thinking, learning, I'd have been just about ready to get it right, right?'

'Right,' said Angie.

'So we all want to join,' said Adam. 'How much are the subs?'

There was a pause.

'We ... er ... we don't actually have any subs,' said David Harris-Jones.

'Oh God,' said Adam. 'You people are seriously naive. Nobody respects anything they don't have to pay for in this country.'

'You decide a sub and we'll all pay it,' said Angie.

'I can't wait for August the twentieth,' said Adam.

'Er ... good,' said David Harris-Jones. 'Good. We ... er ... we're very glad that you ...' The relief was still washing over him in waves, but it was no use getting carried away. 'We ... er ... We're absolutely thrilled that you ... but ... er ... the revolution is really for ... well, I mean, isn't it?'

'David means that the day of the revolution is planned as a mass march of old people,' said Prue.

'That's where, frankly, we wonder if you're right, right?' said Angie.

'I think we are right,' said Elizabeth. 'I think symbolically the image that goes round the world should be of the elderly marching, right?'

'Right,' said Adam. 'No, I agree. The image, Angie. We didn't think of that. That image, going round the world, on that day will ... well, what it'll do, on August the twentieth, is free the human race from the stigma of ageing *at a stroke*.'

214

'Super,' said David Harris-Jones.

'Wicked,' said his adoring wife Prue.

During the rest of the week, the booking of coaches proceeded steadily, but slowly. It was a difficult business, since they could never be booked in the name of the revolution.

Some were booked in the name of fictitious charities: the Royal Society for the Preservation of the Elderly; The Senility Society; The Senior Citizens' Charter; The Twilight Homes Trust; The Evening of Life Insurance Company; The Retired Loom Overlookers' Benevolent Society; The Home for Retired Quantity Surveyors; Octogenarian News; The Anti-Loneliness League. But all these needed printed letterheads. It was a laborious business.

The legatees and a few trusted recruits each booked three or four coaches from their own homes. Some were booked directly from the old people's homes, in the names of residents posing as treasurers and matrons.

When Jimmy opened his eyes on the following Monday morning, he had no idea where he was, but he had a vague feeling that it was somewhere exotic. He felt extremely exhausted. Why did he feel so exhausted?

He turned his head slowly, because it felt thick, and he saw, on the wall beside the door, a rather lurid painting of the Battle of the Somme. He was in his modest bedroom in flat twenty-two, Clement Attlee Mansions. Why had he believed that he was somewhere exotic?

He stretched his weary legs and touched something soft. He jumped. There was something in his bed.

He moved his legs cautiously, to feel what the soft thing in his bed was, and then he remembered. He knew now why he had believed that he was somewhere exotic. He knew now why he was so exhausted.

He turned over, and put his arms round the soft body of Ms Geraldine Hackstraw. How lovely she looked without make-up. She stirred, moaned, opened her eyes, had no idea where she was, and then remembered. There was an amazing look of recollection and disbelief on her face.

He kissed her awkwardly, fiercely, Mars to her Venus.

'Wonderful night last night,' he whispered gruffly.

'Incredible. I can't believe I . . . I can't believe we . . .'

'Wasn't surprised at the time. Am now.'

Last Tuesday, after a slightly sticky dinner – 'Awkward customer, conversation. Never quite got the hang of the blighter' – Jimmy had been surprised when she had accepted his invitation to go out for Sunday lunch.

It had been a late Sunday lunch and it had taken a long time. He had invited her back for tea, having for once excelled himself on the catering front and bought crumpets on the off-chance. They had eaten crumpets and watched the *Antiques Road Show*. It had been a lovely spring day and he had suggested a drive in the Surrey countryside. She had accepted. An idyllic pub had appeared at the right moment, Sod's Law being suspended for the day. They had sat in the garden in the evening sun and drunk passable wine and watched the sunset and listened to the great variety of expressive cries made by those reputedly dreary animals, sheep. When they had driven back to Clement Attlee Mansions, he hadn't invited her in. He had just led her in, as if it had been decided, and she had just come in, as if it had been decided. The rest, as they say, is history.

As it all came flooding back, Jimmy planted an unsubtle kiss on Ms Hackstraw's full, gentle lips, and a shrill bell rang. He reached out to switch off the alarm clock, but the bell continued to ring.

'Postman,' he said. 'Registered letter. Blasted hell.'

His feet found his bedroom slippers. His bath robe was on a hook on the door.

216

'Coming,' he shouted, as he hunted for the front door key.

He opened the door, and discovered that, unless C.J. had become a postman overnight, his surmise as to the identity of his caller had been incorrect.

'What the hell are you doing here?' he demanded.

'I might ask you what the hell you're doing in a bath robe,' said C.J. 'We have our meeting here this week. It was you who suggested it.'

'Oh God, I'd forgotten. Thought it was at Elizabeth's.'

'Well, even if it was, shouldn't you be there by now? It's one minute to nine.'

'Oh, my God. Cock-up on the alarm clock front.'

'Well, can I come in?'

''Spose you'll have to.'

'Charming. What a welcome.'

Jimmy led C.J. into his sombre, shabby lounge.

'Be a good chap, will you, let the others in?' asked Jimmy.

'I didn't get where I am today by being a good chap.'

'Know you didn't, but, damn it, a cove's going to be busy on ablutions fatigues.'

'Of course I will. I was only joking.'

'Joking?? You??'

'Oh, get off and have your shit and shave.'

Jimmy returned to his bedroom and explained the dreadful situation to Geraldine Hackstraw.

'Oh, God,' she said. 'I'll have to ring the office.'

'Yes, but, awful thing is, can't even get to the bathroom, layout of this bloody stupid flat, without going through lounge,' said Jimmy. 'Can't get you out without everyone seeing. Unless you care to shin unwashed down four flights of outside wall.'

'I'm not ashamed,' said Geraldine Hackstraw. 'Are you?'

'No. No. Good heavens, no. No, proud, if anything. I'll get dressed, then you borrow my robe,' said Jimmy.

He hurried through to the bathroom, nodding to C.J. as he went.

By the time he returned from the bathroom, Doc Morrissey Elizabeth, David, Prue, Tom and Linda had arrived.

How they gawped as Geraldine Hackstraw, wearing Jimmy's bath robe, appeared before them *en route* to the bathroom.

C.J. and Doc Morrissey went absolutely white.

Geraldine Hackstraw favoured them both with a sweet, challenging smile.

The doorbell ran again. Jimmy hurried out, fully dressed in his regulation patched jacket, and let in Hank and Joan.

Geraldine Hackstraw emerged from the bathroom just before Welton Ormsby entered. She had combed her golden hair and applied some make-up which she carried in her handbag. She was, even in the emergency rig of Jimmy's worn, torn bathrobe, a splendid ship in full sail.

'Well, it's another glorious spring day,' she said, sounding casual and unembarrassed. 'Almost too nice to spend on a planning meeting, but the work must go on.'

While she dressed, Jimmy addressed the gathering.

'Sorry about that,' he said. 'Bit of a cock-up on the cock-up front. Lovely lady, carried away, forgot to set alarm. Take a smack, that naughty sexy man. What's up, Doc? What's up, C.J.? Why are you looking as sick as two parrots? Aren't you pleased to find your leader's got lead in his pencil? Oops, sorry, breach of security. What happen in bed with wonderful sexy lady, not for public consumption. Sex is a private matter. World's gone sex mad, sex scenes in adaptations of Jane Austen, only matter of time before they have them in the weather forecast, may as well go to bed, my darling, there'll be rain spreading to all areas from the South-West. Sorry, carried away, hobby horse of mine, absolutely disgusting people practically eating each other on park benches. 'Nother plank of our policy, keep sex private, more fun that way. Now Ms Hackstraw, when

218

dressed, will need to phone office. Suggest we have coffee now, start meeting after her departure. Any objections? No? Good. Coffee break.' In a lower, less confident voice, he added, 'Remembered the milk, Sis?'

Elizabeth had, and she and Linda went to make coffee.

Geraldine Hackstraw emerged from the bedroom, fully dressed, and asked to use the phone.

'Go in kitchen if you like,' suggested Jimmy.

'There's no need,' said Geraldine Hackstraw. 'We're all adults, aren't we?' Into the phone she said, 'Hello, Jackie. It's me. Could I speak to Mr Venison, please . . . Thank you . . . Hello, George. It's me. I've been a very naughty lady, but if you saw the man you'd understand.'

Jimmy tried to look modest, but devious facial expressions weren't his forte. C.J. and Doc Morrissey bristled.

'Anyway, we overslept, I'm in Spraundon . . . Spraundon. It's near Coxwell . . . That's rude, George. Anyway, I'll have to go home and change. I've got a Mr Linklater coming in at ten, and I won't make it, and I've let him down before. Will you apologise to him personally and perhaps see him for a few minutes? He'll explain what it's about . . . No, I can't explain, it'd be a breach of confidentiality, I've got a room full of people here . . . That's *very* rude, George, and of course I haven't, and I may have to ask you to resign from the partnership, but first I'll introduce you to my lover. He'll teach you how to be a gentleman.'

She slammed the phone down. Jimmy's efforts at looking modest were becoming feebler by the second. C.J. clutched his heart and winced, and Doc Morrissey emitted a low moan.

When Geraldine Hackstraw had left, Jimmy felt that an expression of modesty might be graceful. On reflection, he felt that he could have done better than, 'Surprised myself, really. Seem to have fallen on my feet. Well, not my feet exactly.'

Luckily for C.J.'s heart and Doc Morrissey's sanity, coffee arrived, and the meeting began at last.

'Big success to report,' said Jimmy. 'Tom and Linda's boy Adam, and his girlfriend Angie, have not only joined us, but have recruited twenty-seven other young people already. We owe a big thank-you to David Harris-Jones, who put them in the picture.'

'He's a good lad,' said C.J. 'I knew that even at Sunshine Desserts.'

'It only goes to show what I've always said,' said Welton Ormsby. '*In vino veritas*.'

'At the risk of sounding pompous,' said Tom, 'I think we ought to make a formal vote of thanks to David, who has discovered a whole new source of manpower – the young. I propose a vote of thanks. Will anyone second me?'

The vote of thanks was seconded by Linda and passed *nem. con.* David Harris-Jones smiled proudly, and Prue clasped his hand lovingly.

'Progress report,' said Jimmy. 'Coaches ordered so far – six hundred and twenty-six. Supporters recruited so far – six hundred and twenty-six. Even I can work out that that is one supporter per coach. Main objective this week – booking more coaches.'

'I'm sorry, but this is ludicrous,' said Doc Morrissey.

'Barmy,' said C.J. 'We're putting the cart before the trees.'

'I must say I . . . er . . . having recruited people, feeling there must be many more people to recruit, I do feel . . . er . . . but there we are,' said David Harris-Jones.

'It does seem a little foolish to book yet more coaches, Jimmy,' said Elizabeth.

'Very foolish. Absurd even,' said Joan, 'so it's probably what Reggie would have done.'

'You have complete insight into his mind, do you, Joan?' said Elizabeth.

220

'Shut up,' said Jimmy. 'Sorry, Sis, but sounds like jealousy to me. Nasty little tyke, jealousy. Green-eyed bloody monster. Can't help wondering if C.J. and Doc are jealous of me. Hope not. Be even more pathetic bastards than I think they are, the bastards.'

'Jimmy, please!' implored Prue. 'We must all pull together at this stage.'

'Thank you,' said Jimmy. 'Only one word to describe you, Prue. Sensible.'

'Super,' said David Harris-Jones.

Prue glared at Jimmy and at David.

'I didn't mean super that you're sensible,' said David hurriedly. 'I mean the word I'd use for you is "super", not "sensible". I mean not that you're not sensible, but you're even more super than you're sensible. Sorry.'

'Wicked!' said Hank.

'Quite finished?' enquired Jimmy bitingly. 'Pity. Got to get down to the nitty-gritty now. Need as many coaches as possible, if we're to succeed. This week, sole task, coaches. Need bums on seats, first job, get seats. What theatre says, "Goodness me. Lot of people booked in tonight, best get some seats or the poor bastards'll have to stand"? Seats first, bums later. Don't like it, sack me. Get leader who hasn't got lead in his pencil. Sorry. Shouldn't boast. Bad form. Right. All agreed?'

There was total silence in the drab little room in Clement Attlee Mansions. Doc Morrissey looked as fierce as Field Marshal Montgomery. C.J. looked as fierce as Lettuce Isobel Horncastle. Nobody spoke.

'Take your silence as agreement,' said Jimmy.

The following Monday's meeting was held in Hank and Joan's high-tech flat.

'Give us the figures, Hank,' said Jimmy.

'Coaches booked – one thousand and sixty-six,' said Hank.

221

'Ten sixty-six!' exclaimed Jimmy. 'It's an omen.'

'Supporters recruited – nine hundred and ninety-nine,' said Hank.

'Nine nine nine!' exclaimed Doc Morrissey. 'It's an emergency.'

'Nice one,' whispered C.J. to Doc Morrissey. 'I got you wrong. I thought you were a bastard. The bastard's elsewhere.'

'I'm happy now. I'm reconciled to my lot,' whispered Doc Morrissey.

'I'm happy now too,' whispered C.J. 'I have other fish to fry.'

'No whispering in the ranks,' thundered Jimmy. 'Right. Our priority this week – booking more coaches.'

Everybody groaned.

When C.J. said that he had other fish to fry, he was speaking of Elizabeth. His first attempt to fry her took place at the Hildon Hall Country House Hotel, which he regarded as an inspired choice, since it would for ever be associated with the happiness of the double wedding celebrations.

They enjoyed an aperitif in the Haig Bar. C.J. chose malt whisky with water, while his companion plumped for a dry martini.

'Well, here we are again,' said C.J., as they studied the menu.

'Absolutely, C.J.'

'I thought you were going to call me Bunny.'

'So I will, C.J.'

'Do you have difficulty in calling me Bunny?'

'Not at all, C . . . Bunny.'

'Good.'

The bar was decorated in pale green. Everything – curtains, carpet, upholstery – was pale green. There were pale green tassels a-plenty, and it was also a haven for lovers of pale green pelmets. There were no prices on Elizabeth's menu.

'I meant, "Here we are again" in the sense of you and I together,' said C.J.

'Yes, Bunny.'

C.J. chose smoked eel with raspberry and horseradish coulis, followed by rack of lamb with rosemary and redcurrant coulis. His companion plumped for game terrine with fig compote, and sea bass with fennel and apricot compote.

'You've gone for compotes, I for coulis,' said C.J.

'Absolutely, Bunny.' Elizabeth allowed herself a wry smile, as she reflected on how often, in C.J.'s company, one found oneself saying, 'Absolutely, C.J.' She felt that she should try to be slightly more original, but wasn't altogether satisfied with the result of her effort, which was, 'It's lucky we aren't all the same.'

'It's the difference between people that makes the world an oyster,' said C.J.

'Absolutely, Bunny.'

In the Auchinleck Dining Room they were given a window table, which afforded a view over the garden. They could gaze out on a mulberry, two sweet chestnuts, a fine plane and a sycamore.

'I wish I knew the names of the trees,' said Elizabeth.

'I didn't get where I am today by knowing the names of the trees,' said C.J.

Maybe you'd have more conversation if you did, though, thought Elizabeth.

Their starters were good, and they discussed them at some length, since they couldn't think of anything else to talk about.

A fine rain began to fall.

'Pity it's not a fine evening,' said C.J.

'A great pity,' agreed Elizabeth. For God's sake, woman, say something interesting, she beseeched herself. 'I do hope we get enough people to fill the buses.'

223

'I never talk business when I'm with a pretty lady.'

'Is that because you don't take women seriously?'

'Not at all. Not at all! But I never mix business with pleasure.'

'This *is* a pleasure for you, then, is it?'

'Well, of course it is, Elizabeth. A rare privilege and a rare pleasure. You're a beautiful woman.'

'Thank you.'

'A very beautiful woman.'

'Thank you.'

Their main courses maintained the standard of their starters.

'This chef knows his onions,' said C.J.

'And his fennel and apricot. This compote is delicious.'

'Very good! You're a witty woman, Elizabeth. I'm not witty. It's not one of my talents.'

'Well, one can't be good at everything, Bunny.'

'That's true.'

Their conversation during the rest of the meal did not quite maintain that standard. The rain grew heavier. It had become a dank, grey, misty evening, sliding almost imperceptibly into night.

Over their coffee and petit-fours, in the Alanbrooke Lounge, C.J. said, 'Do you remember our foreign travels for Eurogrot?'

'Yes, Bunny,' replied Elizabeth. 'Amsterdam, Dusseldorf. Parfait d'Amour.'

'Precisely. I told you I loved you, Elizabeth.'

'I know.'

'I made . . . attempts. But Reggie was alive.'

'Yes.'

'Reggie is no longer alive, sad to say.'

'True.'

'Will you come to bed with me tonight, Elizabeth?'

'I don't think that would be fair to Reggie's memory, Bunny.'

'Will you come to bed with me tonight in a manner that is fair to Reggie's memory, Elizabeth?'

'What sort of manner would that be, Bunny? Would we apologise to Reggie, or pray to him, or just talk about how wonderful he was, as we did it?'

'Of course not.' C.J. had to control his irritation.

'Besides, you have a wife.'

'Luxembourg has fine parks, with a wide range of flowers, and its clothes shops are excellent. The beautiful River Moselle bisects the country.'

'That hardly compensates for an unfaithful, absent husband.'

'It does for Mrs C.J. That's the sort of thing she likes. I'm different. What's caviare for the gander is sauce to the general.'

'I think it's too soon, Bunny,' said Elizabeth.

'That would seem to indicate that there might be a moment when it would not be too soon. Do I read you correctly?'

'I wouldn't want to promise anything, C.J.'

'Of course not. I understand.' C.J. leant forward and stared into Elizabeth's eyes. 'Tell me one thing, though. Tell me honestly, Elizabeth. You aren't just leading me up the garden to keep everything rosy until the revolution, are you?'

Elizabeth held C.J.'s gaze unflinchingly.

'What sort of a woman do you think I am?' she asked.

Well before the end of May, every available coach from Penzance to Wick had been booked for August the twentieth, ostensibly for outings to the seaside, theme parks, butterfly farms, twig museums, water parks, heritage centres, wildfowl sanctuaries, falconry displays, craft demonstrations, Dickensian summer markets, antique fairs, garden open days, traction engine rallies, open-air concerts, canal lovers' fetes, barrel-organ bonanzas and rare bison events that littered what had once been the British countryside.

The next Monday morning meeting saw a return to number thirty-eight, Leibnitz Drive. Jimmy stood in front of the fireplace, where a display of tulips now sat in front of the coal-effect fire, and addressed the founder members of the Bloodless Revolution of Senior Citizens and the Occupationally Rejected.

'Just looked out of the French windows,' he said. 'Absolutely astonished. Smooth lawn. No moles. What's happened to the blighters?'

'I'm very much indebted to Doc Morrissey,' said Elizabeth.

Doc Morrissey smiled modestly, and C.J. tried not to scowl, now that Doc Morrissey was no longer the real enemy.

'It was an idea of a friend of mine,' said Doc Morrissey. 'He put cassettes of Andrew Lloyd Webber's music in their runs with enough batteries for a hundred hours of continuous playing. Long before the end, all moles gone.'

'And it's worked here!'

'Yes,' said Elizabeth. 'Argentina may not have cried, but the moles did.'

'It's an omen,' said Jimmy. 'A sign. We are on the verge of great success, ladies and gentlemen. We have the coaches. So far, we have recruited three quarters of a person per coach. It's not enough. The long hot summer of recruitment is about to burst upon our green and pleasant land. By the left, quick march!'

17 *The Long, Hot Summer of Recruitment*

Every day, that early summer, the legatees and their most trusted recruits were out recruiting. They widened their objectives, to take in a major assault on Britain's high streets, rocked by competition from shopping malls, out-of-town shopping centres and giant superstores. Rumbelows, where three thousand redundancies were taking place, proved fertile ground, as indeed did all the struggling major electrical retailers. They found sympathisers in the banks, where staff were rocked by the collapses of Barings and Credit Lyonnais and the knowledge that technology would gradually render people redundant in banking and might eventually, when everybody was redundant and nobody had any money, make banking itself redundant, and all the banks of machines in the banks would have nothing to do except send amorous faxes to the banks of machines in other banks.

Every day, Welton Ormsby penned press releases and was told by Jimmy, 'Well done. Excellent. These are dynamite. If one word of these gets out, we're done for. Eat them immediately.'

Dan Peters and Barry Kelsgrove, increasingly fearful of the scrap heap, joined, along with their wives Nicky and Niki. Rick Holdsworth didn't join. Jimmy had been right about Nicci.

Hank recruited several more young dealers who were revolted by being burnt out to serve the greed of their masters.

Tom recruited his neighbour Malcom Warbottle, a retired schoolmaster, and he recruited several other retired school-masters, on a law-and-order and Save-Our-English-Grammar platform, and they in their turn recruited still more retired schoolmasters.

Jimmy had great success among the veterans' associations, and they all did good business around DSS offices. Several jazz bands joined *en masse*. The phrase that Adam had used – 'We will free the human race from the stigma of ageing *at a stroke*' – proved a potent weapon, as did 'We will all be moving towards the best years of our life, not away from them.'

Some recruits were able to make an enormous contribution to the cause, and none more so than Leonard Norris.

Leonard Norris had been an industrial psychologist employed by one of the recently privatised companies in what had formerly been the public utility sector. He was a curly-haired, youthful-looking forty-five-year-old from Stoke-on-Trent.

His job had been to investigate staff morale and suggest ways of improving it, and, after he had spent three months surveying all aspects of the company's operations, he had reported to his boss.

'Well?' his boss had asked him. 'How goes it, Leonard?'

'Very well,' Leonard Norris had said. 'I've pinpointed one major factor which could improve morale overnight.'

'Splendid! Congratulations! Fire away!'

'What depresses the workforce is that they are getting a 1.8 per cent rise on their average salary of fourteen thousand two hundred pounds, and you are getting a seventy-five per cent rise in your salary of three hundred and seventy thousand, plus a two-million-pound share deal. Get rid of that anomaly and your problems are solved.'

There had been a long silence in the magnificent office, expensively refitted by a building firm owned by a fellow Mason.

'I earn my money,' his boss had said quietly, smoothly. 'I have to make important and decisive decisions.'

'Such as?'

'Such as – you're sacked.'

The sacked Leonard Norris offered to put his psychological expertise to good use by visiting the staff of retirement homes and other organisations, posing as a civil servant, and assessing which of them could safely be told about the revolution. As a result of his efforts, the management of the Elysian Fields Retirement Home in Slough offered to attempt to recruit all their elderly inmates for the cause, and watched with pride as backs straightened, mouths and hearts lifted, jigsaws remained on shelves and soap operas were transmitted to empty lounges. The matron of a home for retired gentlefolk near Peebles, which had been riven for months by dissension over the quality and frequency of the fish pie, leapt at the idea of the revolution as a most welcome diversion. An impotence diagnostician in Bradford put his patients on an 'erection through action' programme.

Leonard Norris's efforts proved to be worth their weight in gold. By the middle of June there were three passengers for every bus. And the rate of recruitment rose steadily all the time, as rumours of the revolution spread.

Tom and Linda, recruiting in tandem, discovered a happiness greater than they had ever managed first time around. Things remained super between David and Prue Harris-Jones. Hank and Joan grew into a quiet maturity, and shared a mug of cocoa at least twice a week. Doc Morrissey enjoyed his regained contentment and made a batch of vegetable samosas which he truly believed to be his best ever. Jimmy continued to enjoy the miracle of sex with Geraldine Hackstraw. C.J. continued to press Elizabeth to go to bed with him. 'After the revolution,' she said.

It seemed impossible that security should remain solid, and,

229

every day, the Inner Council held its collective breath. But day after day passed without a leak. 'Politicians can't keep anything to themselves, and they exploit leaks ruthlessly. Let's prove that we, the so-called ordinary people, the herds, the masses, the voters, the despised, are actually more honest, more trustworthy, more mature' was another sentiment that inspired people during that summer of preparation.

There was a lot of talk about the disaffection of Middle England. Well, Middle England had begun to find the cause it needed.

Indeed, there was such widespread contempt for politicians that there was a real danger of the force of the revolution being dispersed by passions not strictly relevant to the inner core of its force, which Jimmy described as its 'semi-frugal force'. The squalid greed of top managements, the callous disregard for clean air and safe beaches, the scandal of quangos stuffed with self-interest, the kowtowing to those who contributed vast sums to party funds, these things helped to fuel the growing force of the revolution, but they were not its point.

The young sometimes wished to widen the agenda of revolt. They sometimes wished for a more active role on the day. They had to be dissuaded. They were dissuaded. They accepted that the cause was greater than any individual.

The Monday morning meetings had become quite chirpy affairs, whether they were held in the grandeur of Expansion Cottage, the moleless suburban calm of Leibnitz Drive, the gleam of Hank and Joan's high-tech, high-rise flat, the shabby decay of Clement Attlee Mansions or Tom's old second-floor flat, which was growing steadily more feminine under Linda's influence.

'Recruits so far – twenty-one thousand six hundred and sixty-seven,' Hank would say. 'Recruits so far – thirty-three thousand five hundred and seventy-nine.' By June the twenty-sixth the fifty thousand mark had been passed. By July the tenth the figure was over a hundred thousand. And all the time the rate of increase was increasing, as recruit begat recruit. Adam had proved to be right about the subs. Not only did the money prove invaluable in paying the balance owing on the coaches and in establishing a fund to provide food for the rebels on the great day, but people had much more respect for the movement now that it cost five pounds to join. Even people who had mocked their earlier efforts joined, including nine people who had been on Prue's enforced outing to Bognor, and all the residents of the Verruca Foundation's Home for Retired Chiropodists. 'It'll do our feet good,' wrote their leader, who had once been a refugee from Hungary.

And still the security held.

There was a security scare just before the end of July.

Elizabeth had driven to pick Jimmy up at a retirement home near Norwich, his jeep having broken down. It was a hot, cloudy, sticky, airless, lazy afternoon, and he wasn't there when she arrived.

'Are you looking for Brigadier Anderson?' enquired a retired dental mechanic.

'Yes,' said Elizabeth.

'He's drilling his troops.'

'He's what??'

At that moment, Elizabeth heard a faint cry of 'Left, right, left, right, left, right, left. Left, right, left right, left, right, left,' and Jimmy emerged from behind a row of bushes, marching a group of very elderly people who were almost tottering in their attempt to keep in time.

'Jimmy! Stop that!' she shouted.

'Squad, halt,' shouted Jimmy.

The squad halted fairly creditably, considering their age.

'Squad, stand at . . . ease!' yelled Jimmy.

His squad relaxed, panting.

'Dismiss them,' said Elizabeth curtly, hurrying towards her brother.

'Squad, dissssss . . . miss!' screamed Jimmy.

Some of the old people collapsed on benches, heaving to get their breath back. Others tottered into the safety of the home.

'What's wrong, Big Sis?' asked Jimmy, puzzled.

'"What's wrong?"? "What's wrong?"? He asks me what's wrong,' said Elizabeth.

'Well, yes, I do.'

'Security for a start, yelling over the countryside like that.'

'Oh, Lord. Hadn't thought. Bit of a tricky one, though. Hard to drill people in whispers.'

Elizabeth took Jimmy's arm, and led him towards her car.

'The thing is . . . "Brigadier",' she began.

'Ah. Yes. Sorry. Dramatic licence. Not for personal glory, all for the cause, do assure you.'

'Well, leaving that aside, I really don't think you should be drilling these people at all. How old are they?'

'All over ninety.'

'Jimmy!'

'Think it's too strenuous?'

'I do. It's a hot, sticky day. They'll die.'

'Don't think so, somehow. Tough as old boots. That's why they've lived so long.'

'It's a revolution about respect for life, Jimmy. We can't allow even one person to die unnecessarily.'

'See your point,' said Jimmy reluctantly.

'Imagine the scandal if they did.'

'Right. No more drilling, then,' said Jimmy sadly.

'Well why do you want to drill them?' asked Elizabeth. 'This isn't a military operation.'

'Should have explained,' said Jimmy. 'These are my front line. The human chain.'

'The what??'

'The human chain. Wanted them to look smart.'

'What do you mean, Jimmy – "the human chain"?'

'Thought, march down Whitehall with a human chain of ninety-year-olds, even Michael Portillo wouldn't open fire on them.'

'Nobody's going to open fire on them, Jimmy.'

'What, not even the police?'

'Especially the police. The British police aren't going to open fire on their own citizens.'

'No. Course not. Fine body of men.'

'It isn't that. The eyes of the world are upon them. That's the beauty of this whole operation. Nobody can attack defenceless old people. That's why we'll win.'

Major James Anderson, passing himself off as a Brigadier purely for the cause, no self-glorification involved, perish the thought, turned his head slowly towards his sister as they sat in her motionless car in the car park of the Birches Retirement Home for Gentlefolk, in Norfolk.

'Win??' he said.

'Well, yes, I think so. It's taken off.'

'Yes, but . . . win!!'

'I thought you thought so as well. A cove called Faith. Remember?'

'That was bravado. Leadership. A load of cobblers. Yes, expected some recruits. But . . . win!! That'll change . . . that'll change our lives. That'll change . . . the world.'

'Yes.'

'Good God. Good God, Sis.'

'Yes.'

'Wat Tyler, leader of a rabble of peasants. Lambert Simnel, didn't he invent a cake or something? Briga . . . *Major* James Anderson. Changed the world.'

'Yes.'

'Good God, Sis.'

'Yes.'

Jimmy, unable to cope with the thought of changing the world, changed the subject instead.

'How are things with C.J.?'

'All right. I'm stringing him along till after August the twentieth, then I'll drop him.'

'Almost feel sorry for him. Not quite, though.'

Elizabeth started the engine, and they drove off.

'You mustn't do stupid things like marching nonagenarians,' she said, as she headed towards London.

'Didn't realise they were nonagenarians,' said Jimmy. 'Didn't ask them about their religion.'

'Nonagenarians are people in their nineties, Jimmy.'

'Ooops. Sorry. Bit thick, aren't I?'

'Sometimes. Sometimes you come up with some quite good ideas.'

'Do try, Sis.'

'I do love you, Bro.'

The thought that they might win excited and sobered them. Were they ready for the responsibility? Were their policies sufficiently coherent?

New ideas were coming on-stream all the time. A decent public transport system for those too old to drive. The return of National Service, but in a hugely different guise, not remotely military or hierarchical. Young people would spend the first two years of their pensionable life in young people's theme parks, built largely out of abandoned military establishments. There would be no major rules or restrictions, except one. No computers, no televisions, no videos, no video games, no electronic games, no faxes, no fourteen-lane electronic super highways. They would be forced to do the difficult things in life, to develop those social skills which might all too easily seem to be unnecessary in a technological age – the ability to converse, to relate, to entertain themselves and each other. Those youngsters who already had these skills would spend their two years helping their less fortunate brethren and so would experience all the joys of altruism.

At the penultimate Monday morning meeting of the Inner Council, held as it happened at C.J.'s luxurious home, Jimmy stood with his back to the great Tudor-style fireplace and addressed them.

'Think for a long while we were playing at this. Now we know we aren't. Want you all to be ready for high office. Want you to prepare yourselves. All members of the Inner Council will have cabinet posts, as follows: Elizabeth – Home Secretary; Hank – Chancellor of the Exchequer; Doc Morrissey – Minister of Health; David Harris-Jones – Foreign Secretary. Well, he's Welsh. Joke. Tom – Minister of Housing; Joan – Minister of Sport. Well, she's always been a sport, I'm told. C.J. – Trade and Industry; Linda – Consumer Affairs; Prue Harris-Jones – Education; Welton Ormsby – a new post, Minister for the Media.'

There was a long silence in that great panelled drawing room. On the lawn, a grey squirrel was nibbling at its nuts. Was there a single one of them, if they were truly honest, who didn't envy the squirrel its simple life at that moment? Was there a single one of them who didn't wonder if they had come too far?

But they soon rallied.

'Quite a list,' said Doc Morrissey.

'Super,' said David Harris-Jones.

'Wicked,' said Hank.

'I'm going to be down on estate agents like a ton of bricks,' said Tom. 'They'll wish they hadn't been born.'

'I think we can honestly say,' said Elizabeth Perrin, 'that we know as much about our subjects as do the present cabinet.'

'Yes, but don't get too depressed. We'll get better,' said Joan.

They lived in fear and hope. Fear of failure, hope of success. But also fear of success and hope of failure.

But as the last days before the revolution ticked away, as they considered their potential ministerial portfolios and their plans and hopes for their nation, so they grew more used to the amazing prospect of success. Day by day they gained in confidence. Welton Ormsby wrote press releases that he didn't need to eat, press releases to be issued at the moment of triumph.

The moment of triumph! They grew more elated by the hour. They supported each other. They hoped to win, they were hungry to win, they were ready to win. Now the fear was of a breach of security. Was it possible that there would be no weak link anywhere, that every one of those million and more people would keep his or her mouth shut?

It wasn't possible. There was bound to be a weak link somewhere.

The weak link was a frail eighty-nine-year-old widow and former chicken sexer named Bessie Arnott, who lived in a retirement home near Frome in Somerset, and had a grandson who was twenty-seven years old and worked as a journalist. He had recently joined . . . she couldn't remember whether it was a newspaper or a television company, but it was owned by Rupert somebody, so that narrowed it down a bit, though not a lot, and he was very keen and ambitious.

In fact, he was one of the bright young stars of a national newspaper, plucked from the obscurity of a local paper in Grimsby, he was a golden boy, he had replaced an ageing decrepit drunken legend named Welton Ormsby.

He was a good boy, for all his ambition. He visited Bessie at least once every six months, which was better than most, and sometimes even took her for a spin.

As luck would have it, he turned up on Tuesday the fifteenth of August, five days before the revolution.

'I thought we might go to Weston, Granny,' he said, 'and drive along the front.'

236

He knew that she liked to see the sea above all else. He knew how important it was to many people as they approached death to keep some contact, however peripheral, with the oceans. A sight of the sea, and their spirits lifted, perhaps because its vast timelessness made them realise how insignificant a human life is and how small a matter the leaving of it must therefore be.

It was a warm day, and he kept the roof of his convertible open. The wind in her hair exhilarated Bessie Arnott, and she could almost imagine that she was young again.

'You're looking well today, Granny,' he said, smiling.

She knew that she shouldn't, but he was a good boy and it would make his career.

'I've got a new lease of life,' she said. 'I'm involved in a big new project.'

'Oh yes?' he prompted with rather mechanical interest.

'No, truly, Steve,' she said. 'It's an amazing scheme. It's absolutely top secret so I shouldn't be telling you, so I want you to promise not to tell anybody.'

'I am a journalist, Granny. Can you trust me?'

'Oh no. I want you to put it in your paper. I just don't want anyone to find out it came from me.'

'I promise,' he said, just a little too glibly. 'We journalists never reveal our sources.'

'It's kind of you to take me to Weston, Steve, but I'd prefer you to take me seriously,' she said.

Steve looked at her in surprise. Sometimes she came out with things that were quite sharp. Perhaps he was under-estimating her.

'I mean it,' she said. 'I really am involved on something big, and it'll make a wonderful story for you.'

He was impressed by her tone. She didn't seem, today, to be as old as he expected. Maybe something really was up.

'Tell me, Granny,' he said, trying desperately not to sound sarcastic, 'what is this amazing story?'

Bessie Arnott thought long and hard, but sometimes, when one is old, the harder one thinks, the more impenetrable the fog becomes.

'Er . . .' she said.

Steve felt disappointed and irritated. Irritated with his grandmother for not having anything to tell him, and irritated with himself for believing that she could have.

18 *The Great Day*

Sunday, August the twentieth, felt like the first morning of autumn. Trickles of energy ran through the lethargy of the summer. After Saturday's rain it was mercifully dry, though distinctly cool. Visibility was exceptionally clear, as it often is after summer rain.

Major James Anderson, leader of the Bloodless Revolution of Senior Citizens and the Occupationally Rejected, was awake before five o'clock, after sleeping but fitfully. He was dressed and ready for action by six. His excitement was intense, his anticipation almost unbearably keen. How slowly the digital clock on his electric cooker moved. He sat and watched it, willing the minutes to click up faster.

Jimmy's feelings of excitement and anticipation were slightly muddied by his doubts over his role in the day's events. He had wanted to lead his army down Whitehall, to enter Number Ten himself, but he had been persuaded that he should storm the BBC and deliver a message to the nation. 'This is the age of the media,' Welton Ormsby, Shadow Minister for the Media, had told him, but he hadn't been convinced.

Elizabeth was also awake by five o'clock. She opened her bedroom window, and drank in a great draft of cool, dewy air, filling her lungs with its astonishing early morning purity. The smooth, moleless lawn glistened and sparkled with dew. She looked up into the pale blue unfathomable sky and cried out, 'Oh, Reggie. Oh, Reggie my darling, is there something of you left, in some form or other, to witness what we do in your memory this day?' Tears streamed down her face.

Elizabeth's cry woke David Harris-Jones from an uneasy, surreal world where the distinction between sleep and wakefulness was disturbingly blurred.

His stomach lurched with fear as he remembered that this was *the* day. He wasn't really a man of action, despite his exploits in tailing C.J., and he had a dreadful fear that his nerve would go and he would let the whole operation down. He hadn't been able to tell anyone of this fear, not even Prue. Even in bed beside his beloved, even in their matching pyjamas, he felt very alone that summer's morning.

At breakfast, he was barely able to eat the two free-range boiled eggs provided by Elizabeth for extra sustenance.

'Tell her,' said Prue.

'Oh, really,' said David Harris-Jones, removing the shell off the top of his egg tiny bit by tiny bit. 'She isn't interested in my underpants.'

Elizabeth raised her eyebrows.

'What on earth is this?' she asked, neatly slicing off the top of an egg. 'What about your underpants?'

'It's nothing,' said David Harris-Jones. 'It's just that I'm wearing that pair of Welsh heritage pants you and Reggie once gave me for Christmas.'

'I'd forgotten.'

'They have the Gower Peninsula, the Menai Bridge and Lloyd George's birthplace on them, and the washing instructions are in two languages.'

'And they still fit,' said Prue.

'Well, thank you,' said Elizabeth. 'I'm flattered, and so would Reggie be.'

A tear rolled down her face onto her slightly burnt toast.

'The first thing I'll do with my million pounds is buy a decent toaster,' she said with a watery smile.

Doc Morrissey woke at half past five, and breakfasted on onion bhagees and cold tarka dhal. He felt a delicious mixture of contentment and excitement. The indignity of birth, the agonising long process of learning, the dread mysteries of diagnosis, the decades of unfulfilled desire, the whole stab at existence, at once so deeply astonishing and so utterly insignificant, had been worth it for this day, for this cause, for this belonging.

Tom and Linda stood stark naked at the open window of their flat, looking out over the dewy gardens of their shared estate, over the tiny gravestones of long-forgotten pets, letting their open pores breathe the chill magnificence of the air.

'You're excited, aren't you?' said Linda, stroking his bottom gently.

'Very,' said Tom, 'and I found it hard to obey Jimmy's edict.'

'You're not the man I thought you were,' said Linda.

Tom raised his eyebrows.

'You're much better,' explained Linda.

They had buck's fizz with their breakfast of smoked salmon and scrambled egg. The buck's fizz was made with the very last bottle of Tom's elderflower champagne.

'Well, you don't take over the government of your country and completely revolutionise thinking about old age every day,' said Tom, 'and I've always been a smoked salmon person.'

Joan and Hank had also found it difficult to obey Jimmy's edict, which was that, like Italian footballers before a match, they should abstain from sex the night before the revolution.

They had obeyed the edict, though, and it seemed to have worked, because they had slept as soundly as Members of

241

Parliament at the ballet, and had awoken full of beans, and were soon even more full of beans, because Joan's idea of a nourishing breakfast was fairly primitive, and Hank's idea of good food owed much to the nursery.

'I hope Jimmy obeyed his own edict,' said Hank.

'He'd have had to,' said Joan. 'Ms Hackstraw's in Holland.'

'That's probably why he introduced it,' said Hank. 'What he can't have, we're not getting, the bastard!'

But there was as much affection as anger in his voice.

Welton Ormsby, whose marital shambles had left him no option but to observe the edict, was now busy in his uncouth bachelor flat, knifing on to his toast marmalade which was mixed with the butter from his last seven breakfasts. He felt rather odd. He was shaking. He felt sick. His legs ached. His head ached. His mouth was dry.

He realised what was wrong with him. He didn't have a hangover.

He drank a bottle of Boddington's beer, and felt better straight away.

Even C.J. felt stirrings of excitement as he looked out over the grounds of Expansion Cottage. At the bottom of the garden, seeming to be part of it, although it wasn't, there was a small lake. A heron stood motionless, hunting for breakfast and looking like a piece of garden statuary. Moorhens bobbed anxiously, coots squabbled sourly, C.J. noticed none of it. He saw only largeness, expansiveness, wealth. He longed for the day ahead to be over. He longed to collect his million pounds.

Morton Radstock had also woken early. They call you early in hospital, perhaps out of compassion, because they know how long and uncomfortable the nights are, especially when you're itching all over and have two legs and an arm in traction. The

242

Scottish surgeon, with his sunken cheekbones and gallows humour, had said, 'It's lucky you aren't a private patient. This accident, with five months in hospital, would have cost you an arm and a leg.' Morton Radstock had laughed, but only because it wouldn't have looked manly to cry.

He had been listening to hospital radio since half past six. Another long day dragged before him, utterly wearisome, deeply uncomfortable at best, excruciatingly painful at worst. He had forgotten the smell of a cool, fresh morning. He lived in a world of bedpans and stale sweat.

Something about the date, Sunday, August the twentieth, struck a deep, distant chord in his memory. Every time the almost unbearably cheerful hospital disc jockey announced it, he shuddered slightly, like a ship vibrating, feeling the significance of something that he couldn't quite pin down. He had the feeling that something really important was within his grasp. He had the feeling that it would be interesting if he could remember it. God, how he longed for something to be interesting. Yes, he was lucky to be alive, again and again they told him that, but it was difficult to appreciate the fact with two legs and an arm in traction.

He had suffered the alliterative agonies of coma, concussion and constipation. Today his brain and his bowels seemed more lively. We will draw a veil over his bowels, gentle reader, and concentrate on his brain. Morton Radstock, five months after his collision with a lorry carrying deep-sea aggregates, was beginning to remember how to think.

By eight o'clock Welton Ormsby, Hank and the nine legatees were on the road, driving to the pick-up points for the coaches that they would escort to London. All over Britain, the old folk woke early. The frightened, the bored, the querulous, the confused, the desperate, the lonely, the sick, they all felt needed that morning. They felt the exhilaration of their enormous togetherness, and they felt a joy in their own individual worth. They chatted excitedly about the seaside, the Lakes, the Trossachs, keeping their true destination locked in their brains, loving the responsibility, the discipline, the importance of this day.

All over London, people who had come down to the capital earlier in the week were waking up and having breakfast and preparing for the great day. Some were in hotels, some in boarding houses, but the great majority were staying in the homes of sympathisers and supporters.

All over England, staid middle-class and working-class revolutionaries were washing their cars ready to drive to London.

Every scheduled coach service (though there weren't many on Sunday mornings) would be full. All the trains (though there weren't many on Sunday mornings) would be full. Staff would comment on how busy it was, but wouldn't think too much about it. The vagaries of the travel business were well known.

By eight thirty, as the sun at last began to warm the unseasonably crisp air, more than three thousand coaches were on the move. Some were on their way to their pick-up points. Others were already filled with excited senior citizens. Coaches from Scotland were already well on their way.

In each coach, a carefully selected representative informed the astonished driver that the destination wasn't the Trossachs, or Dunoon, or St Andrews, or Edinburgh, but London.

It was coming back. It was coming back! Morton Radstock strained his rusty, Anglo-Swedish journalist's mind. Goose pimples broke out agonisingly on his back. Sweat poured off him, and his bandages itched. An interview in a wine bar, with a strange name. An interview with a man known by his initials. A mad scheme. August the twentieth.

His tape recorder! Could his tape recorder have survived the accident? In a collision between a lorry carrying deep-sea aggregates and a tape recorder, it seemed unlikely that much of the tape recorder would survive. But it was possible.

He rang his bell. The nurse came swiftly, for it was unusual for him to ring his bell.

'Could you see if there's a tape recorder in my locker?' he asked. 'It's important.'

The nurse hunted through his locker.

'I'm sorry,' she said. 'There's no tape recorder.'

'Thank you,' he said. 'Thank you. I'll just have to think harder, then.'

'You're better today,' said the nurse.

Jimmy made his way down the aisle. It was the moment he had been waiting for.

'Excuse me, driver,' he said. 'Change of plan. We aren't going to Lulworth Cove. We're going to London.'

'I've got my orders,' said the driver, who was twenty-seven years of age, and was sallow, callow and probably shallow. How he would have benefitted, thought Jimmy, from being forced to see the world for ten years before he started work. 'I've got my docket, see. My docket says Lulworth Cove. Lulworth Cove it is.'

'Lulworth Cove's polluted,' said Jimmy. 'Been a big tanker accident. Tricky wallahs, tankers. Tanker went aground negotiating narrow entrance. Awkward coves, coves. Whole Dorset coast out of bounds. Bit of a cock-up on the sea front.'

'I've heard nuffink of this,' said the driver stubbornly. 'And I've got my docket. Can't go against my docket, see.'

Jimmy turned to face the passengers, and called out, 'Ladies and gentlemen, where do we want to go?'

'London,' thundered the senior citizens.

'That's as may be, but I got my docket,' said the driver doggedly.

Jimmy decided to go on the offensive. 'London, or I knock your block off,' he said.

'All right, sod it, we'll go to bloody London,' said the driver. 'But why I couldn't have been told I do not know.'

'Computer error,' said Jimmy.

That satisfied the driver.

'Oh, well,' he said. 'That explains it. There's a roundabout in six miles. I'll turn round there.'

'Thanks,' said the twentieth century's answer to Wat Tyler.

As the coach began to nose its way towards the great wen, the blood began to course even more rapidly through Jimmy's ageing veins.

Something absurd about a revolution, about taking over the government. Pensions for young people? That didn't make sense.

As the sun strengthened, the sky grew a darker, clearer blue. It really did seem to Elizabeth Perrin that she could see into infinity, as she searched for Reggie in that great sky.

A single strand of white fluff appeared over Oxfordshire.

The coach, which had been booked for a tour of the New Forest, with halts to fondle the over-fondled ponies, was heading for London now. Its driver, a fifty-seven-year-old do-it-yourself enthusiast from High Wycombe, had raised but scant protest, and Elizabeth had explained the change of plan very convincingly. 'There's an outbreak of mad pony disease. The whole forest's quarantined off.'

'Oh, gawd,' the driver had said. 'Nasty.'

The single strand of cloud attracted other strands. It began to develop into a thin, wispy, almost transparent cloud. Elizabeth shivered. Could Reggie come back as a cloud, to watch over her? If he did, it would be such a cloud as this, alone in the sky,

246

gathering in size and intensity, watching over them, white and motionless.

Gradually, it all began to make sense in Morton Radstock's mind.

'I wonder if I could have a phone?' he asked the nurse. 'It's important.'

The nurse looked at his serious, Anglo-Swedish face, and smiled.

'Of course you can,' she said, 'and don't look so solemn. It may never happen.'

'What I'm worried about,' said Morton Radstock, 'is that it's already happening.'

All the coaches were heading for London now. Many and varied had been the reasons given to the drivers for the change of destination: 'The Lake District's full'; 'Wales is closed'; 'Chelsea supporters are having their annual picnic in Margate'; 'Grantham is in mourning for Mrs Thatcher.' 'I didn't know she was dead.' 'She isn't'; 'The European Community has closed down the whole British coastline due to excessive discharge of sewage'; 'A train carrying nuclear waste has been derailed at Whitby.' 'I didn't even know there was a railway at Whitby.' 'There isn't now'; 'Cheltenham's too dangerous. They're investigating a huge increase in baldness there, and whether it's due to acid rain'; 'There's a big hole in the ozone layer right above Crieff'; 'The government's closing the Cotswolds on Sundays as an economy measure'; 'The Isle of Wight's completely cordoned off. Sixty-eight people have escaped from Parkhurst, including the Governor.'

It is a telling comment on the state of the nation, and on its citizens' perception of its state, that all these excuses were accepted by the drivers without too much demur.

On other coaches, a more direct approach was employed.

247

'Take us to London, or you'll feel the weight of my fist,' was the comment made by a retired undertaker of hitherto exemplary character on a coach booked to go to St Andrews. The driver, an amateur middleweight boxer from Motherwell, turned round for London immediately. There was an irresistible force about the passengers that day.

Nick Grabworthy, editor of the *Daily Sludge*, was thinking hard. Morton Radstock had been in a coma. He'd had concussion. He might well be deluded.

But he had an old head on young shoulders. He was solemn and serious and hard-working and drank designer lager in moderate quantities and had no moral scruples whatsoever. He was the very model of a modern Wapping journalist. And he hadn't sounded deluded on the telephone.

If he wasn't deluded, and if he'd got the date right, they had lost all chance of an exclusive, and that was tragic. But if they informed the police, and announced to the nation that they had foiled the plot, in the interests of a democracy that they had suddenly discovered to be worth cherishing after all, they could still come out of it with considerable credit.

He decided that he had no alternative but to co-operate with the authorities, and to tell the truth, the whole truth and nothing but the truth. He didn't like it, it went against everything that he stood for, but it was the right solution for this particular, rather extraordinary set of circumstances.

'Injured *Sludge* Ace Foils Wrinkly Rebels.' No, that was altogether too literary and only contained three one-syllable words, but one of his brilliant employees would come up with something pithier.

He picked up the telephone.

Tiny white clouds were forming all over the sky, and growing slowly larger. One or two were developing dark centres, but they weren't really threatening, and the sun was dappling the fields most pleasantly as the coaches thundered on.

A retired civil servant from the Ministry of Transport had planned the timing and routing of the coaches, so that there would not be an absurdly large number on any stretch of road at any time. The departure times had been carefully staggered, so that some four hundred coaches would reach London every hour, a number which wouldn't cause any surprise in the general bustle of the capital's streets.

Several different drop-off points were used, and the coaches then dispersed to the suburbs for the day. Young people were detailed to accompany the drivers and make sure that they had no access to telephones.

Down the M1 and the M6, the M2, the M3, the M4, the M10 the A1(M) they thundered, leaving Sunday drivers far in their wake. Along the A41, A5, A6, A12, A13, A2, A20, A22, A24, A3, A4 and A404 they roared.

Every now and then they passed under a bridge on which the acronym BROSCAR had appeared overnight. What throaty cheers they raised.

Senior metropolitan police officers had already received two entirely isolated reports, which they had not taken particularly seriously. One of these reports had been from a patrol car on the Ml, which reported more coaches than usual heading south. The other report had been from an officer in the Covent Garden area, who had reported that it was busy but peaceful. 'The wrinklies seem to be out in force today, wandering around, killing time, probably can't afford to buy anything, poor bastards.'

After Nick Grabworthy's phone call, they began to wonder whether there wasn't something afoot.

*

Among the supporters of the revolution were many recruits from that underpaid, often elderly and of necessity courageous breed, the nation's caretakers. The caretakers responsible for several key buildings in the vicinity of Trafalgar Square had been persuaded to allow rebels into their buildings for rest and refreshment. Many of the capital's cleaning ladies had donated duplicate keys for the duration. Already, as the police began to awake to the possibility of revolution, rebels were slipping unnoticed into South Africa House, into Canada House, into New Zealand House, Zimbabwe House and the Finland Trade Centre. Others were treating the Lord's Day as a day of rest in the premises of the Lords Day Observance Society. Several friends were meeting in the Friends Meeting House in St Martin's Lane. Others were camped in the premises of the National Bank of Egypt, the National Lottery, the Royal College of Pathologists and the London Yachting Information Centre.

Even government buildings were called into service, although nobody had dared to approach the Ministry of Defence. But senior citizens, given keys by sympathetic cleaners, had taken their fish and food into the Ministry of Agriculture, Fisheries and Food, and were lying on the floor like rows of sardines on a slab, resting. Members of the West Midland Rights for Gay Pensioners Society were even now wandering around and saying 'Hello, sailor' to each other and being altogether rather arch inside the Admiralty.

In all these places there was a cameraderie and excitement, a self-imposed sense of discipline, that was reminiscent of the VE Day celebrations earlier in the year, and even of that regrettably destructive historical event, the Second World War, without which the delights of VE Day would not have been possible.

David Harris-Jones couldn't believe it when his coach was flagged down by a police patrol car. His mouth went dry. His heart raced. He almost ruined his Welsh heritage there and then.

Two police officers boarded the coach.

'Faulty brake light,' said the older of the two to the driver. 'Get it seen to. Where are you bound for?'

'London,' said David Harris-Jones, stepping forward tentatively. 'A trip by pensioners from the Northampton area. Half a day in the capital. Seeing the sights.'

'What sights?' asked the younger officer.

'Well, any sights. I mean . . . er . . . it's not . . . er . . . it's up to people to . . . er . . . you know . . . and . . . er . . . be back on the coach on time.' David Harris-Jones was quaking, but trying not to show it. It would be so awful if his coach blew the whole operation. It would be his nightmare come true.

'We was booked for Skeggie,' said the driver, 'but they forced me to go to London.'

'"Forced"?' said David Harris-Jones. 'That's a good one. "Forced"? What with? That *is* a good one.' He tried a light, humorous laugh. It was a failure.

'Why did you change your destination?' asked the older officer.

'Er . . .' said David Harris-Jones. 'Er . . .' he added. 'Er . . .' he expanded. 'Er . . . very cold, Skegness. Doctor's orders. Outbreak of chestiness, Skegness out of bounds, it could kill them. So I . . . er . . . I decided not to go to Skegness, not . . . er . . . not wanting to kill them.'

'They forced me,' said the driver. 'They're up to something.'

'Yes, and I'll tell you what we're up to,' said David Harris-Jones bravely. 'We're up to London to see the Queen, aren't we, boys and girls?'

'That's right,' shouted the passengers. 'We're up to London to see the Queen.'

'Thank you,' said the older officer. 'Carry on.'

'Give our love to Her Majesty,' said the younger officer.

*

As soon as their random searches revealed that the drivers of coaches had been forced to change direction on the orders of their elderly passengers, the police knew that Morton Radstock had not been deluded.

Hurried phone calls were made. Ministers of the Crown were contacted on beaches, up mountains, in restaurants and secret love nests that weren't as secret as they thought, and even on fact finding missions to Brazil. They gave the authorities the authority to resist the revolution with all force except the use of force. Stop it, whatever you do, but remember, the eyes of the world will be upon you. If you don't do enough, heads will roll, but if you go too far we will not support you. That was the encouraging message.

By lunchtime St James's Park, Hyde Park, and the gardens of the Embankment and St James's Square were full of elderly people, picnicking as if they hadn't a care in the world, waiting for their late-afternoon call to action.

Two hundred and fifty lovable white-haired recruits were packed into BBC Radio's Paris Studio in Lower Regent Street, disguised as the studio audience for a new series of *Singalonga-max*. Several other rebels were blending easily with other elderly members of the Royal Automobile Club and the other clubs in Pall Mall.

Barry 'I shouldn't be telling you this, but' Benskin looked out across his small, ill-tended lawn towards the hop kilns and timbered farm houses of the rolling Herefordshire country-side.

'Fancy popping over to Woolhope and sinking some cider?' he asked his pretty but pale wife Carol, who had not taken easily to the uncertainty of his life in the SAS.

'Suits me, Barry,' she said.

252

'How's your mother?' he asked.

'Oh, didn't I tell you? I can't ring her today. Funny thing. She's gone to London.'

He stared at her in astonishment.

'That's funny,' he said. 'That *is* a thing. Mine's gone to London too.'

They each phoned their mother every Sunday morning. Neither of them got on well with their mother-in-law.

'They never go out,' he said. 'It's funny them both going to London.'

The phone shrilled. Carol looked tense, as she did at every phone call.

'Don't worry,' he said. 'It won't be anything. It'll be Graham asking if we're going down the pub, or Hereford United asking if I'm doing anything at three o'clock next Saturday.'

'Well, answer it!'

He lifted the receiver, and listened in silence.

'Right,' he said. 'Right. What is it this time?'

'I knew it!' hissed Carol, as he signalled to her to shut up.

'What??' he said. 'What?? Good God!'

He put the phone down and looked at his wife compassionately.

'Sorry, love,' he said, 'but it could be worse. At least I don't have to go abroad.'

'What is it?'

'You know I shouldn't tell you.'

'Oh, Barry!'

'Well, all right, but don't tell anybody. We're flying to a very big capital city in the South-East of England. There's a revolution of old age pensioners. Bloody hell's bells! I didn't join a highly-trained specialist organisation based in Herefordshire in order to fight a lot of pensioners,' said Barry 'I shouldn't be telling you this, but' Benskin.

253

'Well, don't shoot mother,' said his pale, pretty wife Carol.

They stared at each other in astonishment, and Carol even forgot to be upset that he was going.

Were their own mothers revolutionaries?

As the afternoon wore on, the sun began to burn off the clouds. The air was heavy and stale and laced with fumes. The crisp pure dewy dawn was but a distant memory of bygone innocence. The world is born innocent each morning, and dies from intrigue, cynicism and fumes each day.

The fittest of the revolutionaries were already on the move towards Trafalgar Square. Twenty-nine retired tax inspectors from Derbyshire, who had formed themselves into a limited company called Joggers for Life (Jersey) Limited for tax purposes, were wending their way, with big boots and rucksacks, from Regent's Park. Forty-five members of the Retired Civil Servants' Ramblers Association were plodding, in high spirits and in triplicate, all the way from Brent Cross.

Keen youngsters dropped other old people off around Oxford Street and Shaftesbury Avenue. Others came in taxis and milk floats and invalid cars and traps pulled by the dray horses of the breweries. No vehicle was too small to be pressed into service, and this Dunkirk was not a retreat.

Gradually the crowds in the parks gathered their belongings together and began to move. They were in no hurry. They had been told to be in no hurry. Everything must seem normal.

The people who had been wandering round Covent Garden began to wander, as if by chance, towards Whitehall. The embassies and clubs and government offices began to unload their temporary guests. Each bus and underground train brought more of the deeply respectable rebels. The elderly of Middle England were on the march.

*

Barry 'I shouldn't be telling you this, but' Benskin was on the roof of Horse Guards, rifle cocked, alert, at the ready, yet bewildered. They had been warned, on the helicopter flight, not to open fire. What were they doing there, then? Insurance, they were told, against things getting out of hand.

The tough nonagenarians hand-picked by Jimmy for the human chain were gathering in Trafalgar Square. Retired doctors were present to look after them but Doc Morrissey had been forbidden to interfere. He was slightly behind them with C.J., Joan, Hank, Elizabeth, David and Prue Harris-Jones, Tom and Linda and Welton Ormsby. David was a little worried because his coach had been stopped. The others were exhilarated, C.J. because it would soon be over, and the rest of them because it was just about to begin. They were blissfully unaware that policemen and soldiers were gathering in force. They were blissfully unaware that Barry 'I shouldn't be telling you this, but' Benskin was on the roof of Horse Guards with his rifle cocked.

Armed with splendidly accurate and detailed maps and instructions from Adam, who had done a magnificent inside job, Major James Anderson led three coaches to Wood Lane. Three other coaches parked at the back of the BBC Television Centre.

Three hundred and fifty-eight senior citizens approached the Television Centre in dribs and drabs. One hundred and ninety-three of them had forged BBC staff passes. The other hundred and sixty-five had forged tickets for the studio audience of a new situation comedy, *Fur Coats and No Knickers*.

By five o'clock, lollipop men and women recruited by BROS-COR were standing beside all the traffic lights in the vicinity of Trafalgar Square. As each set of lights turned red, a lollipop person stepped out into the street and allowed the tide of rebels to surge across the roads. Once begun, there was no stopping them, and hundreds of car horns disturbed the late afternoon air and terrified the pigeons.

At the head of the great crowd as it streamed out of Trafalgar Square and into Whitehall marched Elizabeth Perrin, widow of Reginald Iolanthe Perrin, silver hair glinting in the sunshine. Suddenly she removed from her shopping bag a banner, knitted by Prue Harris-Jones. 'We Shall Overcome' announced the banner, which was fixed between two walking sticks. Elizabeth held one walking stick and Joan the other.

Behind her, C.J. and Doc Morrissey, David and Prue Harris-Jones, Tom and Linda, and Hank and Welton Ormsby shared identical banners, all knitted by Prue.

And throughout the great crowd thousands more banners were produced from shopping bags and rucksacks and picnic hampers. They were fastened to walking sticks and fishing rods and bamboo poles. Many and varied were the messages that were unfurled. Some proclaimed local allegiance – 'Matlock Pensioners'; some announced the name of their retirement home – 'Dedham Vale Sheltered Bungalows'; some gave individual messages – 'Maggie, 76 and still sexy'; some were just eccentric – 'Stubborn Old Sods from Salisbury'; some whimsical – 'Retired wine merchants. We improve with age too'; some poignant – 'Remember the Altzheimers victims. They can't'; some pithy – 'Today's Young Whiz-kid is Tomorrow's Old Codger'; and some heartfelt – 'Don't throw us on the scrap heap. We're people not cars'.

What a crowd it was, vast and cheerful, touched with a sense of purpose, of history. What a pity that our leaders were on holiday, and couldn't see it. What a pity that, in their bars and restaurants and chauffeur-driven limousines, they never met the people they represented.

Past the Ministry of Agriculture, Fisheries and Food the crowd marched. Past Horse Guards, past the Scottish Office, past the

Old War Office Building that great throng streamed. They poured past on either side of the equestrian statue of Field Marshal His Royal Highness George, Duke of Cambridge.

Field Marshals the Viscounts Slim, Alanbrooke and Montgomery watched the rebels come. The much smaller statue of Sir Walter Raleigh observed them gravely.

The police waited at the lower end of Whitehall, blocking the entrance to Parliament Square, holding back as ordered by their masters.

Barry 'I shouldn't be telling you this, but' Benskin also watched the vast crowd gravely from his position on top of Horse Guards, and, to his astonishment, in all that vast tide of elderly people, he saw her. His mother-in-law. Bloody Mildred. One shot was all it would take. He was a crack shot. He could get her, even at this range. 'Why don't you give up all this nonsense and take a proper job?' 'It's not fair on my Carol, isn't all the uncertainty. She doesn't know where she is. She's cooking a nice chicken for your tea, and suddenly it's off to Iraq. It's not fair.' 'You're selfish, Barry. It's a drug, is excitement, and in my book that makes you a drug addict.' 'What do you think's the cause of my Carol's irritable bowel syndrome? You, Barry.' His fingers tightened on the trigger. One little squeeze, and irritable mother-in-law syndrome would be gone for ever. He'd only been playing with the possibility. He hadn't been certain that even a shot as good as he was could kill Mildred without risking killing someone else. Now, seeing her so innocent, so radiant, so *smug*, he suddenly realised that he was going to do it. He felt strangely detached, almost disembodied. He waited for her to come that little bit closer.

Safely inside the BBC Television Centre, the senior citizens made their way, by various routes, down the largely deserted corridors of that strange circular building, following Adam's splendid instructions, which they had learnt by heart and then burnt, or, in the case of a few who had thrown themselves into the spirit of the thing with abandon, eaten.

They loitered in lavatories, admired photographs of the stars, read notices of BBC social clubs, got cups of tea out of machines, stood around in small groups moaning about the bosses, spread wild rumours about resignations and sackings among the top echelons, discussed the cancellation of series and generally behaved in a thoroughly unsuspicious manner until ten past six, or zero hour.

Sweat was pouring down the face of Barry 'I shouldn't be telling you this, but' Benskin. Suddenly he was terrified by what he had to do. He would disgrace the SAS, let down his colleagues, endure headlines and emotional court scenes, be imprisoned for life, destroy his lovely Carol, never drink three pints of cider in the Butchers' Arms again, just because he couldn't take a few home truths.

Six steps more of life for Mildred. Five. Oh innocent smugness, you deserve to die. Four. Three. Two. Delicious terror. One.

He didn't have to do it. This was madness. He was mad.

There wasn't any point in doing it, because Mildred would never know that he had done it. There wouldn't even be a second in which she would say, 'Oh,God. I'm dying. If only I hadn't been so cruel and unfair to Barry.'

It was utterly pointless to kill her, so he didn't. The sweat poured off him, he was trembling, he felt dizzy, he was going to faint. He clung to the parapet grimly.

Elizabeth and Joan marched slowly on, holding their banner aloft with increasingly painful arms – Past Field Marshal Earl Haig they went, past the Privy Council Office, past Downing

Street, the whole street safely locked behind gates which ridiculed the very idea of democracy.

Behind them, C.J. and Doc Morrissey, David and Prue Harris-Jones, Tom and Linda, and Hank and Welton Ormsby clutched their banners with aching, protesting arms.

The nonagenarians marched onwards proudly, resolutely, determinedly.

Behind them, in the vast crowd, Mildred remained calm and smug, utterly unaware of how narrowly she had escaped death.

Ahead of them, blocking their way through to Parliament Square, stood a cordon of police horses.

Elizabeth went white when she saw them, and the nonagenarians slowed down in bewilderment.

Elizabeth looked up into the early evening sky. All the clouds had been burnt off. If Reggie had ever been there, he had gone.

At exactly ten minutes past six, by which time the early evening news bulletin on BBC1 was well into its stride, three hundred and fifty-eight senior citizens set off for the news studio. They walked purposefully, and without hesitation, and so nobody stopped them.

The doors to the news studio were shut. Red lights above the doors announced that the programme was on air, and entry was not permitted.

The senior citizens poured into the studio.

Moira Stuart was sitting alone at the news desk, facing a row of cameras and reading from the autocue.

' "A report that states that the teaching of grammar in schools is not as good as what it used to be has itself been slammed for its poor grammar," ' she read. ' "The report, commissioned by . . ." '

She hesitated, as she saw several senior citizens advancing towards her in determined vein.

'"Commissioned by . . ." I . . . er . . . I'm sorry. I think we have an invasion of the studio.'

'Don't panic, Great Britain,' yelled Jimmy. 'Don't panic, Moira. Violence, out of order, plughole.'

The cameramen continued to point their cameras. Moira Stuart looked puzzled, but showed no panic, even managed a tiny smile of incredulity.

In the control box there was consternation and astonishment.

'Shall we pull the plug, Tristram?' asked the studio manager.

'No, Geoff. Be ready to, but hold on for the moment. This is sensational television,' said the director.

Four strong men in their sixties approached Moira Stuart.

'Sorry about this, Moira,' said Jimmy. 'Have no fear, my dear.'

The four men lifted Moira Stuart out of her seat very gently.

Jimmy slipped into her place, and faced the camera confidently, proudly, exultantly. He realised now how right it was that he had chosen to address the nation through the all-powerful medium of television.

Outside the studio, security men were trying to get in, but finding it guarded, very resolutely, by large numbers of senior citizens.

Inside the studio, Jimmy began his address.

'Good evening, Britain,' he said, in solemn tones. 'My name's Major James Anderson, and I'm leader of the Bloodless Revolution of Senior Citizens and the Occupationally Rejected. We've just taken over Britain, but don't panic. Our aim – create a land fit for the elderly to live in, everyone moving towards best years of their lives, not away from. Good wheeze, sure you'll agree. Land where citizens are never discarded. That will be *our* citizens' charter. Apologise to Moira, lovely lady, even more attractive in flesh than on box, she'll be back soon. Also Jill Dando, another cracker. Thing is, nothing to fear, because

260

we believe in love for all mankind. Except C.J. Sorry, private joke, he's a bod in our organisation, and he's a bastard. Oops, sorry, before the nine o' clock deadline, forgot. So there it is. No more stigma about ageing. Quite simply, a better world. Over the next few days I'll introduce my cabinet to you, and you'll agree that they're a fine bunch of coves and covesses. Er . . . one thing, there will be no more TV or radio today. Well, wouldn't be a coup if we didn't say that, would it? However, don't want to do what those Ruskies used to do, martial music blaring out, scaring the sh. . . the living daylights out of everybody. Love, peace, no violence, that's our motto. So, all BBC channels for the rest of the evening will play Barry Manilow records. Major James Anderson, your new leader, BBC Television Centre, London, goodnight.'

The senior citizens burst into applause, and Moira Stuart shook her head sadly.

Jimmy would have shaken his head sadly, if he had been able to see the scenes in Whitehall.

The great rebellious army had come to a halt. Jimmy's human chain stood in some bewilderment, facing a solid line of mounted police.

Behind the human chain stretched a vast crowd of senior citizens, a sea of cardigans, an army of bent backs, a burning of bald pates, a patchwork quilt of white and grey hair, a brave parade of perms.

Behind the mounted police stretched a great contingent of police and soldiers, young, tough, tense, alert.

Trained marksmen had the rebels covered from the roofs and windows of all the buildings in the area. They were terrified. None of them wanted to open fire on the senior citizens of their own nation.

The police officers were also ill at ease. They had never faced a gathering of the elderly before.

Eight helicopters were circling overhead like vast vultures, increasing the tension that they were there to help dispel.

About twenty yards separated the two front lines of police and rebels.

A senior police officer in the middle of the mounted cordon took a megaphone and began to speak to the crowds.

'It's our duty to maintain the integrity of the British government,' he said. 'They were democratically elected. It's our duty to defend democracy and we will not shrink from it.'

'But we're the people!' shouted an eighty-three-year-old retired bicycle manufacturer.

'And we are the guardians of your electoral representatives,' said the police officer through his megaphone.

'Why don't you get stuffed?' shouted a bankrupt taxidermist.

There were one or two other angry cries, including, 'Oh, drop dead, the lot of you. You're the bastards that stitched up my Sidney. He never even *had* a power drill,' but on the whole the great crowd maintained its dignity.

'We have crack marksmen covering your every move.' The police officer's words echoed back off the empty Sunday buildings, so that it sounded as though teams of officers with megaphones were yelling at the crowds. 'Stay back and no one will get hurt.'

'They're bluffing,' shouted a seventy-seven-year-old retired greengrocer in the true spirit of a man who had been the very first person to introduce paw-paws to Wearside.

It was stalemate on a colossal scale, as the two great groups faced each other. To generations brought up on confrontational films with violent climaxes, it had a weird unreality, like living under water.

And still the helicopters circled.

The crowd began to press forward and lose their discipline. The front line of nonagenarians was pushed forward. Soon there were only twelve yards between them and the police cordon.

'Go back,' shouted the police officer. He looked frightened. '*We* can't go back. *You* must.'

Elizabeth stepped forward.

'May I?' she asked, indicating the megaphone.

He took a close look at her face, nodded, and handed her the megaphone.

Elizabeth Perrin put the megaphone to her lips, and turned to face the great crowd who had assembled as a result of her determination to create an adequate memorial for Reggie.

'Stop pushing,' she shouted. 'Ladies and gentlemen, senior citizens, colleagues, friends, for God's sake stop pushing. The police have no intention of pulling back. If you push forward, our front line will be crushed. They're all over ninety, and you will have killed them. The forces of the state don't play games.'

The human chain, terrified now, was being pushed slowly but remorselessly towards the police cordon.

One of the police horses arched a leg fretfully.

'Stop!' shouted Elizabeth. 'Pass the message back urgently. Tell them to stop pushing forward. The police won't kill us. We won't even be martyrs. We will have killed our own kind by pushing them under the police horses, and that will be the end of our cause. We've had a great day. We've made a great effort. Somebody must have betrayed us, and so we've failed, but we will not have disgraced our cause, if we can stop with dignity now.'

She was being driven backwards as she spoke. There were now only five yards between her and the police cordon. She was speaking in a smaller and smaller space as the human tide advanced. Two or three of the horses were becoming restive. There was nowhere for her to go, and C.J., Doc Morrissey, Tom and Linda, David and Prue Harris-Jones, Hank and Joan and Welton Ormsby were all occupying the same diminishing space, and there was fear on all their faces.

'Please try to move away from the back,' implored Elizabeth through the megaphone. 'Please stop. There are old, exhausted people here. They are going to be trampled underfoot.'

She could feel the heat from the horses behind her. She was terrified, but she didn't show it.

'Stop,' she shouted again.

There were cries of 'She's right' and 'Stop pushing' and 'Move away at the back' and 'I didn't get where I am today by being trampled underfoot.'

And, somehow, the message got through just in time. The human chain, terrified and exhausted, were no longer being pushed.

Gradually, very gradually, the human tide began to ebb. A few old people who had fainted were laid down on the road, where they were treated by the many nurses and ambulance men who had been recruited by BROSCOR and had marched proudly alongside the senior citizens.

The great crowds began to disperse to the pick-up points for their coaches and cars. The pick-up was as well organised as the arrival had been. Once again, no vehicle was too small or too ancient to be pressed into service.

Long and sad were the homeward journeys of the coaches. Long and sad, but also proud, were the faces of the passengers. They were sad, but not despairing. This Dunkirk was a retreat, but they all knew that Dunkirk had not been the end of the story.

The police and the soldiers dispersed. The helicopters were withdrawn. Barry 'I shouldn't be telling you this, but' Benskin clambered stiffly down from the roof of Horse Guards and wondered if he would ever be able to look Mildred in the face again.

264

Not one piece of litter was left by that vast, disciplined crowd. When they had gone, it was as if they had never been there.

Estimates of the number of people taking part in the bloodless revolution that day varied from the four hundred thousand of a government spokesperson to the five hundred thousand of the *Sun*, the eight hundred thousand of the *Daily Telegraph* and the one and a half million of the *Guardian*. It was generally believed, however, that round about a million people attempted to take over their nation and change the course of history that day.

Of that million, twenty-seven died in the course of the day, mainly from heart attacks, although two were crushed by vehicles and one lay down on a park bench and simply never woke up.

The government made great play with that, and criticised the leaders of the revolution fiercely for putting old people's lives at risk.

What the government did not reveal was that, statistically, fifty-three of them might have been expected to die if they had all stayed at home.

19 *Their Ultimate Reward*

Major James 'Bit of a Cock-Up on the Moira Stuart front' Anderson hurried head down through the streets of Climthorpe. He turned up his coat collar and pulled his hat down. It was a gloriously sunny day but there was a keen edge to the little late summer breeze, a mistiness in the mackerel sky, a smell of wood smoke, which must have been in his imagination, because Climthorpe had never been a mecca for wood smoke.

Jimmy was terrified that he would be recognised. He just hoped that everyone had been watching ITV at the time. Taking over the nation! Barry Manilow on all channels!

They should have had guns, of course. The others refused to admit it, the thought horrified them, but they had walked naked into the arena.

'I wish I could walk naked into Geraldine's office,' he thought as he passed the pub where, centuries ago, in another life, he had spent an uneasy twenty minutes with C.J. and Tom.

C.J.! He began to shake. He stood at the pedestrian crossing, waiting for the green man even though there was no traffic, because it was situated outside Mothercare and he didn't want to set a bad example. 'Don't think about Wat Tyler and your lost place in history,' he told himself. (But the thought did cross his mind that Wat Tyler wouldn't have waited for the green man.) 'Think about Geraldine.'

He was disappointed to find that she was with another client.

Damn! He'd wanted to get their personal business over before the others arrived.

He sat in the deserted waiting room of Messrs Hackstraw, Lovelace and Venison. He had no interest in looking at the magazines, which were even more out of date now. He had no eyes for the legal notices on the notice-board. His mind, that habitually sluggish organ, was seething with unpleasant memories of disaster, and excited anticipation of love and money. What was it Rudyard Kipling had said? 'If you can meet triumph and disaster and treat the two bastards the same way'? Something like that.

Joan entered. Damn damn damn! Oh, nice to see her, handsome woman, still got nice pins on her, lucky Hank, but secrecy blown, pity.

'Hello, Joan,' he said. 'How's Hank?'

'Asleep.'

'Oh, dear.'

'No, no, he's fine now. We just had . . .' She looked coy. She was charming when she looked coy. '. . . an active night.'

Jimmy sighed, hardly able to bear the thought of active nights to come with Geraldine.

'Excellent,' he said. 'Well done. Getting over the disappointment?'

'Not really. It runs deep.'

'Know what you mean. History in our grasp, history snatched away.'

'You at least had your moment of glory.'

Jimmy gawped at her. 'What?'

'It's given to few men to interrupt a BBC news broadcast and address the nation.'

'Nice of you to look at it that way.'

Perhaps that was the way he should try to look at it. He had to look the nation in the face again some time. Couldn't skulk for ever.

267

Next to arrive were Elizabeth and David and Prue Harris-Jones.

Elizabeth kissed Jimmy warmly.

'How are you feeling?' she asked.

He wrinkled his face by way of answer.

'Me too,' she said. 'I feel we let Reggie down.'

'I really don't think so,' said Joan. 'It was the doing of it, not the succeeding, that counted with Reggie.

'Mustn't blame yourself, Sis,' said Jimmy. 'Blame C.J. He was the snake in the ointment.'

'You're speaking his language,' said Elizabeth.

'I think . . .' began David Harris-Jones. 'I think . . . I mean what's strange to me . . . I mean, there we were being absolutely astounded at being offered the chance of a million pounds . . . but here we are now . . . and I think I . . . and I'm sure you . . . well, it's strange, isn't it?'

'David means that we did all this because of the money and yet we hardly gave a thought to the money really,' said Prue.

'Absolutely right,' said Elizabeth. 'The cause took over. Oh God, why couldn't we have succeeded?'

'We would have, if it wasn't for that . . . that . . . that . . .' said David Harris-Jones.

'Bastard,' said Prue.

'It's uncanny how she knows what's in my mind.'

'There wasn't anything uncanny about that one,' said Prue.

There was a brief silence, while they thought about C.J.

'Not going to turn the money down, though,' said Jimmy.

'Oh, no,' said Joan.

'Reggie wouldn't want us to,' said Elizabeth.

Tom and Linda were the next to arrive. Linda kissed her mother and Tom sat down with a great sigh.

'Oh, dear. That *was* a sigh,' said Elizabeth.

'I can't handle this,' said Tom. 'I don't want to feel greedy, but I can't forget that I'm about to inherit a million pounds.

I find it difficult. I've realised that I'm just no. person.'

Linda squeezed his hand.

'It's just one of the reasons why I love you, Tommyplops,' she said.

Jimmy sighed. Would Geraldine ever call him lovely things like Jimmyplops?

Doc Morrissey came in almost breezily.

'You seem cheerful, Doc,' said Jimmy, and it sounded so like a rebuke that everybody laughed.

'Sorry,' said Doc Morrissey. 'No, I've felt the disappointment, just like everybody. But the way I look at it is, I might be dead tomorrow, who knows, certainly not me and I'm a doctor, so I'll try to enjoy life while I can. My Asian friends are very philosophical. They've taught me a lot.'

The door opened again. Silence fell as C.J. entered.

He surveyed them all and gave a slightly icy, fixed grimace that hardly merited the description 'smile'. They had all known, after they had read the *Daily Sludge* the morning after the revolution, that it was his betrayal of them to Morton Radstock that had alerted the authorities.

'Good morning,' said C.J.

Nobody spoke.

'Sent to Coventry, eh?' said C.J. 'Well, I can take it. I didn't get where I am today by being upset about being sent to Coventry.'

Still nobody spoke.

C.J. gasped, winced, and clutched his heart.

Nobody moved. They assumed it was play-acting, and perhaps they wouldn't have moved even if they'd believed that it wasn't.

C.J. went to the table, picked up a copy of the *National Geographic* magazine, sat down, and began to turn its pages without seeing.

'I'll talk to you,' said Jimmy. 'Stupid not to.'

'Thank you, Jimmy,' said C.J. 'I appreciate that.'

'Can't call you a bastard if I don't talk to you,' said Jimmy. 'Can't call you a pus-filled boil blocking the arsehole of humanity if I don't talk to you. Don't like that nickname, Conniving Judas. Unfair to Judas.'

'Thank you,' said C.J., 'but people living in glasshouses shouldn't cast beams into the moat.'

'What on earth do you mean by that?' asked Joan angrily.

'None of you took the revolution seriously at first,' said C.J. 'Gradually you did, and in the end, after telling Morton Radstock, I did too. I regret that we failed as much as anybody. I bitterly regret that I was the vehicle that betrayed you. There are . . . there are times when I don't like myself very much.'

'Well, that's the difference between us,' said Tom. 'I don't like you at all all the time.'

Linda laughed and kissed her man.

'I don't want you to feel guilty, C.J.,' said Elizabeth. 'I'd hate you to have to live the rest of your life tormented by feelings of inadequacy and self-hatred.'

'Do you mean . . . do I dare hope . . .?' spluttered C.J.

'Oh, no,' said Elizabeth. 'Not now. There's no hope for you and me now that you've betrayed Reggie. It's goodbye Bunny, and hello, C.J. No, what I meant was, there's a very simple way for you to get rid of your guilt. All you have to do is renounce your claim to your million pounds.'

C.J. went white. His mouth opened, but no sounds emerged. He grimaced and clutched his heart.

Luckily for C.J.'s health, the secretary entered at that moment.

'Ms Hackstraw will see you now,' she said.

They all stood up, none more eagerly than C.J., who forgot his pain in an instant.

Jimmy blushed.

'Er . . .' he said. 'I . . . er . . . I'd like to see her on my own for a moment first. Personal matter. Think I have the right. After all, I am your . . . I was your leader.' He walked to the door, turned, and tried to smile. 'Won't be two ticks,' he said.

'Good luck, Bro,' said Elizabeth.

'Super,' said David Harris-Jones.

'Yes, all the best, Jimmy,' said Joan.

'Go for it, Uncle Jimmy,' said Linda.

C.J. and Doc Morrissey remained silent.

'Looking gorgeous,' said Jimmy, sinking into a chair opposite Ms Hackstraw. 'Gorgeous.'

'Thank you, Jimmy.'

She smiled, and his stomach turned over with love. Her hair seemed more golden than ever to Jimmy. Her grey eyes were wide and wonderful. She was wearing the same tight-fitting beige suit that she had worn at the reading of Reggie's will. Its trim, prim respectability excited Jimmy ten times more now that he knew every inch of the body that it hid. She stood up as he entered. How elegantly she carried herself. How exquisite was her neck, how high her shoulders.

'Won't beat about the bush,' he said, his voice shaking with hope and fear. 'Will you marry me, Geraldine?'

Ms Geraldine Hackstraw's pause was such that Jimmy's heart sank to his boots. In the despair of love the most insensitive of men can develop sharp antennae.

'I've been very happy with you,' she said. 'We've had . . .' She lowered her voice, as if she thought that Messrs Lovelace and Venison might be listening at the keyhole. '. . . wonderful sex.'

'Thank you,' whispered Jimmy hoarsely.

'If you are happy to continue to have . . . wonderful sex . . . until I find somebody I wish to marry, if indeed I ever do, that will be a great pleasure for me.'

'But,' croaked Jimmy, 'why won't you marry me?'

'Because it wouldn't work.' She turned the photograph of her husband away from her. 'I couldn't bear the unhappiness of another failed marriage.'

'But why should it fail?'

'I'm a lawyer. I like my comforts. I know myself too well. I wouldn't enjoy roughing it, scrimping and saving.'

'But I'm going to inherit a million pounds!' There was a long silence. 'Aren't I?'

'That's not something I feel we can discuss without the others being present,' said Geraldine Hackstraw. 'Shall we call them in?'

Ms Hackstraw stood up again as the other legatees filed in. She invited them to sit with an elegant, eloquent wave of the hand.

They seated themselves, as if instinctively, in exactly the same positions as they had chosen at the start of it all, and only then did Ms Hackstraw sit, as if in the judgement seat.

There was a pause. Elizabeth raised a questioning eyebrow at Jimmy, but his eyes were fixed on Geraldine Hackstraw.

Only when they were all looking in her direction did Ms Hackstraw's severe look melt into a dazzling smile.

'You've done brilliantly,' she said.

'Thank you very much,' said Elizabeth.

'It was an awful shame that you didn't succeed.' Geraldine Hackstraw glanced at C.J.

'Thank you very much,' said Prue Harris-Jones.

'Your efforts were extremely well thought out.'

'Super,' said David Harris-Jones.

'I'm sure many of you feel that you are better people than you were at the outset.'

'I admit it. I am, for one,' said Tom.

'Good.' Geraldine Hackstraw turned the photograph of her

husband back towards her, as if she needed his support. 'Unfortunately, I can't release the money.'

Everyone except C.J. tried not to gawp at her. Everyone except C.J. tried to look as if that wasn't what really worried them.

C.J. passed out.

When C.J.'s face had been bathed in cold water, and he had drunk a copious draft, and a bit of colour had come back to his face, Geraldine Hackstraw explained.

'When I visited you I was pleased by what I saw – incompetence, squabbling, no clearly thought-out policies. Since then, you've become quite sensible. Oh, I applaud it. Excellent ideas. A magnificent operation. Millions thought so too, so how could what you did be described as utterly and totally absurd? I would be failing in my duty as a trustee of Reginald Iolanthe Perrin's wishes if I said otherwise.'

There was a stunned pause, as the legatees saw their inheritance dissolving into the mists that had taken away the cause that they had espoused so bravely.

'She's right, of course,' said Elizabeth. 'She's absolutely right, I'm afraid.'

'I suppose we rather forgot about being absurd, in all the excitement,' said Tom.

'But I gave you money in order to make money,' said C.J.

'Hard luck. Shut up,' said Jimmy.

Geraldine Hackstraw rose.

'It's been delightful meeting you all and sharing in your exploits,' she said. 'I hope you won't be too disappointed about the money. After all, most of you forgot all about it as the excitement gripped you. And you do have the ultimate reward, don't you? You know, in your hearts, that what you did was right. I do hope I see you all again before too long, when you've gone away and thought up something a great deal more absurd.'

Nobody spoke. David Harris-Jones almost said 'Super' out of nervous habit, but managed to stop himself.

They filed sadly to the door, where Jimmy could stand it no longer.

'But, Geraldine,' he wailed, 'you have it in your power to make me rich and us happy.'

'I know, my darling,' said Geraldine Hackstraw gently, 'and nobody regrets this more than I. But I can't cheat, can I? After all, there does seem to be a lesson in your exploits.' She glanced at the photograph of the simple old couple who weren't actually her parents. 'Nothing is to be prized as greatly as integrity.'

As they emerged soberly into Climthorpe High Street, a single dark cloud obscured the sun. Elizabeth looked up at it and shivered.

A sudden burst of rain, carried ahead of the cloud on the strengthening wind, pinged on to the dusty pavement out of a blue sky.

Then, when the cloud was overhead, the rain stopped, and the sun burst out in all its fierce glory.